DRAGON'S BABY

NEW & LENGTHENED 2021 EDITION

MIRANDA MARTIN

CONTENTS

Stolen by a Dragon.
My kidnapper is tall, dark and alien....

My dull, predictable life as a scientific researcher is ripped apart the day blood-thirsty pirates attack our space ship. In the confusion, the ship is thrown off course.

We crash land on a planet that can barely support life.
Yeah...things are going swell.

I've escaped the pirates, at least. But I've got a new problem. The planet is home to a dragon-alien, and he has his eyes set on me. Ladon, a powerful Zmaj warrior rescues me from the scorching desert wasteland.

Ladon takes me to the ruins of his ancient city. I'm his treasure. His mate. He loves my curves and my soft, human form. He makes it clear that he intends to keep me and claim me in every way. The moment he touches my trembling body, he leaves no doubt.

This fierce, protective dragon owns me.

Dragon's Baby is a full length, standalone SFR novel with a happily ever after ending, plenty of steam, bloody battles and alien-human intrigue.

 Created with Vellum

GET A FREE BOOK!

Subscribe to Miranda Martin's e-mail list and get the Red Planet Dragons of Tajss prequel Dragon's Origins *PLUS* bonus freebie Ribbed For Her Pleasure!

http://tny.sh/mirandamartinlist

CALISTA

I break into a flat out run, wishing I'd had time to get a cup of coffee. The stuff at work sucks. My tyrant of a boss, Gershom, insists on programming the roast and strength, which is part of his psychotic need to control everything. His taste in coffee is as terrible as his smarmy attitude.

A stitch stabs in my side, a not-so-subtle reminder of missed days in the gym.

It's so much easier to curl up in bed and watch a vid or read. Nothing beats being transported to some imaginary world, experiencing what life was like on Earth or what it could be like on some far-flung planet. Life on a planet. Real gravity. Unlimited space to explore. Horizons! Oh, the horizons are the best. I love the vids where they show a broad, open landscape. It makes my heart ache with the wonder of it all.

Also, it's not like my job as a botanist requires much in the way of physical strength, so skipping leg day is more like skipping exercise, period.

I emerge from a side passage into one of the main thoroughfares of this deck of the ship. Throngs of people move about going from one place to another. It forces me to slow down and navigate my way through the crowd. I glance up at the hologram-covered ceiling that simulates open sky. Blinking twice and looking left, the time appears.

8:37, twenty-three minutes.

I can make it. An opening appears in the crowd, and I don't miss the opportunity. I dart through, then dodge left and right. A lift opens as if it's aware of my burning need, and I jump in with the others rising to the next deck.

"I'm not one to spread rumors, but I heard on good authority that General Rosalind is going to retire," an older man in formal attire says to his companion, a younger fellow with a receding hairline.

"Lady Rosalind? That will be the day. She's never going to give up her position of power. Why would she?" his companion says.

"Word is," the first man lowers his voice, as if that means the dozen of us on this lift can't still clearly hear every word, "she's sick."

"No," his companion disagrees. "She's too tough to ever be sick. If she did get sick, she'd order it to retreat, and it would."

The two men laugh as the lift comes to a stop. I'm counting my heart beats waiting for the door to open. The instant they're wide enough to fit through, I turn sideways and push out.

"Hey!" Another lady huffs in ire as I bump her in the process of moving away.

"Sorry! I'm late," I call over my shoulder.

Almost there. Almost there.

I skid to a stop at the entrance to security. The guy in line ahead of me looks like he's in his eighties, and I guess he forgot his ID. They're going extra slow checking him out. I hop from foot to foot as I wait in the security line.

Damn it, I'm late. Hurry up! He's eighty—who cares! Let him in!

"Hell, I work here. Show some damn respect," the old guy grouses.

"You work here, so you know the rules, Mr. Chamberlain," Bert, the guard frisking him, says. Bert is older, big and burly looking with a gruff attitude to match.

"Here now, you touch the merchandise, you better be ready to finish what you started!" the old man cries out as the guard pats down his leg. I can't hold back a snort even as my cheeks warm. I look away, covering my mouth with my hand.

"Sorry, sir," the younger guard, Charlie, says.

Bert grunts. I shake my head and look up for the time.

8:48, so close. Hurry up. Gershom is going to give me so much shit. Damn it. I need this like I need a hole in my head.

"Bert?" I ask, and he looks up from patting down Mr. Chamberlain.

"Is there any way I could get passed through?"

Bert's pissed, which is nothing new, but today he apparently wants to piss on the entire world too. This becomes abundantly clear when he rolls his eyes.

"Oh, I'm sorry, do you think I asked this guy to forget his ID then expect to get through anyway? Am I putting a cramp in your style by doing my job?"

"Bert, I didn't mean—"

"Didn't mean to put down us poor guards who look after you high and mighty lab techs?"

"I didn't say—"

"Didn't say please? Yeah, I noticed. Thanks for the respect, by the way. Goes a long way. Now get in line, *please*, while we clear this snafu up."

"You never get laid, do you?" Chamberlain quips.

Bert's eyes widen and his face turns purple as his blood pressure soars. His mouth moves and he's making a sputtering noise, but no words come out. My own mouth drops open, and then a laugh slips out. I cover my mouth with both hands.

"What? You think you can talk to a pretty girl like that and expect her to give you any honey?" Chamberlain continues. My cheeks flush, burning red hot.

It's clear that Charlie is doing his best not to laugh as he stands up in front of Chamberlain, but judging by the color of his face and the way he's holding himself, he's about to burst. Chamberlain looks at me with bright eyes and a grin that goes from ear to ear.

"If I was twenty years younger, I'd ask you out," he says. "But hell with that; you need a good time, I got just the equipment to show it to you!"

My skin goes nuclear. Now I'm speechless too. Part of me wants to crawl under the security machines, part says to run, and part is full of admiration for the old man. I don't know what to feel or how to respond. Should I be flattered? Flummoxed? How about embarrassed? Is that close enough?

"You're cleared, sir," Charlie says, pulling on Chamberlain's shoulder and forcing him to take his eyes off me.

"About damn time," Chamberlain mutters and wanders off without another word or look in my direction.

Relief rushes in, and the pressure on my chest eases as my cheeks burn less hot.

"Sorry, Calista," Charlie says as I step up to the security checkpoint and scan my badge.

"Wow," I say, uncertain still how to react or what to say.

"Yeah, he's . . . different," Charlie says.

"You deal with him often?"

"More than I'd like. He constantly forgets his ID, too," Charlie answers.

"I hate that son of a bitch," Bert mutters.

Bert is back at the scanning machine that monitors everyone entering the sector. Why, exactly, we need such heavy security at a laboratory, is above my pay grade. We speculate it about it off and on, but no one really knows, or if they do, they aren't saying.

We do research that I can't imagine anyone really caring about. It's not like we're designing weapons. My team is working on new strains of wheat. Whoopee! Prime target for terrorism, I guess, if you're a wheat hater. Is there such a thing? Does anyone really care what we're doing?

No matter how seriously I doubt it, the security has now made me even later. Gershom is going to put me through the ringer. God, he's such a self-important, pompous ass. Checking the time once more, it's now 8:56.

Bert and Charlie pass me through, and I run for the lift. The ride will take another two minutes, and then I have to go down the hall to where my team works. At best I'm going to be twenty-nine minutes and twenty-four seconds late, just under the thirty-minute cut off, so I don't have a second to spare. Thirty minutes late and Gershom can dock my units by half a day. Anything under that and it's only a reprimand, not that I need any more of those either, but screw losing half my day's units.

The elevator crawls up, and I would swear it's moving at half pace. I dance from foot to foot and watch the number slowly climb. Finally it comes to a stop and then the doors slowly slide open. I dive out the moment they're wide enough for me to squeeze through then run down the hall. Thankfully I wore flats today. Dress code in the lab is casual since we're all either wearing lab coats or the special suits that prevent cross contamination.

"Run, Calista, run!" a high-pitched voice yells down the hall.

My best friend Jolie is waving me on and holding the door to the lab open. Jolie is shorter than I am by a couple of inches and super cute. She has shoulder-length rich, dark hair that perfectly accents her tawny skin. She's also really petite with an ability to eat anything and everything without worrying about her weight, of which I am not at all jealous. Nope, not at all. Ignoring the stitch in my side, I break into a full sprint, heart racing, pumping my arms and legs for all I'm worth.

"Jolie, shut the door," Gershom's baritone rings out.

"Yes, sir!" she yells. "I'm doing just that, holding the door!" she calls over her shoulder then turns back and grins.

I skid to a stop with a squeaking of rubber on tile just barely inside the door. Jolie motions at the time computer and I slap my hand down on the scanner. She had my employee id already punched in and waiting. It's a fudge, but not a flat-out breaking of the rules. The screen flashes 'Clocked In' right before the time changes. I made it! I'm panting heavily. I lean over, hands on knees, then Jolie grabs me in a tight hug.

"Calista," Gershom says, stalking towards me like a cat prowling towards a bird and every bit as creepy.

"Yes?" I ask.

Gershom is an older man, late forties or early fifties, with gray at the temples of his dark hair. He has a deep, tan lined face, and big hands that constantly grip a mug of coffee, which he sips to accent his statements. He seems to think that the gesture makes him cool and hip. As if the suspenders he wears don't kill any hint of hip or cool.

He's our supervisor, but he's not a scientist like the rest of us. I think this makes him insecure and is part of the reason he likes to enforce his authority. Lording it over us every chance he gets.

"You're late," he says, sipping his coffee.

"Yeah, sorry about that. Problem at security."

"I see." Sip. "Well, we have rules around here." Sip.

"Yes, sir," I say.

"Rules that are made to be followed." Sip. "Perhaps you were out too late last night?" Sip.

"No, sir."

I can't help but wonder if he has a crush on me. He's always asking or implying things about what I do on my own time. I'm never sure if he's hitting on me or not, which makes me even more uncomfortable than Chamberlain's comments downstairs.

The worst part is, it's not something he does with anyone else. Apparently, he has a type, and I fit the criteria. I wish he'd not do it. He's my boss for one, and two, he's an asshole.

"I see." Sip. "Well, that's too bad." Sip. "Then you'd have a reason, wouldn't you?" Sip.

"I suppose so, sir."

"Well, half a day's pay." Sip as he turns to wander away.

"I was within the time limit."

His eyes widen and he whirls back. His eyes narrow, making the lines on his forehead even thicker. He motions with his suddenly forgotten coffee then shakes his head without saying anything. He turns to the time computer and punches in his security code. He leans in and reviews the logs. When he turns back, all pretense of control and cool is gone.

"Get to work," he says, pointing with his coffee cup.

I suppress my laughter, nod, and follow Jolie into our lab. I feel his eyes burning into my back as we leave. The clear glass door closes behind us, somewhat shutting him out. I glance over my shoulder to see Gershom disappear into his office. Jolie and I slide on our lab coats.

"That was close," Jolie says.

"Yeah," I agree.

"Where the hell were you?"

"I overslept."

"Again? Hot date last night?"

I snort. "Yeah, right. No one wants the nerdy librarian outside of cheesy Earth vids."

"I call bullshit."

"I call bullshit on your bullshit."

"You need to put yourself out there! Come on, girl, you got the goods, under that nerdy smile and loose ponytail."

"Uh-huh. Well, for now I'm going to stay focused on work."

"Bah, work is boring."

"No, it's not; we're close to breaking through, though."

"True, I do love the science," Jolie says and laughs, shaking her head. "I guess I'm just as big of a nerd as you are." She sighs heavily, placing one hand on her forehead mimicking really old vids of women acting faint. "I suppose there is no help for us. No overly muscled barbarian lord to come take us away from our daily toils."

"Overly muscled barbarian? Seriously?" I snort and shake my head. "I want to see how the new seeds are doing. I'll find you after I'm done in the clean room."

"You'd better," Jolie says.

I head into the clean room and check on all the new seeds we're testing. Biochemistry is fun. Well, I think it's fun. It's also vitally important. If my great-great-great grandkids are going to be fed on their new home world someday, we need to keep evolving better strains of food. Botanist like us ensure the future.

When I return to my workstation, there's a steaming cup of coffee waiting for me. Grateful, I take a sip and the warm, fullness with the hints of nutty overtones fills my mouth. Jolie made this cup. She makes the best cups of coffee.

"Thank you," I say.

Jolie looks up from her work and smiles. "Of course. How were the seedlings?"

"They're ahead of schedule," I say.

"That's great," she says. "The modifications we made to them are working? They're accepting the new soil?"

"So far," I say.

"You need to clean this station up," Gershom's voice echoes through the lab.

I cringe and am unable to stop myself from looking over my shoulder to see who he's bothering. Out of the corner of my eye, I notice Jolie does the same.

"I'm in the middle of—" Terry, another scientist, starts, but Gershom motions with his ever present cup of coffee and makes a tsk sound, cutting the other man off.

"I know, I know," he says. "You're in the middle of something. I know all this, but does that change the rules? Does that change the need for cleanliness?"

"I'm about to—"

"About to clean this up? Riiight, that'd be great," Gershom interrupts then moves on before Terry can speak again.

Terry moves his papers around and straightens his area, muttering the entire time. Gershom looks smug, almost beaming with hubris. Then he sees me looking. I look away as quick as possible.

"Please don't come over, please don't come over," I whisper my soft prayer.

"Oh no," Jolie says. "Look out."

I lean in close to my screen, putting all my attention on it, trying to appear as absorbed as possible in my work.

"Cah-lis-ta," Gershom says, accenting my name in his weird way. "How's the research?"

I count the thumps of my heart before answering. One. Two. Three.

"Huh? Oh," I say, glancing at him with what I hope is a look of surprise. "Fine. Fine."

"Fine," Gershom nods, smiling. "Good, good. We do like fine."

"Yep," I agree, keeping my eyes on the screen. *Go away. Go away.*

"Okay then, that's great, carry on then. Carry on. You too, Jolie. Lots to do. Future generations depend on your work."

"Yes sir!" Jolie says cheerfully, giving him a mocking salute with two fingers. He moves on, and I drop my head onto my desk, groaning. "Cheer up, buttercup."

"He's the worst," I grouse.

"Maybe," she says. "But our new seeds are growing. That makes it all better."

"Okay, Miss Positivity," I say, and we return to our work.

The rest of the day passes as I lose myself in my work. I'm at my desk punching in the results of my latest round of tests and the reports to end the day when Gershom walks up again, ever present coffee cup still in hand.

"So, yeah," he says without preamble.

I look at him over my glasses. There's no one else in the area with us. The way his eyes roam over me, dropping repeatedly to my chest and never quite staying on my eyes, makes me self-conscious. I push my hair back behind my ear, clear my throat, and cross my arms over my chest.

"Yeah?"

Gershom clears his throat, then his eyes dart around the office. Is he nervous?

"So… Calista… Yeah. I thought, perhaps you'd like to go out, to dinner, you know, tonight?"

"Me?" Surprise makes my voice come out higher than normal.

"Well, yeah," he says. "You, me, dinner, maybe some other… entertainment." His eyes drop on the last word, and my stomach clenches tight in revulsion.

"I don't think that'd be appropriate," I say, cheeks burning hot.

"Oh, well, um, why not?"

"Work?" What else do I say? I find you repulsive and slimy? God, months without a date or a hint of one and in one day I have an eighty-year-old man and Gershom. I have the worst luck.

"Ah, right, of course," he says, motioning with his half-empty coffee cup. The scent of its stale contents filling the air between us, the perfect metaphor for him and I. "It's only... I thought... I don't mean..."

"Hey Calista, you about done?" Jolie asks, walking up behind our boss, being my saving grace.

He stiffens, squaring his shoulders and losing the bumbling demeanor. He waves the coffee cup in a figure eight. "Yes, well, very good. Make sure you fill that report in fully."

He turns around and comes face to face with Jolie. The two of them stare at each other, but Jolie keeps her bright smile fixed on her face. He nods then walks off. Jolie and I watch him go, listening to the click of his hard-soled shoes on the tile. When he turns a corner and goes out of sight, she whirls on me with a grin from ear to ear. "Did he just ask you out!?"

"Ugh, yes."

"Man, he's got it bad for you. You could use it later for a raise or something if you wanted to," she laughs.

"No!"

"Hey, just saying," she laughs again. "Scratch that itch and all that."

"I'd rather die," I reply.

"Yeah, can't blame you there. He's really... I don't know... weird, I guess."

"How strange is it when the two of us confirmed geeks are calling him the weirdo?"

"What can I say, it's a weird life," she laughs. "That said, this day's over; ready to go?"

"You bet," I say, shutting off my monitor and rubbing my eyes.

We make our way out of the lab and past security without incident. Outside on the thoroughfare, we walk along quietly. The throngs of people heading home each in their own conversations, going about their lives, create a background hum.

"Dinner?" she asks. "Or straight back to our dorms?"

"Dinner would be great. Think we can get into Cosmos?"

"No clue, but I love that place," Jolie says. "Let's give it a shot!"

We work our way through the end-of-day-rush crowd. When we reach Cosmos, it's not a surprise that there's a line. We take our place in it, making small talk while we wait our turn to see how long the wait might be before we decide to give up on the idea or not.

The hostess is a young, good looking guy who has shaved both sides of his head but has a thin line beard along the lines of his jaw coming to a sharp point goatee. Jolie and I exchange knowing looks but manage to not say anything. He's friendly and says the wait isn't long, offering to let us sit at the bar until a table is ready.

"What are you drinking?" Jolie asks.

"Bloody Mary tonight."

She holds up two fingers and orders our drinks. I grab mine and walk away from the bar.

"I want to see the view," I say.

"Sure!" she says, following along.

The view is what makes Cosmos a hotspot. In general, the ship is designed to make it easy to forget you're on a ship. It's a psychological design choice by our grandparents who created the Generation Ship program. The journey we're on isn't one intended for any of us alive today to live to see the end of. We'll never walk on the surface of a planet, but our own grandchildren will.

I lead us through the packed bar and through the door to the observation room. There are tables, each with three tall chairs carefully arranged to allow a full view of space, but we're waiting on those, as they're reservations only.

A chrome rail divides the back third of the room from the tables where people can stand and see the view, but there are no seats, and the view is intermittently blocked by those at the tables moving around. We can see the stars, though, while we have our drinks and wait for a table so we can eat.

"Lucy in the sky with diamonds," Jolie hums, holding her drink up and swaying back and forth.

"No doubt," I say.

"What galaxy is that?" I ask, pointing at a nebulous cloud that must be a few hundred light years away.

"I'm not sure. I don't know where we're at in the journey right now," she replies.

I sip my drink. Looking into the big black, I feel small and complete all at the same time. The black emptiness is all around. Awesome in its very vastness, but at the same time, we've conquered it.

We're the third generation aboard the ship. Two more generations will live here before the journey is over. I chuckle. Thanks to Grandpa and Grandma, our lives are, and always will be, defined by the confines of the ship.

Something rises. A vague, ill-defined feeling. A sense of something more. As if, out there, something calls to me. Almost like a voice I can't quite hear, calling me to come home.

"What are you thinking about?" Jolie asks, startling me out of my thoughts.

I fix a smile on my face and force myself to look away from the view. "Nothing." I shake my head and take another drink.

"That didn't look like nothing."

I sigh. "I don't know. You ever get, I don't know, a feeling that you can't really define? It doesn't make sense but at the same time... Ugh. I. Don't. Know." I sip my drink and try to figure out my thoughts. "As if there's something more?" I finally venture.

"Of course I have, and there is. Love! In the grand scheme of things, what else is there but love?"

I smile and look out at the black. Jolie has love on the brain. It's all she thinks about. She loves watching romantic movies and dreams of her knight in shining armor, which means she also dreams of me finding mine.

"I think," I say, sipping thoughtfully, "that the nerdy science girl only gets the hot guy in the vids or romance books."

"Bah," she says. "Art imitates life, and life imitates art!"

"I'm not sure that those overly dated romantic comedy vids you love are 'art'."

"Oh my god, how can you say that? They're the best!"

"Yeah," I sigh. "I'm not an actress in one of those vids. Or a romance heroine of any kind. I'm... me. Happy to curl up on the couch and watch old vids or read a book."

"You have no idea how cute you are, do you?"

"What?" I ask, surprised.

"Cute, you," she repeats. "Lots of guys would love to go out with you."

"Sure," I shake my head.

Jolie rolls her eyes. "Trust me, I know what I'm talking about."

"I'll stick with the science, thanks."

"We'll see about that my dearie," Jolie says, laughing.

A flash of light outside the viewscreen jerks my attention.

"You see that?" I ask, staring where I thought I saw it, but it doesn't repeat.

"Hmm? What?"

"Flash of light off that way." I point.

"Nope," she says. She's staring around the bar looking for eligible bachelors and not interested in the slightest.

"I know I saw something," I say, moving closer to the railing to try and get a better view.

"Hi."

I turn to see who's talking, and find another friend, Inga, approaching.

"Hi, Inga," Jolie says. "Good timing. You can help settle the debate."

"What debate is that?" Inga asks, climbing up onto an empty chair.

I can't fully pull my attention off the windows, looking to see... something.

"Romantic comedy vids," Jolie says, fixing Inga with an intense glare. "Art or no?"

"Uhm," Inga says, eyes darting between the two of us. She twists her fingers in her long red hair, pursing her lips, trying to buy time.

"Let her off the hook, Jolie," I laugh.

Inga has the greatest smile. When she does, it makes you really shows her heart and how much she cares. She smiles at me then squares her shoulders and faces Jolie.

"I don't think love is that easy," she says, then her shoulders slump and she looks away.

"Probably right," Jolie says, looking wistful. "But wouldn't it be great?"

"It would beat dating," Inga agrees.

"How are you doing, Inga?" I ask, changing the subject.

"You know," she says, shaking her head. "How's life in the lab?"

"Gershom is hitting on Calista again," Jolie says.

"Oh no, I'm sorry," Inga says, putting her hand on mine.

"It's no big deal," I say. "You know how he is."

"A slimy, wannabe tyrant?" Inga asks, and we all laugh.

"Sums it up," Jolie says.

"You didn't answer how your day was," I say.

Inga sighs. "It's interesting, I guess."

"Oh?" Jolie says, eyes alighting with curiosity.

"I don't think she means that kind of interesting," I say.

"No, unfortunately," Inga says. "There's this guy, Mark. He's one of those guys who you'd think has it all, but he still can't be nice."

"Your own Gershom?" Jolie asks.

"No, not that bad," she says. "But, today he was on a rant about vagrants. He acts like they're less than human or some other race. The worst part is the others seem to agree with him."

"A lot of people seem to feel that way," I say.

"That doesn't make it right," Inga says. "They're still humans. They didn't choose to be born without permission."

"You're right," Jolie says.

"I agree," I say. "Once they're born, what choice does anyone think there is? They're alive, they're humans, they have as much right to live as anyone else on the ship."

"Exactly!" Inga agrees. She purses her lips and frowns. "You know, we've come so far, but I have to wonder, are we really better or only better at hiding the negative parts of our nature?"

"What do you mean?" I ask.

"Look at our history," she says. "Well, the history of Earth. How violent it was, filled with hate and bigotry. We've gotten better, and now we're flying through space to populate a new world, but I have to wonder—how is it going to be for our grandkids when they reach a planet?"

"They're going to be great, we're so much better," Jolie says, raising her glass and taking a drink.

"Or we've only been forced to bury the darker parts of human nature because the planet was on the brink of destruction," I say.

"Wow, dark much?" Jolie asks.

I shake my head and force a smile. "Sorry, it's been a day."

"She's not wrong," Inga says. "History has often turned the focus of one group against another to create conflict and strife. We do better on the ship because we have to. Who knows what it will be like when humanity finally reaches its new home. Will our old bad instincts come back?"

"Your table is ready," a host says, interrupting our conversation and preventing any response to Inga's musings. "This way, please."

"You guys should get to your table," Inga says, standing up. "I only wanted to say hi when I saw you."

"Good to see you," I say as we exchange a quick hug.

"Won't you join us?" Jolie asks as they embrace.

"I'm with some friends," she says.

"Okay, see you soon," Jolie says, and we follow our host to the dining area.

"Are there supposed to be fighter maneuvers tonight?" I ask the hostess.

The fighter pilots drill and train all the time, but that's scheduled in advance. The nights you can see them training from Cosmos book out months ahead.

"Not tonight, no," the hostess says over her shoulder as she leads us through another door and down two steps into the dining area.

Our table is on the far side of the room from the view, close to the railing that divides the room. We take our seats and look at the menu, but I can't shake this uneasy feeling.

"You ever feel like something bad is about to happen?" I ask, not looking up from the digital menu floating in the air before my eyes.

"Sometimes," Jolie says. "What's the matter, Calista? You're pale."

"I don't know," I sigh, setting the menu down. I try to force a smile but can't, so instead I stare out at the empty black. "I've got a really bad feeling."

"Probably because Gershom is bothering you again."

"Maybe," I agree but nothing shakes this sense that something is about to go wrong.

Jolie reaches across the table and takes my hand. "Hey. It's okay. Nothing bad ever happens on the ship, right?"

I take a deep breath and turn my attention away from the black, but out of the corner of my eye I see another flash of light. I jerk my head back, trying to pinpoint it, but it's gone. No one else is reacting, so I'm not sure I even saw it. Maybe it was a refraction. Any light source could hit the viewscreen at a weird angle and make a flash like that. That's what it must be.

"You're right." I force the smile this time and pick up the menu. "What are you having?"

As we order, I can't shake this weird sense of dread. Just because nothing bad ever has happened doesn't mean nothing bad ever will.

2

CALISTA

*T*hree beeps and the smell of fresh Caffe Verona coffee permeates the room. I sit on the edge of my bunk waiting for it to finish, then sip the warm, delightful beverage. As the heat and caffeine spread through my system, I slowly come awake. I step into my bathroom and let warm air filled with ion particles scrub me clean, then care for my teeth and fix my hair.

Dressed and ready, I step out of my room into the common area I share with two other girls. The dorms are all designed like this, just enough privacy to keep us sane, but space is at a premium on a colony ship. We'll only get our own space when we marry and have a family.

Jolie is curled up on the couch with her feet tucked under her while sipping her own coffee. She looks alert and ready to go, damn her. She's always full of energy, and I'm jealous.

"Morning, sunshine!" Jolie smiles.

"Right," I say and roll my eyes as I plop down next to her. My coffee hasn't quite kicked in enough yet, I guess. The vid she was watching is still playing. "What are you watching?"

"It's a vid of a musical," she says. "It's funny, I think. I'm not sure I get all the references, but there's lot of music and you know, the lead guy is kind of cute."

"Huh, too skinny."

Jolie tilts her head to the side and squints her eyes then sighs heavily.

"Yeah. I was going for lithe, but not really, huh?"

"Nope. You ever wish they had found room to build in some vid production on the ship? It'd be nice to not be stuck watching all this stuff from old Earth."

"Yeah, but what would they write about? Another day on the ship. More outer space. No sets, no sweeping vistas. I don't think it would have worked if they had."

"Probably not," I agree.

"Oh, I love this part!" Jolie all but squeals. I look at the vid and see a blue lit scene that looks like a bar. She motions with one hand, turning the volume way up. She climbs to her feet as she belts out the song, miming a mic in one hand. *My little China girl, says oh, baby, just you shut your mouth.*

I cover my ears and hide my hide while she bounces up and down on the couch.

"For the love of god, could you please shut the hell up, it's the weekend," Amara yells, stepping out of her bunk.

"Don't be a bear," Jolie says, spinning on her foot to face Amara.

Amara is loud, brash, and used to giving orders. She has a harsh, almost fiercely, beautiful face with a strong jaw and sharp nose that conveys an air of authority. Her short, dark hair is standing on end, and her eyes are heavy, barely open. She looks exhausted.

"Did you not sleep at all last night, Amara?" I ask.

"No, and Miss Happy is not helping," she grouses.

"Why not?"

"Because she's annoying?" she quips with a glare at Jolie, who sticks her tongue out. Amara rolls her eyes.

"I meant, why didn't you sleep last night?"

"We were assigned extra patrols," she says, rubbing her face. "Someone up lines claimed they detected an anomaly."

The uneasy feeling I went to bed with leaps from whatever corner of my mind it was hiding in like a tiger pouncing on its prey. The hairs on the back of my neck rise on end, and drop of cold sweat trickles down my spine. I motion at the vid and mute the volume.

"Did you find anything?" I ask.

"Nothing," she growls then stalks over to the fabricator.

"Isn't that weird?" Jolie asks.

"Yes, maybe," Amara replies, not turning around. Her shoulders are hunched and she's leaning her head against the wall, waiting on her coffee to be made.

"Well, is everything going to be okay?" Jolie says.

"Why don't you stick to growing weeds or whatever the hell it is you two do? Leave the piloting to those of us who know things, all right?"

"We're bio-engineering botanists, thank you very much, Your Highness," Jolie quips. "If not for our work, you high-and-mighty pilots would starve."

"Right, thanks, the food's been so wonderful of late," Amara says, shaking her head.

"We're not the cooks!" Jolie says, rising to the bait, and I sigh.

"She's prodding you, Jolie."

"Oh, right," Jolie says then shrugs. "Whatever."

"Seriously, Amara, was it something? Should we be worried?"

"I'm sure it was nothing," she says, turning around with her coffee. "Lieutenant Draker was probably on a power kick. He does shit like that."

Amara doesn't complain about her work often, but when she does, it's usually about this Draker guy. She's one of the only female pilots in the history of the Gen Ship.

An honor, for sure, and one that another, now famous woman held in her own time. General Rosalind herself. It can't be easy being inside the 'boys' club, though. If anyone can do it, she can. She's tough as nails.

"Can you rep—" Jolie asks, then the room rocks and we're all three thrown off balance.

I pinwheel my arms, fighting to stay upright. Jolie is knocked off the couch she was jumping on. It seems as if time is moving in slow motion. The coffee flying up out of Jolie's cup hangs in the air, slowly stretching towards the ceiling like an amorphous blob intent to stain the tiles. Amara swears as her own hot coffee splashes across her chest.

I'm spun around and bounce off the nearest wall. Decorations we have on shelves around the room are thrown to the floor, filling my ears with the sound of shattering glass.

I lose the fight to stay standing as the floor bounces, and I'm thrown up then land on my back. My breath is knocked out as stars dance in my vision.

"Whoa!" Jolie cries.

"What the hell?" I gasp.

"Damn it," Amara growls.

"Amara, what's happen—"

My question is cut off as the room's light goes from white to red and flashing. A distant alarm sounds, echoing into our space. My blood turns cold and my stomach clenches into a tight knot. I sit up, staring at the other two women.

"Amara?" Jolie asks, her voice almost warbling.

We've drilled this all our lives, but no one ever expected a real alarm. It's theoretical, because there are only a small handful of events that would cause the alarms to sound. None of which are good.

"You know the drills. We have to get to our life pods," Amara orders.

"But what is it?" I ask.

Amara looks at me with heavy eyes. "I don't know."

She's lying and I know it, but there's no time to argue. The alarms grow louder. The room shakes again. The light flash in a different rhythm. Amara watches it carefully while I struggle to remember the codes we learned in core school.

"Damn," Amara mutters, leaping into motion.

She grabs Jolie and helps her to her feet. The room rocks again, and I fall onto my butt. The room keeps shaking as I struggle to stand while Amara and Jolie are supporting each other.

Holding my arms out wide to help with my balance, I try to reach them. I make it two steps before I fall.

Giving up on walking, I crawl to where they've also dropped to the floor. When I reach them at last, we grab onto one another then work our way to the door.

Amara slides her hand up the wall to the activation panel, and the door slides open. Thick, gray, acrid smoke rolls into the room. It assaults my nose and throat at the same time. I cough, and it feels like I'm choking.

The hall is full of other people, crying and screaming. They're fighting to move through the smoke, which lies along the floor coming to about knee height. Holding onto the wall, I manage to stand, then help Amara and Jolie. The floor bucks and heaves again, and we almost fall, but through sheer dumb luck manage to stay upright.

"Amara, what the hell is it? Smoke? There was no smoke in any of our drills," I ask, grabbing her by her shoulders and forcing her to look at me.

She purses her lips and tenses her jaw. She shakes her head, looking around as other people work their way past us towards their own stations or life pods depending on their assignments.

"Pirates," Amara answers me. "We have to get to our stations. Now."

"You're shitting me," I say. "I thought they were a myth. You know, like the Star Wars Empire or Keyser Soze or something?"

"They're not," she replies.

"Pirates." Three girls who were fighting their way down the hallway overheard Amara and scream the word in unison.

"No, calm down. Get to your stations," Amara orders.

A hollow thwap sound echoes down the hall. Instinctively, I know what that sound is. I have never heard one before, not in real life. I've heard lots of them on old Earth vid sticks but never on the ship. It's impossible. It can't be, but the cold ice racing through my veins leaves no room for doubt.

That was a gun, some kind of laser gun, I'd guess. The sound echoes down the hall, bouncing off the walls and reverberating in my ears, causing a ringing that doesn't stop.

"What was that?" Jolie asks.

"Gunshots?" I ask, hoping against all hope that someone, anyone, will tell me I'm wrong. "You don't use guns in space, right?"

I look at Amara, begging with my eyes. She tenses her jaw, her eyes narrow, and then she nods. Oh Amara, why couldn't you lie to me?

Everything is chaos. People running and screaming. Smoke, blaring alarms, flashing lights, and that repeating, empty thwack sound that Amara confirmed is gunfire.

The three of us stick close together, and Amara falls into a leadership role that I'm glad to let her have. We make our way out of our dorm levels and onto the main thoroughfare, where things go from bad to nightmarish.

The ceiling lights flash bright red in time with the blaring alarms, casting everything into a hellish glamour. The air is thick with smoke. Screaming people run for their security stations, or they run out of fear and confusion.

Jolie's grip on my arm is vise-like, her nails digging into the flesh, but I don't mind. It's something to focus on besides the chaos. I keep one hand on Amara as she pushes and fights her way through the crowds. I don't want to lose her.

A blue flash of light burns through the air over our heads, followed by a zinging, crackling sound a second behind it.

"Shit," Amara curses, pulling all three of us down.

"What was that?"

"Lasers," Amara says, grimacing. "Keep low and don't fall behind."

The screams grow louder as we duck walk our way forward. It's not that far to our designated life pods. We've drilled this all our lives, and it's supposed to take less than two minutes for everyone to reach their life pods in any emergency situation.

It's been much longer than that.

The smoke, the screams, the fear, all contribute, but no one is calmly proceeding like they do during the drills. Everyone has gone insane, running here and there, crying and wailing.

I don't blame them, because I'm barely holding it together myself. Tears press hard against the back of my eyes. I'm nauseous and terrified. The only thing keeping me from being one of them is my death grip on Amara's shoulder and the pain of Jolie's fingernails digging into my arm.

The crowd turns against us, almost a mob. We can't keep moving ahead in our crouch, so Amara stands and Jolie and I follow suit. She fights to clear a path for us until we're against the wall. Then we work our way along it. We're moving against the crowd, which isn't helping, but still we are making progress.

"Run," a dark-haired man screams, grabbing Amara as he appears from the smoke. He's wild-eyed, mouth open as if he's going to keep screaming for no purpose. He shakes Amara roughly. She jerks away from him, breaking his grip. "They're that way."

He lets her go and shoves past us. I turn to look after him then back at Amara.

"Ignore him. They're all in a panic," she says, waving at the pressing masses, and then continues forward.

The crowds thin as we press ahead until we're no longer being crushed against the wall. We go less than a dozen feet more when a blood-curdling scream crests over blaring alarms.

"NOOOO!!!!!"

The scream echoes off the walls and through the smoke. My blood runs cold, goosebumps form on my arms, and my stomach clenches into a hard knot. Acid burns its way up my throat as I freeze in place.

The sheer terror in that cry hits something primal. Adrenaline dumps into my body and I'm stuck between fight and flight for a heartbeat. Amara isn't.

Amara leans in, her hands clenching into fists as she steps forward. The smoke swirls around us like wispy walls that obscure our vision. Amara breaks the illusionary walls with a wave of her arms and keeps moving.

My heart is pounding so hard it feels like a kettle drum in my chest building to the crescendo of bursting free. I twist my wrist to grab Jolie's arm and tighten my grip on Amara's shoulder, letting her drag us forward.

My ears are ringing. Breath is shallow. My steps are heavy, an effort of will to keep moving, but I can't not. Someone is in trouble. Someone needs help. How could I stand aside?

The smoke dampens sound. There are still sounds of fighting, running feet, even screams, but it's as if all of that is happening in another world. There's nothing here but the three of us and the acrid, coppery tang of smoke assaulting my nose and the back of my throat.

Amara speeds up, muttering something under her breath that I can't catch. I'm stuck in awe and admiration of her courage. I only wish I had some of it myself. I'm a researcher. Courage wasn't part of the job requirements.

I feel a cool breeze, then there is a break in the smoke as we step into an intersection of halls. Ahead, I see the outlines of three big human shapes. They must be men by their size; no three girls are that bulky. They're standing in a group with their backs to us, staring down at the floor.

The tension in my chest eases, then I see what they're looking at, and the massive hand clenching my chest tightens convulsively. I squeak. It's not brave or courageous. I don't mean to make the sound, but behind that expression of my fear rushes rage.

It doesn't matter how scared I am. This can't be happening. I can't let it. One of the men turns toward us.

It's not a man. He has orange skin that looks like buffed leather. He opens his mouth to reveal sharp teeth. The mouth has two spiky protrusions coming out on either side. The top of his head is bald, but there are black, dreadlock-looking hair or tentacles around the sides and back with metallic bands up and down each individual strand.

His mouth moves, and a clicking, croaking sound comes out. The other two with him turn. I thought my heart was pounding before, but that was nothing. Now it's triple timing as the crescendo of this nightmare arrives.

My senses seem sharper. I notice tiny details like that they're wearing black space leathers. Outfits designed to double as spacesuits for short jaunts in the cold vacuum. They're armed with clubs, and one of them has a gun that he points at the three of us. There are bits and pieces of metal clipped in various points on their outfits. The shading of each of their skin is slightly different. The one with the gun has more splotches on his face than the other two.

And then I see the source of the scream. On the ground in front of them is a fourth man holding down a woman. The rage rushing in behind my fear fills me. I clench my hands into fists and take a step forward. This is not happening.

"Click-clack-grrr-snikt," the pirate with the gun says as he grins, showing sharp, nasty, yellow teeth.

"Oh no," Jolie cries.

Amara moves so fast even my heightened senses can't keep up with her. She grabs the gun, twists up at the same time she brings her knee up into his groin. There's a loud crack, then his head explodes and he drops to the ground.

Botanists don't go around armed. Regular folks like us don't have access to firearms on the ship, and I've never been interested in self-defense, but I am desperate to find anything like a weapon. There's a fire extinguisher mounted on the wall, so I grab it and run forward, waving it madly in wide, sweeping arcs as I go.

I scream, a wordless battle cry expressing all the rage I've never experienced before. The pirate on top of the girl has his pants around his knees. He looks up just as I swing and tries to roll, but I hit him straight across the top of his head.

There's a loud crack, a moment's resistance, and then a sickening softness as his skull caves in. Wetness splashes across me, and my stomach flips. Bile races up my throat, and it takes all my willpower not to drop to my knees and vomit. Keeping myself under control, I kneel beside the girl, and only then realize I know her.

As I reach for her, someone grabs my shoulders and I'm thrown backwards. My head cracks against the wall. Stars dance across my vision as everything blurs. I hear Jolie yell in rage. There's sounds of more struggling. I try to stand up, but something lands on my legs and I'm slammed back to the floor.

It takes me a moment to realize it's another one of the pirates. The lifeless body stares with empty, glassy eyes. I gulp air, forcing my stomach to not eject its contents, then push it off and pull my legs free.

I'm dizzy and nauseous. The smoke in the air, the blood, the fighting, and the adrenaline combine to make me sick. I don't think I can stand, so I crawl across the floor to Inga, where she's curled into a ball.

"Inga," I say, reaching her and cupping her face in my hands.

She jerks away screaming. Tears stream down her face.

"NO!" she screams, looking in all directions and scrabbling backwards.

"Inga, stop!" I yell and grab her hand. "It's me. You're safe."

Her eyes land on me, wild and crazed. She keeps fighting, but I get ahold of her with my other hand too. She focuses on my hand then looks up at me. At last I see them clear.

"Calista?" she says, her voice quivering.

"Yes," I say, pulling her forward into a tight embrace. "You're okay. We've got you. You're safe now."

She squeezes me and then lets go and pulls at her clothes, trying to cover herself. She's sobbing and shaking. My heart breaks seeing her like this.

"Come on, we have to get to the life pods," I say, wishing to comfort her and hurry her up at the same time.

Amara and Jolie close around and the three of us help her to her feet. I look at the lifeless bodies of the pirates. One eye stares at me as it glazes over. Bile rises in my throat. I gag and turn away.

"You okay?" Jolie asks, placing a hand on my back.

"I'll be fine," I choke out, forcing the bile back down. It's a lie, but I cling to it. He was alive, and I just... no, I can't think about that.

"Let's move," Amara orders.

We form a protective circle around Inga and continue. The ship rumbles. The floor vibrates so hard it feels like a blaring concert speaker beating against us. In the distance, we hear explosions.

"We're going to die," Inga sobs, barely keeping herself upright.

"No, we're not," Amara barks without looking back.

We come to a crossroads that I recognize. It's not one we should have reached. "We missed our turn," I say.

"It doesn't matter," Jolie says. "There's another life pod on this corridor."

"Fine, let's go there then," Amara says.

"How did we get turned around?" I ask, but as soon as I say it the sound of fighting echoes through the hall.

It's close and intense. Cries of pain accent the sounds of flesh hitting flesh. The four of us look at each other. We're scared, and even Amara doesn't seem sure on what we should be doing. Nothing in our lifetime of safety drills prepared us for a flat-out pirate invasion.

Space pirates are a myth, a bedtime story to scare each other with. They're not supposed to exist! Except they're here. I just killed one. My stomach clenches tight and burns with hot bile as I see that man, not that… alien lying there with his head bashed in. I did that. Oh god, what are we going to do?

"We have to push forward," Amara says.

"It's just a few yards that way," Jolie says, pointing the same direction the sound is coming from.

"Right, just a few yards," I say, looking into the swirling smoke. Jolie shrugs and gives a tentative smile.

I must have hit my point of overwhelm. A strange calm falls across me and I'm here. In the moment, sure I'm going to die, but not scared, upset, or angry. There's nothing under my control except what I do in the next moment and then the next.

"Well, if nothing else, we just Han Solo it," I quip.

"What?" Amara asks, looking at me like I'm crazy.

"*Star Wars?*" I ask, surprised she doesn't get the reference. "When they're outnumbered by the storm troopers, so he and Chewie make a wild charge in, blasting, the two of them against a dozen, and all the troopers run in fear thinking they're outnumbered?"

Amara stares blankly and shakes her head, but Jolie laughs. Inga chuckles softly, the first response she's given that makes it seems like she's going to be okay.

"Seriously? You've never seen *Star Wars?*"

"I prefer *Star Trek*," Amara responds.

I shake my head and sigh.

"Vulcans are sexy," Inga says, her voice soft and quavering.

Jolie laughs, a high-pitched, nervous tittering, but I smile, encouraging Inga. The sounds of fighting continue and seem to be coming even closer.

"Okay sure, I agree, but still. Does anyone have a better idea?"

"We have to reach the life pods," Amara hisses.

As if in response, there's a screeching sound and the floor jumps beneath our feet. I'm thrown into Inga, and together we smash into the wall. Looking back where we came, the smoke is flickering orange and red. Fire. Great.

"Fire," I say, my voice sounding hoarse.

The others look where I'm looking, and Amara curses.

"Let's go," she commands.

We crouch down and creep towards the sounds of the fighting. We move ahead, staying close to the wall. The crowds of people running are gone. The sounds of fighting grow louder, accented by distant screams, tearing metal, and a low rumbling sound. As we approach another intersection, it's clear that the sound is right around the corner. Amara holds up a closed fist, and we all stop. She peeks then pulls back and leans against the wall.

"Um," she says.

"What?" the three of us whisper almost in unison.

"I think she's winning," Amara says.

"Huh?" I ask.

Amara shakes her head and glances around just as another explosion rocks through the ship, causing the floor to jump then buckle. It knocks all four of us off our feet. There's a loud whistling sound, and then air is rushing past us like a strong wind blasting through the corridor.

I climb to my feet, then help Inga and Jolie. Amara is already up and looking around. The ceiling is ruptured. A crack has formed in the wall with pipes sticking out, one of which is spewing steam, and another has water pouring out.

Amara grabs the water pipe and works it back and forth until it breaks off in her hand. She looks at me then down at the fire extinguisher I forgot I was still carrying.

"You ready?" she asks.

"Whether you've seen it or not, this is totally a Han Solo," I say, hefting up my fire extinguisher.

We step into the corridor both raising our weapons high, and I yell a wordless battle cry. My heart races and my breath is coming in short gasps. Adrenaline-fueled fear has me in its grip.

I run beside Amara through the smoke. Up ahead is a group of bodies in motion, tearing holes in the swirling mist. The red flashing light glints off black space leathers, but there are glimpses of white too. As we run forward, two of the black-clad bodies go up into the air then land hard on their backs, not moving.

A woman clad in flowing white stands in what looks like a defensive position, facing us across a pile of unmoving bodies. I stop my forward charge, stumbling to a halt. This is not what I expected.

The woman is instantly recognizable. There isn't a soul on the ship that doesn't know her or her story. Lady General Rosalind, head of the ship's fighting force. She's a beautiful woman with long dark hair that hangs past her shoulders. Her hands are balled into fists with one leg forward so that she's in a slight crouch.

"Who are you?" she asks without relaxing.

"I'm Cal—"

My attempt to answer is cut off by another explosion, then the hallway turns sideways and I slam into the wall. The air rushes past us, whistling. I can't breathe. Amara slams down on top of me, and we're tumbling forward.

Gravity switches positions, pushing me against the wall so hard I can't raise my head. My vision grays at the edges. I struggle to not pass out.

I have to get our group to the life pod. This is it. The ship is too damaged. We're screwed. I strain with all I've got and manage to raise my head, but there's another explosion, and the last thing I feel is my head slamming back against the wall.

3

LADON

*S*canning the horizon, I close my protective lenses to filter out the harsh rays of the suns. The sands around my city are empty. As they should be, but vigilance cannot be set aside. This is my territory, and I will protect it.

My tail twitches reflexively, and the sound of it dragging across the sand and dirt of the rooftop blends with the hot breeze. I turn a full circle until I'm no longer looking at the desert but across my city.

The past is a gray fog that eats away at memory, slowly dissolving the images and recollections. I know, on some level, that once this city bustled with life. That I was not alone, there were others like me.

That was before the Devastation. Now, I am alone. It is as it should be. This is my city, my territory, no other may rule here. The twisted, broken buildings rising towards the sky are the bones of what was. What was is gone. There is only now. Only me.

Satisfied that no threats are approaching, I walk to the edge and look down. The wind gusts and I leap, spreading my wings and riding the drafts down in a spiraling descent. I land lightly and then walk towards home.

The wind whistles through broken windows and between piles of rubble. There's a scratching sound from my left and I stop, one hand going over my shoulder to grasp the shaft of my lochaber. The scratching scrabbles into the distance and fades. Once I'm sure it's gone, I resume my journey.

On my right are the rusting framework of a playground. I pause, something tugging from the fog, the bijass, that covers memory. Laughter. The memory blossoms so fully that it's as if I hear it instead of recall it. Ghostly images of young Zmaj playing, chasing one another.

The bijass rises and takes the memory away. Relief follows it. All that matters now is protecting my territory. Survive another day. One day that will bleed to the next. There are and will be no more children. My prime cock is hard and throbbing. I ignore it. It will fade soon enough. I gave up all hope of fatherhood long ago.

When I reach my sleeping quarters, I set my lochaber to one side and begin my evening routine, starting by checking every floor for intruders. It has happened that another has sought to challenge me for my territory.

The lower floors are in the worst condition, but I've done my best to fortify and secure them. Piling rocks to block holes in the outer walls, moving heavy machines and using those when available. I did that so long ago now all I have to do is look for tracks in the dirt that has settled since.

On one floor I note tracks. They're small, padded feet with four claws. Too small for another Zmaj, so no real threat. I debate hunting down the animal that has intruded but decide to let it be. Small rodents such that make these tracks can be helpful. They'll eat encroaching vines and insects. They're also too small to be useful for meat.

Thinking of meat, I finish my inspection then head towards my supplies storage. The box I keep meat in is slowly rusting but is still serviceable for now. I open the lid. Inside are three oil-skin wraps. I pull out the bottom one, and unfolding the leather, I inspect the meat. Holding it up to my nose, I sniff it then taste it with the tip of my tongue. Satisfied it's still edible, I toss one of the bite size chunks into my mouth and chew.

Once I finish my meal, I add the leather wrap to the pile next to the box. Tomorrow I will need to hunt and replenish my supplies. At the edge of my thoughts there is an echo of futility and despair. Those thoughts I push far away, and the bijass races in to fill the void.

I retreat into the bijass, grateful for the relief it brings. Simplicity. Survival and dominance. That's all the bijass allows for, no need for complex thought. No need for emotions or loss.

I growl, a low rumble that comes from deep in my guts, and head to my sleeping space. I pass by the technology of the broken and all but forgotten world. The clear walls of the individual booths lie dormant except for one that flickers to life, reacting to my presence.

I pause and look at the screen. My hands ball into fists as my tail rises straight up. Rage fills my head, fire burns in my throat, and I swing. In these moments it's as if I am two people in my own head. The primal part of me that is the bijass is reacting, destroying that which threatens its control. The other me is the me that thinks, and to some degree, remembers. That part of me stops the other part from destroying the offending screen. I know I might need it someday.

My fist strikes empty air and I growl, struggling for control. The screen flashes its images. Showing, over and over, when I lost everything. Struggling to remain in control against the rage and primal urges, I force myself to turn and walk away.

Tomorrow I hunt. I will survive because I don't know what else to do.

4

CALISTA

My head is pounding like a double bass drum being played by someone trying to break the sound barrier.

Double beat, single beat, double beat, single beat. I'm hot, really, really hot. I try to open my eyes, but it's too much effort. My mouth and throat feel like I've been eating sand, and my eyes are glued shut. I give up. I must be trapped inside a sun. It's so damn hot, and I just don't care to even try. I tell my hand to move, but it feels like it's a million miles away.

Someone moans, then someone else is crying. A grunt of pain echoes through my head, cutting through the pounding. My hand responds at last, slowly rising until it touches my forehead. I rub across my eyes. There's grit all over them, so I wipe it away the best I can. Everything feels distant, disconnected, and hard to accomplish. The simplest of tasks take monumental effort to push past the pulsing pain in my head. I don't want to be here. Don't want anything to do with this body. I try to retreat into the black unknowingness, but it won't come.

Giving up on blacking out, I force my eyes to open. My eyelids tear their way painfully across my eyeballs like they're sandpaper. When they open at last, I'm assaulted by bright light, which temporarily blinds me.

"Gah!" I cry out.

"Calista?" Jolie's voice comes from somewhere close by.

I blink repeatedly, trying to clear my vision so I can see my friend. "Yeah?" My voice sounds tentative even to me.

"Are you alive?" she asks.

"Maybe?" I still can't see, so I wipe at my eyes furiously until at last my vision clears.

I wish it hadn't. I'm on my back staring up at a red-orange sky with wispy clouds that look like purple bruises. Two blazing red suns glares down like the eyes of an angry god punishing me for having the audacity to look. I push off the ground, trying to rise to my elbows. As I do, my arms sink in to my wrists.

Sand, red sand dotted with massive chunks of steel, debris, and bodies, for as far as I can see. In the distance are rock protrusions that rise high above dunes, breaking the skyline and my line of sight. It looks like we're in some kind of valley in the middle of a desert.

"Wow," I exhale heavily.

A horizon. A real, honest-to-goodness horizon. In this one all too brief moment the pain and horror pauses, swept aside by the beauty and enormity of what I see. It's unbelievable.

"Damn," Amara says, whistling.

The momentary pause ends with a crash. Everything either hurts or aches, pulling my attention back to my body. I struggle to finish sitting up, and turn to see Amara on her feet and shielding her eyes while turning in a circle. I lie back down as my head explodes worse. It's so bad I'm sick to my stomach.

"What happened?" Jolie asks.

"We crash landed on Tatooine," I groan.

"It's Vulcan," Amara says.

"Is not," I grouse. "Sand, fucking sand everywhere. That's Tatooine."

"It's red and there's mountains, that's Vulcan," Amara replies.

"Fine." I fold to the *Star Trek* lover. "Get Scotty to beam me up so Bones can do something about this pain in my head."

JOLIE KNEELS BESIDE ME AND INSPECTS MY HEAD. Where she touches, sharp pain stabs through the regular pounding, and I cry out in surprise. She purses her lips and shakes her head.

"You got cracked pretty good," she says.

"I can tell," I say, rolling over and getting onto my knees.

"Be careful," Jolie says, helping me steady myself.

"Sure, all the time in the world for that," I say, standing up like an old, old woman.

Jolie holds on to me, and Amara comes and helps on my other side. I lean on them gratefully until the dizziness passes.

It takes a few moments for me to be able to stand and not feel that weird, woozy feeling. Once I can stand on my own, the three of us silently inspect the area. It's obvious we've crashed on a planet and not a hospitable one, but we're breathing. So there's that. The atmosphere supports human life, at least. That's a long shot right there.

A massive section of the colony ship is partially buried into the sand, rising up hundreds of feet into the air. There are other shards of what was our home dotting the landscape. Some of them might be whole enough to use for shelter.

"Damn," I exhale.

Bodies dot the landscape that might be alive or dead. Some are moving. A few people are on their feet, looking around lost and confused. I can't believe we survived the crash. Those of us who have are either the luckiest people in the universe or the worst off.

I can't embrace the enormity of what's happened. The degree of loss. Our home, everything we've ever known is... gone. None of which I can do anything about or with. A black swirling hole is in the middle of that which will swallow me whole into its unending despair.

Rejecting that, I embrace my scientific training. Logic. Logic and handle the immediate problems. The rest will wait for later. The heat is going to be the first thing. We can't survive long in this heat. We need shelter and water. My throat is as dry as all this red sand, and my skin is burning. I look at my friends and see they're flushing bright red too.

"We need to find shelter," Amara says. "Now."

"Yeah," I agree.

"That big section looks pretty whole and stable," Jolie points at part of the largest surviving chunk of the ship. It's a few hundred yards away.

"Probably our best bet," I say. "We can gather survivors on our way."

The three of us trek across the hot sand. The first person lying on the ground we come to didn't make it. Propriety makes me want to bury them or do something, but survival has to come first. The next one we come to is Inga. As we approach, she jumps to her feet and looks around wide-eyed.

"Inga!" I call.

She whips her head around so fast it makes my own head hurt worse.

"You're fine," Jolie says, running over.

"Where are we?" Inga asks, her voice cracking.

"Tatooine," I say.

"Vulcan," Amara says right on top of me. I glare at her and she returns it. "I won that debate, remember?"

"Right," I agree, sagging. "Vulcan."

Inga looks between us with tears welling in her eyes. Her fair skin is bright red and blistering already. We have to get to shelter and find water, or nothing else is going to matter. With Inga in tow, we continue on our way towards the broken piece of the only home any of us have ever known. Inga silently cries as we go. My head continues pounding.

We find a handful of others, but most of those we come to didn't survive. The survivors who are in better shape support the ones who need it as we form a train of the last of humanity.

As we reach the shadow of the ship, I'm dizzy, my knees feel weak, my stomach is cramping, and I'm nauseated. The others are not faring any better. The heat is incredible, too much to be dealt with.

I haven't seen any signs of life on the planet yet. Idly, I wonder about adapting our own plant life to survive here. Did any of it survive the crash? Are our labs in this section of the ship? We're going to need a reliable food source and water. If our labs are in this section, we might have the tools to handle one of those basic needs.

If not, then we have to find it on the planet. Which leads me to wonder if there is other life here. Are there aliens on the planet? Did any of the pirates survive? Did they crash with us? Are we facing other dangers besides the heat? Or are we alone on this planet and doomed to die?

"Finally," Amara sighs as we pass fully into the shade.

We work our way along the cool metal of the ship, trying to find an opening. It's huge, probably three to four hundred yards long and towering at least a hundred into the sky. It looks like a triangle with one point buried into the sandy ground. The sun is behind it, and the shade it casts is at least twenty degrees cooler than the blazing direct sunlight, but still hot.

A few times, someone faints, forcing us to stop and help them back to their feet before we can continue. Our progress is slow, too slow. If we don't find water soon we're all going to be passed out on the sands and dying shortly after that.

"I think that's the edge up there," Jolie says, pointing with a shaky arm.

Amara and I nod. I can't bear the idea of speaking anymore. My throat is too dry. I work my mouth, trying to force moisture into it, but get nothing. My sinuses are even burning, making me not want to inhale the air. I blink, trying desperately to at least force the grit out of my eyes.

We reach the edge of the ship and I lean against it, trying to soak up the small comfort of its coolness. Amara pushes forward and disappears around the edge. I dig up the willpower at last to follow and make my way around the corner. The sand pulls at my legs with every step, making everything even harder. This place sucks.

Once I clear the corner, the ship goes on for quite a way, but the first thing I notice is there's a tear and there are people moving in and out. They stop to look at Amara and me, and then a few of them rush over and embrace us. I fall into their arms, and they carry me and the others inside. As we pass through the flapping sheets of plastic into the interior of the wrecked ship, it's cool and dark and the most wonderful feeling I've ever experienced.

It's perfect. Cool, no sun, thank you all the stars in heaven, there's no sun beating on me!

They get our small group inside, and then Rosalind, the woman in white we met just before everything went to hell, walks up. She stands imperiously tall and perfect, like even the sun can't break through her defenses. She's flawless. I swear she's not even sweating, which is just weird. She stares and I stare back, too stunned and out of it to consider the rudeness or social implications.

It strikes me, suddenly, that she's not sweating because her outfit is space leathers. Those space leathers will also have an internal temperature control. Nice. I'm jealous, can I have a set too, please?

Rosalind finally purses her lips and frowns as if choosing her words carefully. "What is your specialty?" she asks.

I blink several times and squint. That's not anywhere in the realm of questions I expected, and I'm having a hard time making sense out of it. "Huh?" I ask in a display of utter brilliance.

"Your specialty? What was your job?" she repeats, speaking slower.

Maybe it helps, because it does penetrate the constant throbbing in my head, even if it's not the question I would have expected. "Bio-engineering," I answer. "Specifically pertaining to botany."

"Good, we'll need you."

"Good?" I repeat numbly. What does she mean good, I wonder? What if it wasn't good? "We need to find water."

The Lady General motions with one hand, without taking her eyes off our group. She is asking others the same questions, cataloging who has what skills. Some of the people already inside come over with containers filled with cool water. All of us grab them and gulp. The cold hits my throat like a soothing balm.

"Slow down," Rosalind orders.

My stomach cramps hard as the cold hits, and I double over in pain. Amara was smarter and sipped her water, where the rest of us gulped. The pain and nausea recede, and my headache returns with a dull pounding roar.

As I struggle to survive my own stupidity at taking too much water too fast, Rosalind questions the others with us on their specialties. She's assessing what assets she has to work with. Cold, calculating, and no nonsense. It lines up with everything I've ever heard about her. She has her job for a reason. She's one of the best tactical minds the ship has ever produced. Or so the hype around her says.

I stand up to face Rosalind. She has now turned her attention back to issuing orders to the other survivors. I clear my throat, and she looks in my direction.

"What happened? Where are we? How did we get here?" I ask.

She turns as the small group that came with me gathers closer. Jolie and Inga are clinging to my arms on either side, and even Amara has moved closer to listen. Rosalind sighs as she turns her full attention on us.

Some of the other survivors have stopped their gathering and organizing to listen as well. Rosalind looks around, pursing her lips, then comes to a decision. She moves a couple of feet away, climbs on top of several crates of supplies, and holds her hand up, waiting for the noise of conversation and people carrying crates to stop. We gather closer around her to listen.

"All right, all of you," she says, and her voice carries easily. "Here is what we know for certain. Our ship, our home, was attacked by space pirates. They damaged the life support and sent the ship into an emergency survival condition. This means sections of the ship were sealed off to try to save as many people as possible. Unfortunately, because of the damage done, the sections broke off from each other. Our section crash-landed on this inhospitable planet. Survival is our first and only priority."

"What about rescue?" someone in the crowd asks.

"There will be no rescue," Rosalind says.

Gasps and cries of despair rise from those gathered. My stomach clenches into a tight knot as the enormity of the situation settles on me. I turn to Jolie, whose eyes fill with tears. Inga is gripping my arm tight enough to cut off the blood flow to my hand, which is tingling and numb.

"Damn," Amara says softly.

"We can survive," a beautiful blonde says, stepping forward to stand in front of Rosalind. Her hair is so light as to appear almost white and halo-like in the red sun piercing the shadows of our shelter. She smiles, and it's like a cooling balm passes over the crowd. "We have to organize. Work together and we'll be all right. Someone will rescue us eventually, but until then we have to work together."

Rosalind looks down at her and says, "Mei is right. We have to focus on immediate needs.

Gathering survivors, fixing this shelter, food and water. After that we'll handle those who didn't make it, but for now survivors first. In this heat we must be careful. Does everyone know the signs of heatstroke?"

Several people acknowledge they do among scattered mutterings.

"Who put you in charge?" a man asks from the crowd.

Rosalind looks for the source, but no one is stepping forward.

"I am Lady General Rosalind, Head of Armed Forces and Security. If anyone else feels they are more qualified than I to lead this mission of survival, then I welcome them to step forward."

"Right," a familiar voice says, and cold nails trace down my spine. "About that."

It can't be; of all the dumb luck. I scan the crowd, looking for the speaker, not daring to hope it's not him. He steps forward to stand in front of a group of angry looking people.

Gershom. I glance to Jolie, and she's as agape as I. This isn't Vulcan, Tatooine, or any other science fiction place. This is flat out hell.

"How can you be so sure there isn't going to be a rescue?" Gershom says. "There were contingency plans in place on the ship for such emergencies."

As my eyes scan the survivors, it's almost as if I can see rifts forming. None of us can be thinking clearly. We're all hurt, lost, and I can't even begin to grasp the enormity of what we've lost.

"I am sure," Rosalind says, "because rescue will be impossible."

"But there were contingencies? Safety protocols? Plans for emergencies. Did we not drill all our lives for every possible scenario?" Gershom asks, squaring his shoulders and meeting Rosalind's cold stare. The crowd around him murmurs, giving him their support.

"We did," Rosalind says. "And there were."

"Then you can't *know* that there will be no rescue," Gershom says.

My stomach clenches into a tight ball of worry, fear, and loss. I can barely breathe watching the two of them face off. What is he doing? She's the Lady General!

"No," Rosalind admits. "But to wait on rescue would be foolish."

"Oh, I don't disagree," Gershom says, switching his tactics like a snake.

He's agreeing with her, but the gleam in his eyes screams it's all part of his plan. He's always craved power. I've never seen it so clearly as I do now. In our lab he was a miniature tyrant, lording his power over everyone he could, but there it was more comical than dangerous. That's no longer the case, and I'm afraid.

"I'm glad to hear it," Rosalind says, turning away from him. "Now that that is settl—"

"Except," Gershom interrupts her, "your plans are a bit out of order, don't you think?" The crowd with him nods, and soft whispers of agreement rise from them. "The supplies that came down with us are undoubtedly very limited. I was in charge of the Biogenetics Research Lab, and I see some of my workers are," he's staring at me with wet lips and gleaming eyes, "with us."

"What's your name?" Rosalind asks, narrowing her eyes.

"Oh, I apologize," he says, taking another step towards her so that now he too is in the center of the survivors' attention. "My name is Gershom. On the ship I was in charge of all the researchers, so I am not only used to leading people, but I am also intimately familiar with food chains and the skills of my workers towards ensuring we have an adequate supply."

"*Bullshit*," Jolie coughs into her hand.

"Good," Rosalind says. Her face is inscrutable, but the calculations happening are clear. "I appreciate your help."

A girl with auburn hair steps forward from the crowd. I know her from the ship; her name is Lana. The moment I see her I feel inadequate. Even now, surviving a shipwreck, she's beautiful. Her full chest, ample curves, and perfect freaking skin. She's the girl guys go for, she's the one that gets the hunk in all those old vids. I'm so far out of her league we're not even in the same galaxy. She looks back at the crowd then up at Rosalind.

"What about the pirates? Did they crash too? Do we have to worry about them?"

"I've had a few scouts sent out, and we've seen no sign of their ship or them," Rosalind says.

"But does that mean we are safe?" Lana asks.

"What's your name?" Rosalind asks.

"Lana," she responds, one hand on her hip.

"Lana, I'm putting you in charge of a small team that will scout the area specifically to seek out any threats, pirate or otherwise, we need to be aware of."

"I don't—" Lana protests.

"Thank you, Lana," Rosalind says, cutting off her objections. "Your contribution is appreciated. Calista?"

Rosalind is pointing at me now, and my heart skips a beat.

"Y-yes," I stutter.

"You said you are a botanist—"

"Yes, she was one of my people," Gershom interjects, stepping closer to Rosalind.

Rosalind purses her lips then a tight smile forms on her face. She gazes across the assembled survivors. I follow her gaze and realize that more of us survived than I would have thought. The crowd is really big, big enough I can't see how many of us there are. Even so, it seems that a good chunk of people are listening to Gershom.

I swallow hard, trying to push down my revulsion. I don't know what it is they think he is. Maybe it's shock. How can any intelligent, thinking person want to follow him?

"I am a bio-engineering botanist," I say.

I don't miss the side-long glance that Rosalind gives Gershom or the way her eyes drift across the crowd. It's as if she's gauging his support and who is supporting her. I could be reading more into it than is there. My head hurts so bad and I'm still dizzy too, but I don't think I am.

"Okay, you three," Rosalind says pointing at Amara, Jolie and another person I don't know, "you all work with Lana. Patrol the immediate area looking for any threats or signs of our attackers.

"Gershom is right too, so Calista, I want you to get to study the local flora. We do need to establish food sources. Don't go out of sight of the ship. We don't know what is out there, but we've got limited man-power and need to accomplish many things at once. Any other questions?"

"I'm a botanist too, I could go with Calista," Jolie says, stepping up.

Rosalind gazes at her for a long moment as if considering it. "Okay, you're also looking for possible food sources, but split up. You will cover more ground that way. Anyone else?" Rosalind looks over the crowd imperiously.

"I'm used to dealing with these lab techs, have them report back to me," Gershom says.

Rosalind's eyes narrow, but Gershom is standing with his group of supporters surrounding him. Rosalind smiles, but there is no joy in it.

"Fine," she says. "Everyone get to your assignments! We've got a lot to do. Once we gather and store most of the supplies, we'll set up teams to care for those who didn't survive. Be careful—we know nothing of this planet and all our computers are gone. We're working blind."

The crowd disperses, and I turn back to my friends.

"Well, that was interesting," Amara says softly.

"Yeah," I say. "Guess we all have jobs to do."

"Someone has to take charge," Inga says.

"Jolie, it would be best if we go in different directions, cover the most ground," I say.

"I don't want you on your own," Jolie says.

"Yeah, me either, but I don't know how long our supplies are going to last," I shrug. "Besides she's right. If we're going to survive this, we have to divide up and get a lot done, or we won't last a day."

Jolie frowns then nods. Impulsively she grabs me and pulls me into a tight embrace.

"Be careful," she whispers in my ear.

"I will," I say. "What's the worst that could happen? A big, rugged barbarian going to grab and run off with me?"

She snorts. "Hey, could be fun."

"You two are impossible," Amara mutters, breaking the moment.

We part ways, all heading towards our assignments. I gather some water, salt tablets, and rations, as well as finding a poncho made of reflective cloth that will help disperse the heat.

I take it all, gear up, and head out.

Hopefully I won't get eaten by some crazy alien sand monster.

5

LADON

The herd of bivo circles, then stops and roots into the sand with their protruding tusks. I watch and wait. I've dug myself into the top layer of the desert, grainy dirt and sand covering my scaled skin. The alpha of this herd is larger than most I've seen, with a multitude of scars and broken spikes showing how many times he's defended his position.

Excitement swells in my chest, and I suppress an urge to hiss. I learned to control that impulse long ago. The slightest of sounds could alert the herd to my presence. This will be an excellent challenge, and his meat will be all the more succulent for his experience.

The sands drift beneath the constant warm breeze, shifting along the dunes as the huge animals search for food. Unexpectedly, the wind shifts and the alpha bivo lifts his mighty, fur-covered head and stares in my direction. He paws the ground and snorts, shaking his head violently. He's picked up my scent.

Knowing I've been exposed, I rise from my buried position, letting the red and white sands slide from my back. I stop in a crouch and adjust my grip on the lochaber in my right hand.

The alpha glares in my direction, snorting, and I meet the crimson eyes of my prey. He snorts again and shakes his head. I hiss, spreading my wings, my tail rising behind. The herd alerted to danger, but waiting for his signal, slowly moves away. He's the only fully adult male, and his females will not fight unless I attack their calves. Their defense is on him.

He stomps towards me, four steps, then stops and snorts again, shaking his heavy head. He's so close I can smell the animal scents of manure and dirty fur. He raises his head as far as his massive neck will allow, baring his root-stained teeth and bellowing a howling roar.

I hiss louder, flapping my wings and brandishing my lochaber. I shift my weight, bracing myself for his charge, leaning forward onto the balls of my feet. He's at least three tons of stampeding meat. If I'm not quick enough, he'll trample me, and then some other Zmaj will claim my territory and my city.

This is a challenge of dominance. The primal instincts of the bijass rush in, laying claim over my mind. *Mine.* No one and no thing will stand against me. Nothing will threaten that which is mine. I won't allow it.

The lochaber's long shaft is comfortable in my hand, extending ahead and behind me. I raise the blade that is mounted to the forward end so that the tip is facing the alpha. I rustle my wings, slap the sand with my tail, and hiss.

The alpha snorts, stomps, then bellows, meeting my threat. The muscles of his shoulders tighten, his eyes narrow, and his mouth curls back as he snorts. He charges. The ground trembles as he pounds across the shifting red sand. I hold my position, lochaber ready, muscles tense, my tail lashing back and forth. I pull my wings in close to my back.

Closer. My hearts slow as time itself does. I notice the way the sand jumps with each pounding of the alpha's hooves. I smell his foul breath. Feel the vibration of his hooves up through my legs. Not yet. I hold.

When his red eyes are so close I see their white edges and the grit gathered in the corners, I leap up. I spread my wings, catching the air, and for a moment I hang in the sky above the charging alpha, lochaber angled down, bladed edge gleaming in the sun. As the bivo passes beneath, I slam my tail onto its head between its eyes.

It roars in anger, but then gripping the lochaber in both hands, I drive the sharp point down. The edge slides into the bivo's vulnerable neck.

His roar shifts higher and becomes a bellow of pain and surprise as the weapon cuts through his hide. The blade lodges in his spine, and I can't keep my grip as I drop down.

I land for only a brief moment on its back. At the same time it bucks, convulsing as it tries to escape the pain. I'm thrown back up. Snapping my wings and shifting my tail, I twist in the air. I land to one side in a crouch.

A bivo is most dangerous when he's wounded, so I'm not going to take chances. The alpha bucks and stomps, charging blindly then whirling in a new direction when he doesn't make contact.

Blood runs over its eyes from the lochaber lodged in its neck. It's fighting blind, trying to free itself from the pain of the lochaber. He turns, snorting, then roars and charges forward in the wrong direction again.

He's slowing with the loss of blood. I do not want the creature to suffer, but I cannot risk trying to retrieve my lochaber while it's in the maddened state. The primal instincts of the bijass recede. Rationally I know there is nothing I can do to end this quicker, so I crouch into the sand and move in the subtle ways that partly bury me in the dune. It keeps my temperature adjusted and provides camouflage from any other predators while I wait.

The bivo charges at nothing and turns. His herd mills and lows in the distance, lost without their leader. Some other male will come and pick them up and the cycle will continue, so I pay them no mind. The alpha stumbles, falling to his knees, but then fights his way to his feet once more. He sniffs the air and must catch a hint of my scent, because he turns and faces me. My hearts beat faster and I tense, ready to move or attack.

He stomps forward. He makes it five steps before falling onto his knees. He huffs, snorting, but this time he won't be getting back up. He falls to his side, and I rise from the sand.

Grasping my lochaber with both hands, I jerk it free, then clean the blade with sand. I pull out my hunting knife and field dress the bivo so that the meat won't spoil. This will feed me for many months. Cleaning and dressing it takes time. I watch the herd as I work, making sure they don't take an interest, but they decide to wander off.

The suns move toward the horizon as I work. The temperature is dropping, and the cooler air leaves me feeling sluggish. I am harvesting the last of the meat, carefully wrapping the chunks in the oiled leathers and piling them onto the sled I brought for the purpose.

Some of the meat slides off the sled. I bend to retrieve it and then restack the packages. Then the world flashes so brightly that I'm blinded for a moment. I whirl around with hunting knife in hand, ready to face this new threat. Afterimages burn across my vision, making everything seem unreal and strange, but I don't see the source.

BADABOOM!

I'm thrown backwards by a wave of force, landing roughly onto my sled, knocking packages across the sands. Above me in the sky of Tajss is a spreading white ring, and something massive is falling towards the ground.

I climb to my feet and shield my eyes, closing my protective lids, and stare into the red sky. Another flash so bright it rivals the sun itself blazes. There are small white streaks streaming across the horizon, but the first one holds my attention. It must be massive, judging by how big it appears.

I tighten my grip on the lochaber while keeping an eye on the streak. Something massive is falling. I distantly remember such things happening. So long ago my memory of it is hazy. I know without any specific memory of it that once we traveled and traded with the stars. Now the stars look to return? If so, then I'll have whatever treasure is there first. No other can have it. This is, after all, my territory.

Looking south towards my city, I debate how far I will have to travel. My kill is mostly harvested, but the meat will only last so long without being cooked and properly stored. Still, the pull of treasure is strong, and I can hunt any time. There is no doubt that other males will have seen this event and want to claim the sky treasures for themselves.

Rage burns through my veins, and I hiss. The treasures from the sky will not wait. I must get there first. Decision made, I quickly secure the packages on my sled. The wrapped meat will be safe enough for now. Finishing that, I run across the hot, red sand. I spread my wings, using them to allow me to move across the sand with ease.

I'll investigate, gather whatever treasures I can carry, and take them back to my city. The center of my territory, my home where once there were so many of us. I wonder what it is that has fallen from the stars. As I run, it occurs to me, what if there are survivors?

Others came here, before the wars, before the Devastation. I hiss, thinking of the aftermath of war. The ancient cities like mine that are now ruins. My once proud race destroyed. How many years has it been since I've seen another Zmaj?

Too many, and there are no females. The females didn't survive the aftermath of the Devastation. My tail stiffens and shakes, thinking of females. I am among the last of my race. The handful of us who are left live with no purpose but our territory and the treasures we collect, with no heirs to hand them to. My thoughts spin while I run, racing to stake my claim.

At last I crest a dune and see the object on the horizon. The sun glints off its massive metal sides. It's so large it looks like it could be part of a city of its own. The structure looms high, standing over the dunes and hills in the distance.

There is debris scattered across the sand between here and there. I crouch down and study what I see before deciding to move closer. There are… things… moving across the sand. Creatures that are looking at the debris. They're dressed strangely, and despite the distance, I know they're not Zmaj. What they are I don't know, but I'm going to find out.

I move forward stealthily. The strangers wander across the sand, fighting it instead of working with it. They sink in and push their way forward. As I get closer, I see they have no tails for balance and no wings to offset their weight. They are very poorly made for survival.

Covering myself with the sand, I settle in and watch, studying them. They wander around, gathering items and carrying them back to the giant object. Scattered amongst the debris are other bodies, like them, which are not moving. A group of those that are walking go to them one at a time and poke at each of those lying down. Sometimes the ones lying get up, but most of the time two of the mobile ones grab the fallen by either end and carry them back to the object.

The suns lower overhead and still they wander around. One of them breaks off from the rest and marches straight off on its own. This one catches my attention. It's coming in my direction, looking around, oblivious to my presence.

As it comes closer, I see enough to define details of these new creatures. As soon as I do, I recognize by some primal instinct that it's a she. The features of its face are small, without ridges or scales. Delicate, like a fine milky glass, but pink from exposure to the sun. She has long hair that comes down past her shoulders. Her lack of a tail and wings is fascinating. It forces her to move much slower than would be ideal. She marches over the dune, so I follow, staying low to the ground so I won't be noticed.

Her hips sway as she walks in an enticing way that stirs thoughts and emotions I've not felt in ages. Not since before the war. I watch each movement with great interest as her hip moves left then right, left then right, swaying with each step. She pauses and glances around, then pulls a bottle from a bag at her hip and raises it to her lips. She has full, red lips that purse to take in the liquid, and they are as beautiful as the rest of her. Moisture beads on her brow and runs down. She wipes it away with one hand then shields her eyes and looks out across the dunes. Why is she leaking precious moisture like that? That is very wasteful.

She spots a plant in the distance and says something in a language that I don't comprehend before quickly moving towards it. Well, quickly for her, with her poorly designed body. Poorly designed, maybe, but it's fascinating. I want it. It's been so long since I felt my dragon stir with more than anger or need for dominance, I don't recognize at first what is happening.

Mine. Treasure.

Only then do I realize my claim. It's impossible. She's not Zmaj. I can't lay my claim. Rational thought pales before the certainty of the dragon. She is mine. The one meant for me.

I follow as she approaches the plant. She kneels then pokes at it and does other things with her fingers I don't understand. Apparently satisfied, she stands and looks around again. I hold still and let her eyes pass over me as I blend in with the landscape. She wavers after standing up, different this time than when she walked. It's not enticing but worrisome. Her skin is flushed a deep red, and moisture is no longer forming on her brow. She takes a long drink of the bottle from her bag, then fumbles and it drops to the ground.

She speaks, and the sound of her voice is the sweetest music I've ever heard. It stirs and warms my dragon. I would kill to hear her speak more, no matter I don't understand what she is saying.

She grabs the dropped bottle, shaking her head, then turns and walks back the way she came, but the sway is gone. She staggers and barely keeps herself upright. I debate revealing myself to her now but decide it's best to wait despite the dragon's urging to take her. I want to see what she is doing and ascertain her and the others' intentions. I'd like to know why they are here. Have they come for the epis? Is this the beginning of a new war?

I stalk her as she walks and staggers her way along, then suddenly she stops and stands up straight. She cries out, a wounded sound like a bivo that has been pierced, then she collapses to the ground. My hearts skip a beat. Is she hurt? Is that sound one of pain or pleasure? I hold my position just long enough to see if she moves again. When she doesn't, I rush forward and drop to the sands beside her.

Her eyes are closed, and her face and arms are flushed. Her lips are dry and chapped. It's clear that the heat is too much for her. She's not built for survival on Tajss. I look around and see no others of her kind. I can't leave her here. She needs help, and her companions are no better off here than she is, so they cannot do it.

I'll save her. I touch her face, then her hands. She's soft; incredibly so, it's strange. Oddest of all, her temperature is the same as that of the sand. Her skin lacks scales, so I assume she cannot be transferring heat efficiently. I dig into her bag and find the bottle I saw her drinking from earlier. I pour some of the clear liquid across her lips. It flows into her mouth, and at last she swallows. I pour some of the coolness across her face, then I gather her up into my arms. I look around, but none of her companions are near.

If I take her to them, I don't know how they'll react. They might try to take her from me. I can't protect her and fight them. No, the only answer is to take her home. She will be my greatest treasure.

6

LADON

The suns are close to setting. I'll need to find shelter soon. In the distance I can see the spires of my city, but I'll not make it before nightfall. After dark, the desert is far more dangerous, and I won't risk her safety. Looking around when I reach the top of a dune, I plot a course towards an oasis.

Shifting her in my arms to make sure she is as comfortable as possible, I run. It's a race to reach my goal before the dropping suns. If I don't reach it before nightfall, we're more likely to come under attack. The guster and the sismis are both cunning and hunt in packs. I can stand against them alone, but I can't protect her and fend off a pack at the same time. The ground trembles beneath my feet and I stop, dropping to a crouch. Resting one hand on the sand beneath me, I concentrate, trying to detect any shifting, no matter how subtle. A zemlja would be the worst thing that I could run into right now. They are enormous sandworms that live deep in the earth. They are the most dangerous predator on Tajss.

The sun drops lower as I wait, but it's a risk I have to take. The guster are less of a threat then a zemlja.

Zemlja hunt by vibrations. Their senses are keen enough to detect the breathing of a Zmaj if he's winded and breathing heavily. Carefully, I control my breathing and keep her off the ground to prevent the worm from detecting her. I curse the suns' steady descent as the shadows around me lengthen.

Nothing happens. The tremor doesn't repeat. I rise from my crouch and take a step forward, then another, pausing and listening after each, waiting for a telltale tremor. Nothing happens. A few more steps, pausing each time, and at last I'm satisfied that it was not a zemlja, so I resume a faster pace. I spread my wings and flap to gain speed. It's tiring and will drain my energy more quickly, but now I'm racing full dark. As I run, the stands of baoba trees grow larger as I get closer.

I slow down and come to a halt a short distance from the trees. Kneeling, I sift the sand with my hands, letting it fall between my fingers. I want to make sure there are no sand snakes hiding before I lay her down. I'll also need to deal with any cvet that are sure to be growing near the water. There might be other things to worry about as well. I won't go into the stand of trees unprepared. Satisfied that the ground is safe enough, I lay her down carefully. Her soft skin is an even brighter shade of red, but there is no moisture. I touch her cheeks and stroke along the lines of her jaw. She murmurs at my touch, making some sound that might be words. She's hot, too hot. I know by instinct alone if I don't cool her soon, she'll die.

I hiss almost involuntarily as I realize she needs epis. I cup her face in the palms of my hands, studying her. I don't have any epis. I haven't taken it in recent memory, and it doesn't last long once harvested. Gathering epis is dangerous and not something I can do easily.

Water first. Water I can give her, and there is a pond in the oasis.

I dig into her bag and pull out the small bottle of liquid, but it's empty. She'll have to wait until I get her into the oasis. Water will help. It has to; she has to survive. I want to know more of her, to understand her. How did she get here? Where is she from? Why is she so different from me and my kind?

I pull sand across her body to shield her from the fading sun and hide her from any casual predators. Taking some mesh cloth from my bag, I form a shield for her face that will protect her while still allowing her to breathe. Satisfied I've done all I can, I unhook my lochaber from my back and approach the oasis.

The baoba trees are arranged in a teardrop shape around the water. The cvet has grown at the base of a massive baoba that's larger than I could wrap my arms around. The plant trembles as I approach, its long leaves shifting slightly. The leaves and vines extend from its massive orange-and-red center.

I creep forward, my lochaber at the ready. Its tendrils slide on the sand, making a soft sound as they drag. A small bird chirps and darts down to enter the oasis, and the cvet attacks as it flies over the plant. The long leaves shoot up from the ground, snapping closed. The bird dodges and manages to avoid capture, but the tendrils are longer, like long green fingers, and more shoot up to grab the bird. It struggles, flapping its wings wildly, but to no avail. The long leaves that protect the center of the planet fall open, and the tendrils pull the squawking bird into the center. The bird goes silent as it passes through the trembling fronds of the cvet. The paralytic poison has taken hold.

The cvet is distracted with the snack, and I use the opportunity to strike. I leap up and forward, using my widespread wings to float down. I keep my lochaber held two handed before me with the point down. I thrust as soon as I'm in range, driving the point straight through the plant's mouth into its simple brain. The cvet trembles and shakes while its tendrils and leaves flop around violently, trying to find me. Two of the tendrils grab my right leg, and one closes around my throat. It squeezes, cutting off my air. I pull my lochaber back and twirl it around, sweeping the blade across the tendrils in a long, severing stroke.

They fall free, and I gasp in air as I flap my wings to carry myself past the plant. Landing in the center of it would result in my being paralyzed for several hours. Dangerous for me in the best of situations, but it would certainly spell doom for my rescued treasure.

I land lightly and turn towards the cvet, crouching to make sure that my aim was true. It trembles one last time, then all its leaves collapse and it is still. I poke it with my lochaber to make sure, but it doesn't respond. Only then do I know for certain it presents no more danger. Satisfied, I return to where I left the female. She remains unconscious, so I uncover her and lift her into my arms. I carry her into the oasis, picking my way around the cvet. Inside the trees I hear the soft bubbling sound of water.

As I pick my way through the trees and undergrowth, getting closer to the water, I see there are fresh tracks in the wet sand surrounding it. Bivo and guster have both recently been here, but that's good. If they've recently had their fill of water, they'll be out hunting. That lessens their threat for the moment.

Gently, I lay her down beside the pool and cup cool water in my hand. I pour it slowly across her forehead and then drizzle it into her mouth. She swallows reflexively, and a soft moan comes from her chapped lips. I brush her hair from her face. It's soft. Softer than anything I can recall ever having touched before.

The suns are setting, casting a purple-orange glow as they dip below the horizon. I hear the first cries of sismis as they take to the air to hunt. Here, under the shade of the baoba, we'll be safe from them, at least.

I harvest the fronds of the cvet I killed, and then I cut some low branches from a tree. Using the limbs, I make a frame over where she lies and cover that frame with the fronds. It's a rudimentary but effective cover, big enough for the two of us to shelter in. Once I'm satisfied, I sit next to her and dribble water into her mouth every so often. It's the best I can do for the moment. She needs epis, life force, but I can't leave her to go and harvest it.

She's wearing layers of clothing. I take the cloth and rub it between my fingers. It's thick and not designed to allow for breathing. Instead of exchanging heat with air, it's trapping heat inside, which is making her hotter. I must remove her clothing to expose her flesh to the cooling night air.

The light is fading, so I lean in close and examine her clothing. Her scent is delightful. As if she is bathed with hints of the most pungent of delectable flowers. It's distracting, pulling my attention from my purpose of cooling her. I pull my attention away from such luxuries and focus. Her chest bulges strangely, and for some reason this also seems enticing. It rises and falls with her breath.

I force myself to focus on the task at hand and see that there are small fasteners down the front of her covering. They are shiny, glinting in the fading light of the suns. I take hold of one and turn it back and forth to determine how it functions.

It's attached to one side of the cloth then forced through a small hole. Interesting. I break three of them before figuring out the correct motions to release these clever fasteners. They do not take nearly as much force as I expected to be undone.

As each of the fasteners releases, more and more of her skin is exposed. It's a pale pinkish color, still without scales or protection. It's smooth, so smooth and soft as my fingers brush against her. Fascinating.

Gently I pull aside the cloth, not intending anything overt except to help her body to cool itself. Her breasts swell, peeking out from beneath the soft cloth of her covering. It seems they are external all the time. Different from Zmaj women, whose breasts were protected by scales that opened only for the feeding of children or mating.

Hers are protected only by some more cloth, which is stretchy in nature. When I pull on it, it snaps back. Studying it, there are straps that run up across her shoulders and around to her back. Once more I'm leaning in close, examining this feature and trying to figure out why such an inefficient system was developed. It makes no sense.

The straps going up to her shoulders also stretch and snap when I pull on them. No matter where I look there do not seem to be any connections where it might part. Almost it seems as if it has been sewn directly on her to form the cups that protect her breasts.

I frown and continue my exploration. It must be attached somewhere, as this is obviously not part of her body. She groans again, so I dribble fresh water into her mouth then return to my exploration of this difficult cloth. I trail my fingers along the mounds of her breasts. They're so soft and full. Desire stirs as they mold to the pressure of my fingers.

Gripping under the cloth cups, I pull down, and the flesh springs free with a small bounce. Dark circles rest in the center, and my desire grows. My prime penis extends and hardens. Oddly, I wonder what they taste like, but I push back that urge.

Leaning in closer to study the dark circles, I trace them with my fingers, and the middle point stiffens and extends upwards, straining out.

Mine. The dragons claim is strong, and I growl involuntarily. A shudder runs down my spine and my hard primary cock stiffens even more, desiring to take her, but that is not my purpose. I am saving her, not having her. I sniff between her mounds, and the smell of her is exotic, enticing, and makes my mouth water.

It takes an effort of will to tear my attention from the flesh mounds, but she groans once more, reminding me of her condition. Her soft, pale skin is hot to the touch. The lack of scales leaves her vulnerable to damage and heat. I dribble water across her, and rivulets run down her breasts, cooling her skin.

Giving up for the moment on removing the protection over her breasts, I turn my attention to the rest of her. Her sides curve in, then swell out where her pants sit on her hips. At the lower part of her stomach is a hole that does not look like new damage. Is this a scar? It rests just above the waistband of her pants and goes into her flesh. I push a finger into it, and it only goes a very small distance. She wriggles as I do, and I look at her face, thinking perhaps she will wake, but she doesn't.

The waist of her pants is stretchy with no fasteners I can see. She is still burning up, so I grab the pants and slide them down. The way her hips swell out then slim down at her legs is interesting and sexy. As the pants slide down, fur is revealed at the cleft of her legs. It gives me pause. How strange she is! An enticing, musky scent wafts to me as this fur is exposed, and my currently erect cock throbs with pent-up need and desire. How long has it been since I've been with a female? The memory is fuzzy and distant. Before the Devastation. After that, the females all grew sick. That's all I remember of that time. Time and the bijass has covered those memories with gray fog, but it's okay because there are some memories I don't want.

Tossing the pants to one side, I let my finger trail along her legs. Still no scales; interesting. No protection, no system for heat exchange—no wonder she's doing badly.

Epis is the only thing that will keep her alive. I'll have to harvest the epis alone. It's too dangerous to do with her. What will I do with her while I do? I can't leave her like this. She must wake up. Unconscious and unable to fend for herself, I have no idea how I will keep her safe long enough for me to harvest any epis. In order to do so, I'll have to go underground and travel the zemlja tunnels.

Facing the earth dragons is foolish but not the only danger. Sismis use the caverns as well, and sometimes the guster use them as a place to lay their eggs. It's mating season for the guster, so the odds of running into a pack underground are high.

I have no choice. I must get her awake then get the epis for her. I know I will protect her. She is beautiful, a perfect treasure. The scent from her fur pulls me in. I move closer, pushing her legs apart so I can get a better look. The flesh under the fur has folds that slit down the middle. It's fascinating. I touch along the edges of the opening. The fur is soft and curly to my touch. The light pressure of my fingers pulls at the point the flesh meets, and it opens up to reveal glistening pink. I move in closer still; the heady scent is almost overwhelming me with desire and need.

Placing my fingers on either side, I pull apart, and the opening unfolds before me like the petals of a flower. Inside it's moist and pink with the most amazing smell. Using my thumb and forefinger to keep the flower open, I then touch the interior folds with my free hand. Gently I probe at the soft folds, and to my amazement find a tunnel that leads into her. This must be her reproductive channel, different from a Zmaj, but not that much. Less protected, more open, but everything about her is more open and less adapted to life on Tajss.

She moans and squirms as my finger slides into her, and I hope that this will cause her to wake, but as I pull my finger out, she stops. It is the most reaction I've been able to get out of her yet. Leaning back, I contemplate. If I continue, will she awaken? Is this a peculiarity of her species?

This is very bold and forward. If she were a Zmaj female, this would be of a mating nature, but she's an alien. Is it the same for her species? I cup her face in my hands and feel she is still burning. The water is not enough; she is not awakening, but she is breathing and obviously alive.

How do I protect and care for her? I need her awake, alert, so I can put her into a safe space then go and get epis. She's flushed, and her breath is shallow if steady. I could take her into the water, but there is danger in cooling her too fast. A rapid change in body temperature might be too much for her.

Desire rages in my core. I can see we'd be sexually compatible, and I want nothing more than to mate with her, to be joined with her in the ritual of mating. She is my treasure. The other half of me thinks Tajss brought her to me, but more important than that is ensuring her survival. There will be time for mating once I've gotten her safe. First and foremost I need to get her awake.

Having no better ideas and only one thing raising a response, I trail my finger around the soft folds lining the tunnel. I prod along, examining the structure. A bit of flesh at the top of the opening protrudes out like a button waiting to be pushed. Uncertain of its function or purpose, I touch it lightly. She startles, moans, and shifts her hips from one side to the other. My cock jerks hard, and the first hints of my sperm leak out. My second penis stirs from within the sheath of my tail as well, preparing for its duties in response to the leaking of the first. My tail lashes involuntarily. I breathe deeply, concentrating on remaining in control of my physical desires.

Having gotten a response, I run my finger lightly over the button, and she moans loudly, then jerks upright. Her eyes are wide as she looks around.

When she sees me, she screams with a wide-open mouth and crawls backwards until she's at the rear wall of the shelter I built. She is shaking her head and her mouth is moving, making sounds I'm sure are words, though I don't understand them. I hold my hands up, open, facing her to show I am not a threat.

"You're safe," I say. I motion towards myself. "I will protect you."

She pulls her legs up against her chest and wraps her arms around them, looking around and continuing to say words that don't communicate anything to me. I hiss and shake my head with frustration.

She pulls at her clothes, covering herself. I wait a moment, watching. She's awake, but now what? How do I communicate with her? How do I get to know her? The container with water she had lies on the ground beside her. I move to reach for it.

She screams and I jerk back, almost falling out of the shelter.

7

CALISTA

My body shudders, then I jerk to awareness. Confusing signals overwhelm my foggy thoughts. My mouth is dry, so dry I can hardly swallow. My head bounds and my eyes ache, but still something feels good. Pleasure barrels through my brain in contrast to the exhaustion, dryness, and mild nausea. Opening my eyes, it feels like the lids are tearing across my eyeballs and dragging sandpaper across them.

My eyes don't want to focus. I blink several times before my vision clears. I must have passed out, but that's not open sky over me. I was in the desert. Why does it look like leaves overhead?

I'm not sure if I'm awake and alert or trapped in some weird dream. This can't be real. We crashed. I went out in the desert to try to find some plants, not far from the shipwreck. That's the last thing I remember, so this must be a dream.

Waves of pleasure crash across my body. This must be some kind of sex dream. A moan slips out of my lips, because damn it feels good. I'm really horny and this is a dream, so why not go with it? I move my left hand to my pussy, responding to the half-awake urge.

I close my eyes and move my hips into the source of pleasure. Then it hits me that my hand isn't there yet. I snap my eyes open and rise onto my elbows. Then I see him, and I scream.

There's a man between my legs looking up the length of me in surprise. He's not a human man either. My heart leaps into my throat and I barely manage a scream as my breath rushes out. I scrabble backwards, totally in flight mode as I try to escape.

I back up against something solid, and the roof of leaves rustles as I hit it. Now it hits me that I'm mostly naked. My shirt is open, my bra has been pulled down, and my pants are gone. This isn't a dream, it's a nightmare. Except, god help me, I'm pretty sure I'm awake. I wish I wasn't.

He looks at me and then holds his hands up, palms out, facing me. We stare at each other. I pull at my clothes, trying to cover myself. I've got so much adrenaline pumping through me I might be able to take him. I pull my legs up then wrap my arms around them, trying to cover myself the best I can.

He moves towards me and I scream once more. He immediately stops, jerking back so fast he almost falls over. He holds his position, barely inside what I'm realizing is a makeshift shelter. I attempt to swallow to force my heart back down into its proper place. It's almost impossible, my throat is so dry.

"Who—no, *what*—in the hell are you?" I ask, my voice cracking.

Only thing I'm sure of right now is that he's not human. I blink rapidly, trying to force moisture into my eyes. My throat is scratchy and hurts. I'm dizzy, light-headed, and still nauseated. The muscles in my shoulders and back are cramping, and I just woke up naked with this alien man between my legs. To say I am confused is an understatement.

He leans forward like he's going to come closer.

"NO!" I scream, shaking my head. "Stay back, stay away from me."

I scrabble, but can't retreat any further than I have already. He stops moving forward then scoots backwards. Does he understand me? His mouth moves and a hissing sound emerges, like someone speaking with a lisp dragging out *s* sounds. I shake my head, not understanding. He seems to frown, or maybe he's thinking about eating me. Maybe in more ways than one. My pussy clenches at the thought.

"Give me a minute, just stay there, don't eat me," I say as much for myself as for him, having no idea if he understands me or not.

He settles into a sitting position and stays there. I relax a little and try to assess the situation. This is like research—observe, evaluate, decide. Emotions have no place in research, and they are not going to serve me well here either.

Mentally I cloak myself in my scientific background, like the donning of mental armor.

Outside my armor, I'm freaking out, but here on the inside it's nothing but logic and calm. I'm channeling my inner Spock. Amara would be proud.

Okay, I'm on a planet for the first time in my life. My heart speeds up and my breath comes faster as the outside maelstrom of fear and worry seeps through my protective shielding. No, no emotions. Focus, observe, evaluate; my training kicks in again. Okay, observe.

I'm in a structure that seems to be made of sticks that are covered with some kind of plant material. It's not large, about the size of a pup tent, barely big enough to accommodate the two of us. So, temporary. Odds are he built this shelter recently as protection. If he built a shelter and placed me in it, that means eating me is off the table. Okay, that's good. Well, maybe not good. His... exploration... probably combined with multiple near-death experiences, has kicked in my most primal instincts. Logically I know that's what it is, also known as being horny, not logical at all, but my clit is throbbing. Focus!

The alien is watching closely but doesn't move, so I continue my observations. It's the obvious conclusion that I had a heatstroke and passed out. I last remember being surrounded by sand as far as I could see. The ground I'm on now is solid, more dirt-like, and there is a rough-bladed species of grass. I run my hands around myself. The grass is thick and almost sharp on the edges. A hardy breed, which also means logically this must be an oasis. Grass and plants can't grow without water.

Looking up, I study the leaves and the sticks that form the shelter he made. The sticks are not thick, but they look very strong. They have a thick bark but have grown crooked, waving along their length. Some parts of it are thicker than others, and I'm sure if I studied it in my lab it would show different amounts of water having been available during different growth stages. All of which further supports the oasis theory.

The leaves are very thick and shiny, almost rubbery in appearance. Deep greens with strong orange tints along the midrib and running out across the veins. I'd love to take samples to my lab and look at them under a microscope.

My lab. Gone.

The loss hits as if someone drove a massive ball of pain into my guts. Instantly I'm crying. Tears streaming down my face before I have time to process what is happening. I sob, shake my head, and rub at my eyes, trying to stop myself. Desperate, I claw back the protective mental armor of logic, trying to don it once more.

The alien shifts, leaning in. I yelp in surprise more than fear and he freezes, staring. He has sharp eyes that are a beautiful green shade, but the pupils are not human. They're slits like a cat or lizard. A lizard makes sense, looking at him. Scales, tail, even wings.

I can't let my thoughts wander or I'll lose my shit. So I focus on him, the alien. Scales—he has a light pattern of scales around the edges of his face that gradually grow larger as they go back. They shimmer in reflected light that must come from a moon outside our small shelter. There are horns that protrude from his forehead along a hard ridge of bone. He has dark, almost-black hair that lies close to his head and falls back to just above his shoulders. They run along the edge of his head and down the back out of sight.

The skin beneath the scales is a light tan-ish color with yellow and blue accents along the edges. It's fascinating and scary all at the same time. He's also big. Really big. He must be seven feet tall at least. The tips of his wings protrude above his shoulders, and I saw a tail when he was falling out of the shelter.

He's wearing a soft, loose-looking shirt that billows out around him. It looks like it's made of some mesh material that lets it breathe. Makes sense for the environment. Okay, so observe then evaluate. What do I know? He's particularly adapted to heat and sand, so logic says he's a native to this planet.

Logically it would seem where genetically my race is descended from apes, his is descended from some kind of lizard. Does that mean he's cold-blooded? Wouldn't that be fascinating?

Hmm, yeah, he is sexy in a strange kind of way. His face is finely sculpted, perfectly proportioned with a strong nose and gorgeous eyes. He's shirtless, I assume by choice, but it makes it really clear he's humanoid, at least where I can see. His overall shape is humanoid and the exposed flesh of his chest and arms is definitely human-ish. If said human was freakishly tall, super fit, and muscled to the extreme, but human enough.

They're legitimate observations, I justify to myself. It has absolutely nothing to do with the distracting and almost right on the edge of overwhelming biological urges of my body going crazy, thinking it's going to die without having left a mark on the universe.

Which brings my attention back around to what probably should have been my first concern. Why am I naked? Kind of an important question, I think. Naked, and was he... The thought veers off, because I don't know where it can't be that. He's an alien on a planet millions if not billions of light-years from where my race originates. He couldn't have been, could he? Was it some kind of foreplay? Exploring? Getting ready to rape me?

Factually, I did come to consciousness horny. Really really horny, and he was between my legs. Right up close and personal with my pussy. It isn't a big leap of logic to think that he might have been...

No data and facts only. Observe what is, no speculation allowed. Focus, observe and evaluate. I'm naked, fine. I look around and see my pants are next to where I woke up. A surge of relief hits, making my head spin. I grip the grass, close my eyes, and wait for it to pass. I didn't realize how worried I was about not having any protection from the sand and heat of this planet.

Before I open my eyes, I sense him moving and I yelp, eyes springing open as I curl back against the makeshift wall. My heart races but I'm frozen, nowhere to go, completely at his mercy.

He stops, staring. Neither of us move. I don't even see him breathe, and I'm sure I don't. Nothing happens as the moment stretches. My lungs burn but my heart rate finally slows.

He points with his right hand, never taking his eyes away from mine. His mouth moves and a soft sound emerges that might or might not be words. My ears are ringing and I'm acutely aware of the pain in my head. All signs of dehydration and a heatstroke. He makes the same sound again and motions with his hand.

I make a furtive glance towards where he's pointing, keeping him in my peripheral. My water bottle rests on the ground next to the leaf wall. When I look back at him, he makes the sound again and then slowly reaches past. He picks up my water bottle and holds it out.

He doesn't come any closer than he has to, the bottle hanging halfway between us. I eye it carefully, looking from it to him, then I reach out and take it. He nods as I uncap it, then drink greedily of the cool refreshment inside. Nothing has ever tasted so good. I gulp it until I'm lightheaded and have to stop to breathe. Wiping my mouth, I hand the bottle back and watch as he takes it, sips, then puts the top back on and sets it to one side. He scoots closer and this time, despite my heart pattering faster, I don't exclaim out loud.

He doesn't come too close, which helps, only enough so that he's inside the shelter he built and not half out of it. Nervously, I smooth my shirt then fasten the buttons. I'm acutely aware of his eyes watching every motion, as if he's committing the actions to memory.

Shirt fastened, I meet his eyes for a moment, but I can't hold his gaze. I'm still antsy and I don't have on any pants, which is awkward at the best of times. I force a smile, because being friendly is always better when dealing with an alien.

Calista's rules of alien first contact, coming to a reader near you soon.

I snicker and his eyes widen, then he frowns. I place my hand over my mouth to keep myself from sliding into a mix of heatstroke and hysteria. Slowly the corners of his lips turn up. Surprisingly, his lips are soft looking and full. I wonder what they might taste like? What would it be like to kiss an alien dragon-man?

It's the heat. I've lost my damn mind when I had the heatstroke. Kissing the alien? Seriously? I mean, he is sexy. Exotic too, but get real, Calista. He's an alien with alien biology. I have no idea how he procreates, our compatibility, or hell, even his name!

"Who are you?" I ask, my curiosity aroused.

He watches my mouth move, so I repeat the question. He leans closer, his eyes fixated on the shapes of my mouth, but he doesn't speak or indicate any understanding.

On board the ship, we all spoke Galactic Common. Everyone does, though some old holdouts keep their native language too. Everyone in the galaxy speaks Common. Where the hell have we crashed that he doesn't know it? Vulcan, right, well if only I'd been geek enough to learn to speak Vulcan. He doesn't look like Spock, though, and I sure as hell ain't Captain Kirk.

"Name?" I ask, trying again.

Tentatively I point at him. I can only hope that a pointing finger isn't an insult to his kind. The way my luck has been so far it could be a rude gesture that will anger him.

He cocks his head to one side then opens his mouth and makes a sound that contains a lot of *S* sounds and a bit of hissing. I shake my head, not understanding. I'm confident he's intelligent and relatively sure he has a language. He waits for me to respond, then repeats the same sounds again, making me certain that he does have a language. It's not one I understand, but obviously it is one. I shake my head in frustration.

"I don't understand," I say, motioning with my hands like that will help.

He slides closer, and my stomach tightens and my pussy grows wet. There's an exotic musk coming from him that is causing my body to react beyond all rationality. He'd been... examining me, and he really is quite attractive. I can't keep myself from wondering what he'd look like without those pants. Despite the obvious lizard slash dragon descendant marks, he's not that different from a man, at least from what I can see.

Sure, he's got a tail, wing, and scales, but he's man shaped. His bare chest is formed the same as any guy. Well, any guy who is really, really buff. His arms are forearms, biceps, triceps, like any human. He's got scales covering his exposed skin. He was made for surviving a desert.

He repeats the series of sounds then motions towards me. I shake my head and sigh. The motion of his hand is a grim reminder I still don't have my pants. Which calls even more attention to how turned on I am.

In some really weird way it feels like I know him. Absolutely ridiculous and impossible, but still. It's kind of like when I met Jolie. In minutes of meeting each other we knew we'd be friends for life. We were finishing each other's sentences, loved the same things, we were like life-mates that were meant to find each other.

There's no science to that, but even though I'm a scientist, I know there are some things we don't understand yet. Human relationships is a wide open field with a million little things no scientist can explain.

All of which is justifications for the fact I'm having dirty thoughts about banging this alien I just met. As if I'm the kind of girl that does that on a first date. Well, first kidnapping, sort of. I mean, did he technically kidnap me? I was passed out in the desert, and there is not a doubt in my mind I'd be dead if he hadn't captured me.

It's wrong, though! What the hell am I thinking, getting off on an alien?

He motions, lightly tapping his chest, then gestures with his open palm towards me. He speaks, more syllables which I assume means more words. He touches his chest once more then he moves his hand towards me. Partway to me he pauses, as if waiting for me to stop him.

I should—rationally I should, but I'm not feeling rational. If anything, I'm feeling primal. I can blame all that I've gone through in the last two days. I can blame the heat. I could blame a lot of things, but the truth is I want this. I want him to touch me.

When I don't stop him, he continues his reach and touches my thigh. His hand is cool on my skin. A thrill runs along my nerves. His touch is exciting, enticing, and so damn wrong. I shouldn't do this.

I shift to break the contact, but the delay in my action seems to encourage him. He touches my other leg just above my knee. His eyes are locked onto mine, watching for any protest. If I say no, he'll stop. I'm as sure of it as I am my own name. Only problem is, I don't want him to stop. Not in the slightest.

He traces a path along my thighs up from my knees to the sides of my hips. Electric chills race along to my spine then up and through my core as he moves closer to my erogenous zones. I'm really wet and ready to go.

I shiver and he stops, looking into my eyes. He says something, but who the hell knows what. This is nuts, insane even—I can't let this man, this alien, do this to me. Well I can, obviously, but I shouldn't. But I don't want him to stop. Desire is a pulsing need in the tight ball of my lower torso, and I want nothing more than to be pleasured by him. No matter how wrong it is. He runs his hands up and down my legs, light strokes that leave my skin burning in the wake of his fingers. He goes up and down several times then up across my arms. I'm breathing in short gasps, and my heart is racing. I shake my head.

"No," I whisper, biting my lip. "No."

He doesn't stop. His strong hands grip my knees and push down. I want to resist—I try, but my desire outweighs rationality. I give to his gentle, but insistent pressure and straighten my legs, leaving me exposed.

I cross my arms over my chest in some reactive aspect of modesty. His intense eyes bore into mine then drop to between my legs. He trails a finger across the top of my foot. Warmth flushes my skin beyond the heat of this place.

He speaks again, and it ends with a soft hiss. Strong fingers knead the muscles of my calves, working up past my knees and onto my thighs. My legs part as he massages, almost like they have a will of their own. He's in control, and I don't stop him. I should, I should want to, but it feels so good as he works up closer and closer to my sex.

"I can't," I protest. "This is wrong. I don't know you, know if we're even compatible."

He looks up, pausing and cocking his head to the side. In this moment I know I can stop this. I'm in control; he's not going to do anything that I don't want. I understand this somehow. We may not be able to communicate with words, but he seems to get that I'm protesting, and he waits for my assent to continue.

I bite my lip, knowing I should say no, but my clit is pulsing with a desperate need I can't ignore. I don't say anything else, and he moves again. With one hand he uses thumb and forefinger to form an upside-down V that pulls my silky folds apart. Slowly, so slowly it drives me mad, I watch the index finger of his other massive hand approach. When it reaches my wet silk, a shudder rips through me as he drags that finger up through the layers of my sex and then lightly grazes across my clitoris.

I hear myself moaning, and my hips buck forward, wanting, needing more. I need to be penetrated. He presses against my clitoris and rubs in a circular motion that is perfect. It's as if he knows my admittedly alien body. He's an expert playing my body to a symphony of his own creation.

His hands stop and pull back, then he's stroking my hair, my face, my arms. His touch sends thrills through me as he continues exploring my body. I drop all my defenses, giving myself over to his gentle ministrations. I reach out and touch his face, which makes him smile. His eyes light up as he runs his hands down my sides to my ass. He grips my waist and lifts me up easily, as if I weigh nothing. He moves me to rest on his lap. One of his large hands cups the back of my head while the other roams down across my breasts. Even through my shirt when he touches my nipples and they both stand erect like small diamonds ready to cut glass.

His fingers glide across my stomach and down between my legs. I'm wet and ready as he plows through my folds. When he slides across my clitoris, I cry out in surprise and joy, unable to contain the thrill that pushes me over the edge. Then he buries the tip of his finger inside me while keeping pressure on my clit.

He moves his finger back and forth, creating a rubbing pressure on my sensitive nub while giving me the full sensation inside. It's amazing, and I move my hips in time, letting him have his way with me. I need this, I need to get off, clear my head, and then I'll be able to think.

"Yes!" I cry out, rocking.

He says something back. I bury my face into the glorious coolness of his neck, and only then do I see the backside of him. The first thing I notice is his wings. They're folded against his back. My rational mind, the part that wanted to protest what I'm doing, studies the wings as compensation for losing that battle. They don't look like they're big enough to let him fly, but they probably would allow him to glide.

I rub my face against his neck and shoulder, then run my hands through his hair while studying the wings, then looking down, I see his tail. It's standing stiffly out from his back, shifting back and forth almost like a rattlesnake. It vibrates in time with the motion of his hand inside me, and for some reason, seeing that drives me right over the edge. My body stiffens, stars explode in my vision, and I buck up against him hard, my hands gripping his shoulders tight.

"AH!" I cry out as the orgasm rips through.

He holds me tight until it passes, leaving me panting and sweating in his arms. I hold him until my breath and heartbeat slow to something resembling normal, then I sit up. My cheeks flush, and I feel awkward that I just got off with an alien that I can't even speak to. He lifts me up and sets me back down on the ground, then rises on to his knees. He's wearing something that mostly resembles a kilt, which makes me giggle.

"You're like an alien, dragon Highlander," I say in my best Sean Connery accent. Not that he's going to appreciate the humor.

He cocks his head to the side then shakes it, clearly indicating he doesn't get it. Who knew that some gestures are universal? Nod up and down, agreement, shake your head side-to-side, negative. Huh. I smile and shrug, and then he pulls the kilt aside. From between his legs protrudes the strangest cock I've ever seen. My eyes go wide, and I scoot back as I realize he wants to put that thing inside me. I shake my head.

"Oh no," I say. "No, not yet. I'm not ready for that."

I point at his cock as I talk and shake my head. It's not only big, but there's a bony ridge along the top like it's a weird condom—ribbed for her pleasure, almost. I don't know if I can accommodate such a thing inside myself without severe damage. I'm certainly not ready to find out! He looks from his cock to my pussy and back again, clearly disappointed, but he doesn't move closer or make any kind of threatening move.

He takes his cock in hand and makes a few quick, jerky strokes. A strangled groan escapes his throat as milky come jets across the sand. My belly tightens again, and almost I wish I'd let him have me. God, that was sexy.

No man has ever gotten off like that only looking at me. In some strange, exotic way, it made me feel beautiful. Combine that with the respect, the tenderness, and that he didn't try to force himself on me after I had to have given him a universe-sized case of blue balls? And try? Who am I kidding, he's almost three times as big as me; if he wants me, that's what's going to happen.

We stare at each other while his cock softens in his hand. At last he replaces the kilt and sits down. He offers me more water that I take graciously, then he shifts closer. I flinch, just a little, but he moves to one side of the shelter and lies down on his side.

He watches me, waiting. I don't know what he's waiting for, though. I need to get back to the other survivors. Jolie and Amara at least will be worried about me. I look out of the shelter longingly, but there's no way I'm going out there alone. This place is too dangerous for that.

He pats the ground beside him. He wants to sleep, again its pretty universal sign language. He wants me to rest as well. I am exhausted from the day—and the orgasm—so I lie down next to him. He lays an arm across me protectively, and his body provides relief from the blazing heat of the planet. A few minutes of lying in his arms and it strikes me that, for the moment at least, I feel safe.

It isn't long before I feel his chest rising and falling steadily. Still, I lie awake, full of inner turmoil. I've gone mad; that's really all there is to it. The only home I've ever known is gone. God knows how many lives were lost, and surviving this planet isn't going to be easy.

Will the surviving humans miss me? Will Rosalind send anyone to look for me? If they do, how will my new jerk-off buddy slash captor react? I can't imagine he's going to react well.

One thought crashes into the next. Outside the shelter there's a constant buzz and the soft splashing of water. Eventually the steadiness of that noise combined with my total exhaustion pulls me into a fitful sleep.

8

CALISTA

When I wake up, I don't want to open my eyes. I'm dimly aware of being cool and comfortable. Sleep calls, and I want to answer. I hate mornings; always have. Sleep is so nice. I want to pull the blanket up around my neck and sleep for another hour.

I'm in a half-dream state, mostly aware that if I don't get up I'll be late for work again. Gershom will be pissed, as usual, and I'll have to walk a tight-rope for the rest of the week. Screw it, I don't want to deal with him.

I stretch my legs, working blood back into circulation, and then roll my neck while stretching my arms over my head. My back is cool but my front is warm. The dream world recedes like a heavy fog slowly dissipating. There's something cool and hard behind me.

Reality crashes through the remnants of sleep's fog, and it hits me where I am and what I've been through. I sit bolt upright, adrenaline dumping into my body. I look around wildly, my heart pounding, breathing in short gasps. Every muscle vibrates, ready to fight or flight. My eyes land on my ~~captor~~ rescuer lying beside me.

He's real. The alien-dragon man pushes himself up onto an elbow, supporting his head in one hand, and looks at me with his odd green eyes. He says something, or I assume it's words he says. It could be good morning or a yawn. What do I know about alien-dragon men and their language? He shakes his head in frustration, or maybe he's still considering eating me.

"Yeah," I say. "I agree."

What do I agree with? Why did I say that? I shake my head, I don't know. I'm alone on an alien planet, and hearing the sound of my own voice brings some kind of comfort.

Have my friends missed me yet? Are they okay? How are they surviving the heat, and what about food and water? Will they come looking for me? How am I going to get back to them? Will he let me go? Is this going to be a problem?

"Okay, look," I say.

He stares with unblinking eyes. His wings rustle and his tail shifts, softly slapping the ground. I lose my train of thought. He's so... alien, yet so enticing. I've not been captive long enough to have Stockholm syndrome, so what is this feeling? I feel connected to him, but that's crazy. Stupid, even. I give myself a mental shake. He says something. It's long, and he hisses loudly at the end. I shrug and shake my head.

"I don't understand," I say. "I have to get to my friends."

I point at myself, then stop and look around. I'd intended to point back to the crash, but now I realize I have no idea where I am in relationship to it. I'm lost. My stomach sinks and tears swell in my eyes.

"Shit!" I exclaim, slamming my fists against the ground.

He sits up so fast I barely see him move. He's in a crouch with his arms out front like he's ready for an attack, and his head is swiveling side to side. He's looking for an attack or any kind of threat. He's protecting me. Warmth forms in the pit of my belly. Me. He's caring for me. I've not had the best luck with dating and never had any guy that would jump to my defense like this.

"No, no," I say, making a downward motion with my hands to try and calm him.

He stares with his still unblinking gaze, then looks at my hands. He relaxes at last, and I take a deep breath. Okay, now what? My belly grumbles, and a wave of dizziness hits me. Now that I'm not next to him, I'm getting hot again. I close my eyes and breathe through the dizziness. One problem at a time. I don't know when I last had a meal. Maybe I can handle that. I could really use a win, one thing that I can fix.

"Food?" I ask, using my hands to mime eating.

He watches closely, then slowly mimics my motions.

"Yes!" I nod, excited that we're actually communicating, if only at a fundamental, baby-talk level.

His mouth broadens, and his eyes light up with what is unmistakably a smile. It reveals sharp pointed teeth. He eats meat. Teeth like that aren't for plant eaters.

I hope he's not a cannibal.

Though I guess technically it wouldn't be cannibalism, would it? We're not the same species. Great, Cal, come up with some more justifications why it's okay for the alien dragon-man to eat you, why don't you? No, if he wanted to eat me, he would have by now, and I refuse to believe that any creature in the galaxy would have sexual interactions with their prey before eating them, literally. That's too weird to even contemplate.

He touches my cheek with two fingers. My cheek tingles and my blood pressure skyrockets. I'm instantly thinking about our sexual encounter last night and how hot it was. It brings the pulsing need to the fore of my thoughts. No, push that aside. Food, water, then getting to my friends —that's what matters. I can't be spending my time playing touchy-feely with the alien. I smile and then mime eating again.

"Food," I repeat slowly.

My stomach grumbles loudly and his eyes widen, dropping to look at it. He makes an erratic gesture, shakes his head, then crawls backwards out of our rudimentary shelter. I follow, gathering my clothes as I do. I pull on my pants and have to duck back inside to find my shoes.

While I'm putting them on, bouncing on one foot while putting the shoe on the other, he ducks into the shelter himself. He emerges with a satchel that looks like it's made of buffed, well-worn leather. It's more like a really large purse than anything, with a long strap and a flap that covers the opening. He rummages in the bag for a moment before bringing out two objects wrapped in what looks like oilcloth. He kneels and carefully unwraps them to reveal succulent-looking chunks of meat. He raises his hands before me as if he's making an offering to his queen or goddess, looking expectant.

The strangest feelings spin through my thoughts. I have no idea what to make of any of this, so I smile. My mouth is already watering despite the fact that the meat is raw. He picks one up and motions with it towards me. I take it. It has the appearance of beef. It's a red meat, at least. Still feeling tentative, I sniff it. It has a rich almost spicy scent that smells delicious, but it looks raw and I'm not that hungry. Yet, at least.

Frowning, I look around trying to figure out some way to cook it. I don't want to risk getting sick. Spotting two sticks lying next to the shelter, I grab them up and after laying the meat carefully to one side, I gather a small bit of leaves and grass-like material into a pile. I put one stick point down in the pile then start rubbing the other stick across it, hoping to create enough friction to spark a flame.

He kneels and leans in, watching with great interest. He doesn't say anything, but his eyes move from the sticks to me then back. I keep rubbing, and the one in the pile is getting warm, but I have no idea if it will ever start a fire or if I'm wasting my time. I'm a bio-engineer, not a Girl Scout!

My arms are getting tired, and the hot sun is beating on my back. Sweat is dripping off my forehead and falling into my tinder.

"Damn it!" I yell and throw the sticks in frustration.

My belly grumbles loudly. All I've succeeded in doing is making myself hotter, thirstier, and even hungrier than when I started. Frustration overwhelms me, and then tears fall unbidden, which frustrated me even more. I drop onto my ass, and slap my hands against the ground, shaking my head.

Everything is screwed. I've lost my home, my friends, and now I can't even start a simple fire. What is the point? How am I ever going to survive here?

He moves closer, speaking softly. Tentatively he reaches towards me, and when I don't move back, he wipes a tear from my cheek. He holds the tear up on his finger, examining it, then says something. He has a quizzical look on his face as if he expects me to answer.

"I don't know!" I yell. "I'm hungry and thirsty and I can't eat that raw!"

I point at the meat then at my failed attempt to make a fire. He looks at the meat, at me, then at my pile of tinder. I swear that understanding dawns in his eyes. They widen and light up, then he says something again and points at the meat, then at my pile of tinder. He repeats the same words and motions twice more, until I shake my head and shrug, tears streaming down my face. Tenderly he wipes the tears from my cheeks again and makes a sound that is so similar to a soothing shush that it gives me pause.

He turns to my pile of tinder. He places one hand against my chest and pushes until I scoot back to an arm's length from him. He leans over the tinder inhaling deeply. He lets out the breath with a loud hiss, and a small ball of flame bursts out of his mouth to hit the tinder. It catches fire!

"What!" I exclaim, staring with my mouth open. He's actually a for-real, fire-breathing dragon!

The alien dragon-man grabs some of the twigs I'd gathered and feeds them to the flames until the small fire is burning steadily. He looks back and smiles over his shoulder. He grabs the raw meat, spears it on a stick, and holds it over the flames. He drives the other end of the stick into the ground so it holds the food on its own. In moments, the soft sizzle and aroma of cooking meat fills the air, and my stomach growls louder.

"Thank you," I say, wiping away the last of my tears. "Thank you. God, if only we could actually talk."

He speaks and then goes into the shelter. When he comes out, he hands me my water bottle. I take it and drink gratefully. He points at his eyes, then at mine, then at the water bottle. He repeats the same sounds again. The inflection of his words makes me believe it's a question, even if I can't understand him.

"I'm sorry," I say, apologizing for I don't know what.

Crying, I guess. Frustration, being a baby, whatever. He's been nothing but kind to me. He's actually been the nicest, kindest man I've ever interacted with. Who knew I would say that about a massive alien-dragon?

Home, on the ship, men were so different. There is... no, that's not right. There *was* a carefully monitored ratio and an expectation that everyone will pair up and breed, so that the next generation will be strong and in the right number. The attitudes of men, human men, are so much more... cavalier, I guess?

Most men expect you to just do what they want, that you'll give them what they want, and that's just the way it is. Like Gershom. He's been hitting on me since I was old enough to have sex, but not once has he ever actually been kind to me. Just simple, basic kindness. Like getting me food, offering me water, or wiping away my tears with a surprising amount of gentleness.

He turns the stick so that the flames are on the opposite side of the meat, then spears the second piece. He's so different. Huge, much bigger than any man I've ever seen. He's probably bigger than Dwayne 'The Rock' Johnson at the height of his career. If the Rock was a foot taller and grew everywhere else proportionately, he'd probably be about this size. Of course, The Rock doesn't have scales, or a tail, or wings that flutter every so often on his back.

His wings are fascinating. They look like leather almost, but they have a beautiful shine that draws the eye. They can't be big enough for him to fly, though. In comparison to his size, they're much too small for that, just going by the basic laws of physics. I study them and think about what I've seen of this planet, then it hits me. They're not for flying—their purpose is to make him lighter. The planet is mostly sand—well, all sand from what I've seen. And as I can well attest, crossing that sand is a bitch. During the small trek I made, I was sinking in the entire way and having to fight my way forward with each step. If those wings just gave him some lift, they'd make him lighter, enabling him to move his large bulk across the sand much easier. Which means the tail is designed to help guide!

I chuckle as my thoughts turn to the scientific. Discoveries have always brought me the most joy in my life, and figuring out the nature of his evolution is fascinating. He looks over his shoulder and smiles, hearing my laugh. I return his smile.

"Thank you," I say.

He nods. We just communicated! Elation fills me. I can do this. I can talk to an alien. Okay, that's a start. Good, hmm, how about some names?

"I'm Calista," I say, pointing to myself. "You?" I ask, pointing to him.

He frowns, or at least the ridges along his brow drop down and his mouth becomes a sharp line.

"Calista," I point to myself, saying my name very slowly. "Ca-lis-ta."

I sound it out while repeatedly pointing at myself. He stares with an intensity that in any other situation would probably creep me out. He's watching my mouth move like he's memorizing the motions as well as the sounds. I repeat myself dozens of times hoping to get through. This is the most rudimentary form of communication, but any language can be learned if you can find a starting point. I repeat and point then he nods and points to himself.

"Lay-dun," he says slowly.

My eyes widen as I jump to my feet and whoop for joy, pumping my fist in the air. "Yes!"

He jumps up as well, looking around with his hands up and his wings spreading. His tail shifts back and forth, avoiding the fire.

I shake my head. "No, it's okay. It's okay."

He looks around once more before settling his eyes on me.

"It's okay," I repeat.

He looks carefully around the area, then he kneels and turns the second piece of meat. He leans in closer and looks at the first piece, sniffing. Apparently satisfied, he pulls the stick out of the ground and holds the food out to me.

"Ca-lissss-ta," he says, dragging the 's' sound out in my name.

My heart leaps into my throat, and I'm grinning from ear to ear. My own name has never sounded so beautiful coming from anyone's lips before.

"Yes!" I exclaim, nodding excitedly as I take the meat.

He smiles and I sit down, tossing the hot piece of meat from hand to hand. I blow on it in my hands, cooling it to an edible temperature before attempting to eat it. When at last it isn't burning hot, I take a first, tentative bite.

It's delicious. Moist and succulent, with a surprisingly rich flavor. I swallow the first bite, and it's almost like taking a shot of some strong liquor. Warmth trails down my esophagus to land in my belly, where it slowly spreads across my limbs. He watches me eat expectantly.

"It's good," I say, wiping some juice from the corner of my mouth. "Really good."

I motion the meat around in my hands and smile, which he seems to understand. He gets his own piece of meat, and no matter that it has to be burning hot, grabs it off the stick with his bare fingers and pops the entire chunk in his mouth. He chews it quietly, looking out into the distance.

"Laydon," I say, and he looks at me.

The scale over his right eye rises independent of the other, just like a human might raise an eyebrow to indicate a question. I point at him and repeat his name slowly, wanting to make sure I've got it right. He smiles.

"Ladon," he says, pointing at himself and nodding. "Calisssssta." He points at me, still dragging out the 's.'

I feel a strong sense of satisfaction. It's not a deep, intellectual conversation, but we're talking. I grab my water bottle and take a drink. It's much emptier than I would like, but we're in an oasis so hopefully I can fill it soon.

"I need to get to my friends," I say, standing up and looking around, trying to get my bearings.

I'm lost. Well, maybe that's a stupid way to think of it. I've been lost since crashing on an unknown planet, but now I've got no clue how to return to my friends. Ladon watches me with his normal great interest. I don't understand it, but I trust him. That sense of connection, or sense of familiarity, is so strong. Impossible, since I know full well he's never been on the ship and I'd never been off it, but it is so much like I know him.

I shield my eyes and stare around, looking for anything that would serve as a landmark. The shelter is on the edge of an oasis. The area is lined with trees. The trunks of the trees are really wide at the base, some of them up to fifteen feet at least, but they grow smaller the higher up the tree goes. The tops are no more than a foot across. The leaves are massive palms that grow right around the top only.

The grass is yellow, almost a rust brown. The ground is covered with fallen leaves, and there are other small plants. Groups of insects flitter through the trees, creating a soft buzz.

Beyond the trees to my left I see there's a small pond, maybe a couple of hundred yards wide and about a hundred long, with lush green grass that has wide blades and thick, heavy roots extending to it from the trees of the oasis.

Water is good, but no sign of anything that would direct me to my friends. Beyond the edge of the oasis is the desert. Red and white sand stretching for as far as I can see, rising in dunes that limit sight.

"Friends," I say to Ladon.

He watches my mouth closely, then shakes his head, showing he doesn't understand. I try motioning with my hands, pointing to myself, then moving my hands in an hourglass figure next to me. I have no idea how to communicate the idea of friends to him. He shakes his head after I try again several more times to no apparent avail.

Ladon grabs my hands and shakes his head negative, and then he gathers up the few things that are left in the shelter. He hands me my bag and slides his own over his shoulder. The last item he pulls from the shelter surprises me. It's similar to a spear, but instead of ending in a sharp point along the top, there is a curving two-foot blade embedded into it. The blade looks razor sharp and shows a level of craft and skill I wasn't sure he would have. Working steel is an advanced ability. Ladon notices I'm looking at the weapon. He looks at it, then at me again before holding it out between us.

"Oh, um, no, I have, uh, yeah," I stutter, holding my hands up and waving it away.

I've never held such a thing, and it intimidates the hell out of me. He smiles, nods, then twirls it. The blade and shaft swing through the air, whistling as it slices through. He moves through several motions, all of which look very deadly, before bringing it around and sliding it into a leather holster of sorts on his back. Well, I guess at least I'll be well protected.

I look around once more. There's a large flower behind the shelter. It's massive, with long fronds that flow from its red-orange eye. The center looks like it has a hole in it. The leaves and fronds have a rust color to them and lack any shine I would normally associate with life. I walk towards it, but he puts a hand on my shoulder and pulls me back around to face him. He shakes his head and says something, pointing at the plant.

I don't understand his words, but I get the meaning. He doesn't want me near it. I shrug, and he smiles. He points into the distance, says something, then starts walking. He goes four paces, then turns and looks at me. I debate what to do, but my options are stay here and die or follow the dragon-alien. I think it's pretty clear-cut which way to go. I adjust my bag on my shoulder, then move up next to him and do my best to keep pace.

I need to return to my friends, but that's not going to happen if I'm dead. My best hope of survival is with Ladon. Hopefully I'll be able to enlist his aid for them too. I've only been here a day, but I'm growing surer by the moment that this inhospitable planet will be the death of my entire race without his help. All I have to do is get him to help them before it's too late.

9

LADON

C alista, I think to myself as we walk.

I like the sound of her name; it's feminine and feels nice on my tongue. She stumbles, so I catch her, holding her until she pushes me away. She says something, but her words are too fast and full of hard sounds that I can't follow. I smile as she points behind us, then at herself, and then makes some other motion that makes no sense. I love her energy. She's full of life, though her pale skin is already turning pink. I offer her some more water, and she drinks it greedily.

I have to get epis soon. It will adapt her to live here. I want her to live very much. I like her softness. When I scratch my nose, I catch wafts of her scent on my fingers, and it's pleasing. Her soft folds, her wetness, the smell of her, the soft exposed mounds of her breasts—she is beautiful. Strange. Different. I want to give her pleasure again. In time, she will pleasure me in return. I'm certain of this. She is not ready yet, but we have time. Once she has epis, we'll have as much time as it takes.

She stumbles again, and I catch her. She shakes her head.

"Are you okay?" I ask.

She smiles and wipes her forehead, so strange with its lack of protective scales, and then moves her head up and down. Her eyes are bright and shiny, and they have no protective lids. Any wind will blind her easily, but the sharp blue of her eyes is gorgeous, like perfect shimmering scales. I smile back, and then resume walking.

She stumbles once more and falls to her knees. I watch as she struggles to her feet, waving me away. She steps towards me, and her feet sink into the sand. She has to fight for each step, pulling a foot up, placing it forward, letting it sink in, then extracting the back one. It looks exhausting. She needs wings and a tail, but barring that, maybe she will accept my help. I move beside her and put an arm around her waist.

"Put your arm around my shoulder," I say.

She pushes and pulls, but eventually she figures it out as I guide her arm to where I want it. Spreading my wings, I walk forward, taking some of her weight. She's still doing most of it, but I'm making her lighter, and we begin to make much better time. Judging by the position of the suns, it will be almost nightfall by the time we reach the next oasis where we can rest.

We travel and my female talks incessantly, and I try to follow along and learn her words. Her language is difficult for my tongue, and she speaks fast.

The ground trembles beneath us and I freeze, dropping to a crouch. She takes a step further, forcing me to grab her by the waist and lift her off the ground. I can't risk any more movement.

"Still," I hiss, holding her over my head in one hand while feeling the sand with my other.

She says a string of words too loudly. Desperate to make her understand, I shake my head, but she keeps talking. The trembling moves closer. She doesn't understand how much trouble this is, so I do the only thing I can think of.

I place my hand over her mouth and force her jaw shut. Her beautiful eyes widen and I recognize her look of fear, but I have no choice. She must be quiet. I'll try to explain to her when there's time, but now? This is survival.

She struggles against my grip, forcing me to tighten it until I'm sure she's feeling pain. Tears form in her eyes, and her mouth moves against the palm of my hand. I want to let her go, to explain, but the ground is trembling more.

It's moving directly underneath us. The slightest sound could attract the monster. I've fought and killed zemlja before, but it's not easy, and last time I was severely wounded. I barely survived. There's no way I could protect her while fighting one, so I don't let her go.

It makes me feel bad. I know she doesn't understand. She probably thinks I'm being cruel, the exact opposite of what I want. I want to make her feel good. I want to hear her moan, especially beneath me as I pleasure her. My tail stiffens as my thoughts turn sensual, but I need to focus.

I extend my senses into the ground, trying to picture the giant worm's location. The tremors are receding. Good. It's almost gone, we're almost safe. She struggles harder, and my grip slips. She wiggles free, falling towards the ground.

I see it in slow motion. If she hits, the zemlja will sense it and strike for sure. Spreading my wings to support myself, I lean forward and catch her, just inches above the ground.

"NO!" I hiss loudly, trying to imitate a word I've heard her say while shaking my head.

I think this is the proper meaning. I've seen her do it before. She's lying in my arms, staring at me with her mouth open, but I shake my head, willing her to silence. Something I do works, because her mouth snaps shut and she lies still. My arms burn with the effort of holding her off the ground as I wait for the zemlja to get further away. A tremor runs through my arms, the muscles burn with the strain, but I will not let her go. She is my treasure. I will protect her. No one and no thing may have her.

At last, I no longer sense the tremors. Only then do I lower her gently to the ground. She lays there looking at me without moving until I rise up, and she does the same. We stare at each other and she says things. I watch her mouth move, but nothing makes sense.

"No?" she says, shaking her head while she holds her hand up between us, palm facing me.

I tilt my head to one side. "No."

I repeat the word and shake my head. Using my hands I mime walking by placing one hand after another down on the air in front of me, and say the word no. She watches me closely, then nods her understanding.

"Zemlja," I say.

I mime my meaning by holding my left-hand level like it's the ground, then bring my right fist and arm up from behind it, waving it around like the worm creature the zemlja are. I open and close my fist to mime a mouth snapping at the air.

"Zelm-ja?" she says, and I shake my head.

"Zem-l-ja," I repeat, still miming the monster.

"Zemlja," she says correctly, and points at the ground with a questioning look.

"Zemlja," I agree, nodding and smiling my enthusiasm.

She's smart and quick. I open my arms and pull her into an embrace, showing her that I will protect her by wrapping my arms around her and holding her close to my chest. The heady scent of her hair fills my nostrils. My hands rest on the swell of her ass, and my thoughts turn back to pleasing her. She puts her arms around my neck, snuggling against me. She's warm… too warm. I push her back to arm's length and look at her closely. She's red, and her skin is chapping with an unhealthy look to it. There are cracks along her soft lips, and her eyes are not as bright.

Pulling out my water bottle, I offer it to her again, but I know it's not going to be enough. She needs epis. We have to get to the cavern soon, or my greatest treasure will not survive. I can't have that. She is mine, and I will protect her.

She drinks the water greedily, wipes her lips, then smiles. A warmth lifts my chest, making me feel lighter. I'll save her. There is no other option.

"Zemlja," she repeats and points to the ground.

I nod then get her arm around me, and we continue towards the oasis. Our water supply is low now, but I need much less than she does. I can go without for days, but I don't think she can make more than a mark of the sun before she'll need more, which is only staving off the inevitable. Her body will shut down from the heat in days without epis. No scales, no heat exchange, fur in strange places—it's exotic and enticing, but completely unsuitable for life on Tajss.

THE SUN HAS MADE FOUR MARKS WHEN WE COME across the tracks of a pack of guster. I stop and kneel beside the prints, studying them. I'd put the pack at six members, but one of them is dragging behind with a bad foot. I look at Calista and smile. Guster meat is a rare treat. It's tasty, and also should help buy some time for her survival. I normally don't hunt them because they're dangerous and are meat eaters, unlike the bivo. The danger is offset by the fact that it will help her.

Their meat is very restorative. They sleep in the caverns where epis grows. I don't know if they eat the plant or not, but I do know that their meat is infused with its essence.

"Guster," I say, pointing at the tracks.

She watches with interest and works at saying the word. It takes a few tries, and she's still weak on the soft sounds, but she gets it.

I take my lochaber off my back and whirl it around, then drop to a ready position. I point to my lochaber than back at the tracks.

"Guster," I say, and she repeats it then says another word.

I watch her mouth, looking at the shapes as she says the word. Then she mimes taking something out of the palm of one hand and putting it in her mouth. She means food! I smile and nod, watching her repeat the word. I listen carefully.

"Ffffood," I mimic, and she nods excitedly.

"Food!" she exclaims, and her voice is like the tinkle of shiny bells, beautiful.

"Food," I repeat.

I motion her forward, and she puts her arm around my shoulders. Then we hunt. The tracks are so fresh that I don't think they'll be far ahead. Based on the direction of their travel, they're probably going to the same oasis we are, and we should get there shortly before nightfall.

If we can catch the guster and kill one, we'll have dinner ready when we stop for the night.

I move my wings and increase my speed by taking on most of her weight. Her legs move along as I keep us going, but she's barely touching the ground most of the time. Her poorly designed body just doesn't move well across the sand. Having my wings fully spread also shades her from some of the sun. As we move, the tracks become fresher. The wounded one is dragging further behind the pack. Its tracks are now off to one side. It will be moving off on its own soon to die. Guster are pack creatures, but the weak ones sacrifice themselves rather than slow down the group. Once they die, the pack will feed on them. Though they won't kill their own, they're not above scavenging the remains.

The suns are dropping low when I hear the soft lowing sound. I drop to a crouch, pulling her down with me. I creep forward, staying low to the ground while keeping one arm around Calista's waist.

When we reach the crest of the dune, I see it. The wounded guster has a gash in its rear flank that is leaking blood. It's lowing and mewling as it turns in a circle. I'm not sure how close the pack itself is, but this is the one I want.

Sliding back down the dune, I remove Calista's arm from my shoulders and motion her to sit down. It takes a few minutes of motioning and repeating whispered words, but at last she is lying on the ground and watching me. I take a layer of cloth off and lay it over her to camouflage her into the sand from any predators that might come our way.

Once I'm satisfied she's as well hidden as I can manage, I lay flat and work my way back up to the top of the ridge. Once I get there, I shift back and forth, sinking myself into the sand with the help of my tail, then move ahead until I see the wounded guster. It's moved off a short distance, and now I see the pack too. The pack is a fair distance off and entering the oasis I've been leading us towards. The wounded one stops and walks a circle, unsteady on its feet. It makes a plaintive, lowing sound.

A guster is a large, razor-mawed lizard creature with hulking mounds across its back and four legs that have wide, webbed feet. Spines stick out at various points along the hard leather skin to help ward off any predators. Not that guster have any real threats. The only thing that hunts them besides a Zmaj like me is the zemlja, and nothing the guster does is going to save it from one of those. The spikes might injure a zemlja's gullet, but by then it's too late for the guster anyway.

I work my way closer, keeping myself partially buried and out of sight. The wind is blowing towards me, keeping my scent away, which is important. The guster may be wounded, but it's still very dangerous. Possibly even more dangerous than if it wasn't. My only advantage is that now it's alone. I'm within thirty feet when the guster stops turning and stares in my direction, reptilian tongue flickering.

The left back leg has the gash in it. Being closer, it looks broken too, judging by the way it's twisted and swollen. That will keep it from charging, their normal form of attack, but its teeth are its main weapon.

I hold stock-still waiting to see if I'm spotted or if it only suspects my presence. It lashes out with its tail and darts forward. On its last step, the injured leg hits the ground, and the creature cries out as the limb gives way. Its rear half drops hard to the ground.

I leap into the air, whirling my lochaber. I won't get a better opportunity. I bring the weapon around and aim down as I spread my wings to slow and guide my descent.

The guster looks up as I glide in. Its broad mouth opens, revealing row after row of long, bladed teeth. It opens wide, as if it intends to swallow me whole. I adjust my direction so that I glide across its open maw instead of straight into it. As I pass over, I swipe the lochaber blade through its mouth, slicing the tendons that control its jaw. The bottom half of its mouth falls open, unable to maintain tension, and it howls in pain.

I land a couple of wingspans to one side. I whirl around and stab into the lizard-creature's side, threading my way through the defensive spikes. My aim is off—I hit a rib. It whirls towards the new source of pain and rips my lochaber free of my grip. I crouch to make a smaller target. It glares, distended jaw hanging open. It makes an angry gurgling sound. It doesn't hesitate to charge.

I wait, letting it come closer. If I jump too soon, it will be able to adjust and catch me with those deadly spikes. My concentration is broken when I hear a distant scream.

Calista!

Calista is standing up on top of the ridge. Even as my eyes focus on her and I form the question of why she is standing, the guster slams into me. There's nothing but teeth and saliva and spikes. The razor-sharp teeth slice at my skin. The spikes stab in. I'm carried along with it as I struggle to find a hold on the monster.

Two long spikes protrude from its head above the eyes, and I grab those, using them to gain some leverage. The momentum of the monster carries me backwards across the sand. I use the horns to keep the teeth from finding further purchase in my skin. My protective scales have stopped most of them, but I have several small cuts where they made their mark.

I pull back on the spikes, forcing the guster's head backwards. It can't close its mouth properly because of my earlier cut. It falls open wider as I force its head back, but I'm in trouble. In a desperate move, I shove my hand down its throat, choking it. It struggles and fights, unable to breathe until at last it drops dead at my feet.

I stumble back, taking a moment to catch my breath, but the moment I do, I look for Calista. As if on cue, Calista runs up and moves her hands over my chest, down my sides, and along my arms, then cups my face.

Desire and arousal spring up, and my tail is straight out. She looks at each small cut, and then tears a piece of cloth from the cover I'd used to shield her, the one that was supposed to be keeping her safe, and uses it to dab at my small wounds. A constant stream of words flows from her. I grab her hands, forcing her to stop. She looks up into my eyes.

"Calisssssta," I say, speaking slowly so I get her name right.

Moisture wells in the corners of her eyes. Inefficient, even silly, and yet it only endears her more to me. It must be some way of showing she cares.

"Ladon," she says, then reaches up and touches my cheek.

The instinctual anger I'd felt at her putting herself in danger melts before her obvious concern. I mimic her gesture. The softness of her skin amazes me, but the awareness hits me hard —she's too warm. Burning hot, and her face is flushed an angry red. The dryness of her lips, the lack of shine in her eyes—it's obvious she needs epis. Tomorrow, she just has to survive until tomorrow.

I break the moment and turn to the guster. I have to field dress it before the smell of it attracts any other predators. I set to work harvesting the meat. We'll eat well tonight. I watch the oasis as I dress it, making sure the pack has moved on. They don't come out this way, which is good. Packs of guster never stay in one place for long. They're always moving, hunting endlessly across the sands.

Calista sits off to one side while I dress the guster. When I set to work harvesting the meat, she moves over next to me. She rests one warm hand on my shoulder then kneels. She takes over wrapping the meat in oilcloth to keep it fresh as I slice off chunks. It's messy work, but with her help it doesn't take long.

We can't harvest or carry all the meat, but I take enough to last us several days. The rest of the meat will be consumed by Tajss, returning the guster to the planet's cycle.

Once we've gathered enough, we resume our journey to the oasis, but even with her arm over my shoulder, she stumbles and falls to her knees. She looks up and says something as she struggles back to her feet. I give her water, but she looks weaker and very red. She's no longer losing moisture like I expect. No beads of it on her face or arms. Her eyes are barely open and her lips are very chapped.

I sweep her up into my arms and carry her the rest of the way. I make better time this way anyway, not having to slow to her pace. She makes protesting sounds, but as soon as I have her in my arms, she curls into my chest. In a few moments she wraps her arms around my neck.

My hearts thunder and the dragon rumbles. I could run forever if it means holding her like this.

Once we get to the oasis, I build a shelter. I place Calista inside the shelter to let her rest out of the suns. She's awake, murmuring something, but doesn't resist staying in the shelter.

I build a fire and get the guster meat cooking. The smell of it fills the air. Calista sits up in the shelter and watches it cook, licking her lips. When it's done, I hand her the first piece and watch as she blows on it then pops it in her mouth.

Her eyes widen as she chews, and then she's smiling and chewing fast at the same time. She says words with juices running down her chin. I don't understand the words, but I do get her meaning. The flush on her skin recedes as the magic of guster meat works its way into her system. I give her the next piece as well, waiting to eat myself until she's had her fill. She needs it much more than I do, and the effect is dramatic. Her skin pales back to its normal hue, and her eyes become bright again. Her lips are still cracked, though. The effect is temporary. There are only traces of epis in guster meat, not enough for the full effect it should have.

She gets her fill, then I eat as well before extinguishing the fire. I fill her water bottle, making sure she drinks lots of it, then we crawl into the shelter. She lies down on her side. The beautiful curve of her hips call to me, and I struggle for a moment to control my desire.

I want to please her, but I'm worried she's too weak. When I pleasured her before, there was so much moisture in her feminine parts that I'm sure it contributed to her dehydration, so I resist the urge.

I lie down, uncertain what she wants, so I put a distance between us. She has her back to me but looks over her shoulder when I don't scoot up close to her. She frowns, then scoots across the small space until she is pressed up against me. I place an arm over her and rest my head on top of hers.

I LISTEN TO HER BREATHING. IT'S SHALLOW AND has a ragged edge to it. In the morning we'll reach the caverns with the epis. So many things could go wrong. I play out every terrible scenario in my head, preparing a response for anything that might go wrong.

The one thing I know: she is mine. I will get the epis for her, because if I don't, she will die. She has infused my long, empty life with purpose. Given me meaning. No matter what, I can't lose her.

10

CALISTA

I wake up cool and comfortable. Cool, mmm, I snuggle closer to the refreshing temperature, enjoying it. This place sucks, but here, close to Ladon, it's nice. He's so cool to the touch that it's like having a personal air conditioner. He stirs and moves against me, which is nice in a whole different way. Damn, but he's sexy. I want him, but as soon as I think about that, my friends come to mind. I'm sure they must be scared, lost in the desert somewhere out there.

How do I get him to understand? Our rudimentary communications are nowhere near enough to get across a complex idea like going back for them. Though I have no logical reason for it, I'm sure he'd help them if I can make him understand.

He stirs awake then pats my side and crawls out of the small shelter. I roll onto my side and watch as he makes a fire then cooks breakfast for us. When I see him get out more of that delicious meat, my mouth fills with saliva and my belly grumbles. I've never had anything that tasted so good before. It was refreshing and made me feel alive again. Even my headache was gone after eating it.

I watch as he pulls a few pieces of it out, spears them on sticks, then sets them over the fire. Smiling, I crawl out and join him, wanting to be closer to the smells. He doesn't seem any the worse for wear after fighting that crazy lizard dinosaur crossbred nightmare monster. I run a hand down his biceps and then across his chest. He smiles broadly.

"Calisssssta," he says, still dragging out the 's.'

"Ladon," I respond.

We eat mostly in silence. The sun is already hot, and I know it will only get hotter as the day goes on. As we eat, I look at all the plant life growing around this oasis. It's fascinating, and I really want to take time to study how they've adapted to both the heat and the soil.

I'm not stupid enough to believe there is any hope of rescue. Even if a distress signal was sent, which is doubtful, it will take generations for help to arrive. If my people, my species, is going to survive, we'll have to adapt. Ladon finishes eating, packs the supplies, then carefully puts out the fire. He stands up, says something, and motions into the trees. I rise to follow, but he motions for me to sit down. It's clear that he wants me to stay here.

"Okay, sure, you go. Me stay, no problem, Lone Ranger," I quip like he'd have any idea who the Lone Ranger is, or I would if Johnny Depp hadn't made a vid. I love old vids. So much easier to stay home and watch a vid then go out and deal with dating, people, and all the noise.

Ladon nods then heads into the trees, disappearing out of sight as he moves close to the water. Since we're on the edge of the oasis and nothing has been trying to kill us for a bit, I decide to use the opportunity to explore. My mission from Rosalind was to find edible plant life, and there are more plants here than I've seen yet. I might as well gather some for research.

The first plant I inspect is similar to a miniature cactus with a red hue to it. It has sharp spikes that seem to react to its surrounding environment. As I approach, it trembles and vibrates. When I stop moving, it stops. I find a small stick and poke towards it, and it leans away. Fascinating!

I gather samples where I can, but much of the flora is alive in interesting ways with built-in defense mechanisms. I lose myself in my wanderings as I investigate until I hear the sound of splashing water. The closer I get to the water source, the more varied the plant life becomes. The sand and sparse yellow grass gives way to a lush vegetation that is closer to Earth grass but with wider leaves and tougher stalks. It's green, though, which is nice to see. Scattered across the green are these small, vibrantly yellow flowers that grow in clusters, similar to camphor weed. Carefully, I inspect them then gather a few.

The water splashing is louder as I move through the odd trees with their massive bases. We weren't allowed to grow very many different trees on the ship, but we did have lots of seeds for when we reached our destination. These remind me of the baobab tree that grows in tropical zones on an Earth-like climate. Which makes sense; they're a hardy breed of tree that doesn't need a lot of water.

Stepping around one, I find the pool that is the heart of the oasis and a lot more. Ladon is in the water, splashing it up on himself. The water only comes up to his thighs, leaving every inch of him exposed in a glorious display. He's beautiful, amazing, even stunning. I don't have enough adjectives to describe his sexiness. As I watch, he cups water in his hands and then pours it over his head. As it runs down, the sunlight glints off wet scales and the glorious perfection of his muscles. The scales cover most of his body. Overall his scales are a rich tan, but each is edged with soft colors that range from yellow to blue and make a beautiful pattern.

His cock hangs flaccid between his legs, but even soft it's impressive. Scarily so. I've never seen a penis so big, but it looks normal on his enormous frame. It's a good thickness, and the top has that series of ridges which angle up towards his groin.

The bulging muscles of his chest flex and relax as he bends down for more water, tightening the hard lines of his abs. As he straightens, I stare openly, in awe of his physical perfection. He brings water high over his head, pours, then bends once more and emerges up with two handfuls of sand that he uses to scrub himself clean.

My pussy is pounding, my lower torso a knot so tight it might implode. I'm wet and really need to get off. Absently, I let one hand drift over, wanting to touch myself for relief. No, I want *him* to touch me, to bring me the relief I'm craving. Like he did that first night. The memory of our encounter sends desire into overdrive.

I don't only want him to touch me. I want him. I want more. So much more. I want to feel his cock sliding inside, filling me. Forcing my body to accommodate it. I want more, but what am I thinking? I don't know if we're really compatible. Sure, he's got a cock, but it's big! It looks like it might even be too big. I'm not sure, but I can't take my eyes off it.

I press my hand against myself, desperate for some relief. I shudder as the rough cloth of my pants presses against my clitoris. Suddenly I realize he's stopped bathing and is watching me. His massive cock rises upright and stands at attention. My cheeks flush hotter than even the burning suns can account for.

"Um, hi, uh, yeah, Ladon, uh," I stutter. Caught with my hand all but in my pants, literally. Talk about taking the cookie jar metaphor to its dirtiest extreme.

"Calisssssta," he says the 's' in my name more pronounced than ever.

I look down, embarrassed, but I hear him splashing towards me. I shift from foot to foot, stuck in this insane moment. I want to flee, run away and hide, but where could I go? My only retreat is a tiny makeshift shelter. Anywhere else is too dangerous. I'm frozen by indecision and lack of options.

He stops right in front of me. I can't look up, but now my vision is filled with his hard cock pointing up towards me. There's a glistening at the tip of the head as it leaks droplets of precum.

I close my eyes, cheeks burning hotter than ever. He wants me; there's no doubt of that. How can that be? No one wants me, not really—I'm the nerdy science girl. Hot guys like this, even if he is an alien, don't want me. They want the beautiful girls. The ones who know how to do their makeup. Who own dresses, as in more than one dress. I own one, which I only bought because I had to for a work event.

He's close. Too close. It feels like there's not enough air. I can't catch my breath. My eyes snap open, and the V of his lower abs, his hard thigh, then his cock are there, large as life, filling my view. Hard, stiff, and beautiful as the sun glints off colorful ridges. He growls and takes me by my shoulders.

"Calisssssta," he says, my name like a mantra.

Fear and desire war. He wants me, but this is crazy. He places his fingers under my chin and lifts until I meet his eyes. His strange, odd, enticing eyes awaken things inside me I can't even pretend to understand.

I want to give in to him. I want him to take control. To own my body. To give me pleasures I've yet to experience. He nods slowly. He runs his hands down my arms, soft and gentle. A shudder runs down my spine, causing me to shake. He pauses, staring into my eyes, then he resumes stroking up and down. He runs his fingers through my hair, then cups my face in his massive hands. He leans in closer, then closer still.

He's going to kiss me. Aliens kiss? Kissing is universal? I want him to. I want him, but no, I'm scared. Too scared. I yelp and jump backwards. It's intimate. How can I do this with him? My friends, my fellow humans, are alone, and I'm kissing an alien? As if a kiss will make this more than a flight of fancy, a fantasy, or a thrill. And there is the deeper truth. Kissing him makes these feelings too real.

He hisses and leans in, reaching. My eyes widen as fear fills my stomach with acid, and I'm shaking all over. He's huge, and the urge to run is too much. I can't resist it.

I turn and run as fast as I can. Running blindly, crashing through the trees, I flee with tears streaming down my face. No destination, no clue where I'm going or why. I run, hoping for a savior. I run until I trip over some roots. Falling forward, I throw my arms up to catch myself. I hit the ground hard, hands scraping across the thick, rough grass. I collapse in a heap and cry.

Tears wrack my body. I sob, overwhelmed. I've lost everything. My home. I may never see my friends again. Memories of Jolie and Amara and even Gershom dance through my grief. I lie and I cry until at last I'm drained. I've nothing left to give. I feel empty and yet, amazingly, still horny.

I also realize how thirsty I am. Somewhere in my mad dash through the plants and trees I've lost my pack which had my water, supplies, and plant samples.

"Damn it, you idiot," I berate myself. "What now?"

I talk out loud to keep myself from panicking. Standing up, I take stock of my surroundings. I'm lost, really really lost. I didn't think, and even if I had, I didn't think the oasis was that big. How hard could it possibly be to find my way back to him?

"Okay, well running blindly around the alien planet away from the one guy who could help you the most is stupid. Got it. Note to self, next time don't be scared of the big dick, okay? So he's hung like a... dragon. So what?"

I shake my head and silently continue my self-beratement. There's a stand of those trees a few yards ahead. They don't have any lower branches, but the top ones are thick and plentiful with lots of leaves that shade from the sun. Some of them are close enough that maybe I can shimmy my way up between them, if I'm careful, and get high enough I might be able to look out over the desert and get my bearings. Or maybe I'll see him. Right now my odds of survival are diminishing by the moment. I know if I'm going to make it, I need to get back to Ladon.

"Damn, I'm like one of those stupid teenage girls in a horror vid. Oh god, a monster penis, run through the woods screaming!"

Jolie loves stupid old horror vids like that and forced me to watch them over and over. Jolie. I hope she's okay, and all the others are too. Are they looking for me? They've probably written me off for dead. That makes me sad, but if they're alive, it's okay. Once I manage to find Ladon again I'll figure out how to get him to help them. Once I do and we return to the other survivors, I'll be a hero. He'll help my people and we'll all figure out... what?

I haven't thought about it and now isn't the time, but the enormity of that question leaves me cold. It's been a non-stop attempt to survive the next moment with no time to think any further into the future. What is our future? What will we do here on this alien planet?

None of that matters, because right now I'm not sure I'll be alive in an hour much less a year. I have to get to Ladon, and he will help us survivors. I know it.

"Do I?" I ask myself as I step between the trees. "How do I know he will?"

I don't know, but I feel like he will. I mean, he's been so gentle and kind with me. He's been... sweet, I guess.

"Sweet?" I ask no one. And having no one, I of course answer myself. "Yes, sweet, like I'm a princess."

I laugh. Maybe the heat is getting to me. I'm dry as the stupid sand and my headache is back. I know that no matter how much water I drink, I'll still be dry. The meat he gave me last night is the only thing that's helped. When I ate it, it sent a cool chill through my limbs, spreading from my belly in a pleasing sensation. It was amazing, and damn, what I wouldn't give for some more of it.

"So, yeah, I'm the princess of Vulcan, and now I'm lost. Ladon can be my prince and come find me any moment now."

A stick breaks to my side, then the trees rustle above my head. I jump and freeze, crouching low, fists raised before me as I look for the source. When I see it, I scream.

A huge, sort of gorilla-looking thing steps out from behind one of the trees. Massive arms that look like small tree trunks pound the ground as it walks forward. Then it stops and bares ugly teeth, rising up on its hind legs to pound its chest while emitting a thundering roar. The creature drops to the ground, glaring its challenge.

Thick fur hangs over its shoulders and down the top half of its arms, but the bottom half is bare skin that's a rich blue color. It has sharp, brown eyes that watch my every move. Bent over and resting on its hands like it is, the thing is still almost as tall as my own five foot six. I stand frozen, trying to not provoke it.

"Um, sorry?" I say. "Didn't know this area was claimed."

I back up a step and it doesn't move, so I take another step backwards. Then the tree above me rattles and something falls down. I catch sight of it out of the corner of my eye and scream. I drop into a crouch while throwing my arms over my head, trying to protect it.

There's another one behind me. The trees go crazy with their rattling, then more of the creatures drop to the ground like falling coconuts, except it's raining massive primates. They call to each other as some of them hit their chests or slap the ground. A couple of them shove one other, but my main concern is that I'm surrounded. They keep their distance, but they also keep me in the middle. I turn in a slow circle, trying to see all of them at once.

"Shit," I mutter, then the first one steps closer, and I whirl to face him. "Hold it right there!"

I yell and point a finger, but it doesn't matter. It comes closer one step at a time. He reaches for me with his massive hand that looks big enough to crush my head without a second thought.

I freeze. I've got nowhere to go. Fear takes a firm grip and I'm unable to move. Every muscle locks and all I can do is mutter and do my best not to cry. It touches my hair and runs a finger through it. When it pulls back, I breathe a sigh of relief that turns to a scream as it moves with blinding speed and grabs my hair in its fist and yanks down. I'm thrown to the ground, hitting my head with enough force that I see stars. I keep screaming, praying for rescue.

11

LADON

I hiss a curse and pull my pants back on then gather my bag.

I want her, and I know she enjoyed my pleasuring, so why does she run? She makes no sense. She has no sense! No protection, no weapons, not strong enough to lift a baoba limb on her own, and she runs off blindly. Stupid and dangerous. I have to find her before she runs into something. A cvet or that guster pack from last night. There is little here that won't kill the unsuspecting. Tajss is not a forgiving home.

Clothes back on, I run into the oasis, picking up her trail and rushing after her. Anger pulses with every beat of my hearts. When I find her, I must make her understand she can't do this again. She is my greatest treasure. Tajss is too dangerous for her to be alone. She is unprepared, no weapons, small, and unknowing of this place. I can't allow her to die.

Her tracks are clear and easy to follow. Looking ahead, I see a thicker stand of baoba trees. I hiss a curse, recognizing the stand. Majmun make their homes in the top of those trees. My only hope is that maybe she turned aside. I run, knowing in my hearts that she didn't. Her scream pierces the air and I spread my wings, leaping with every other step to move faster.

"LADON!" She screams my name and anger surges in response.

Whatever is threatening her will feel my wrath. I will tear it apart with my bare hands. She is mine; nothing may harm her. I leap over a fallen branch and at last reach the stand of trees. The majmun tribe has come down to the ground and are circling her. Their alpha has her by the hair and is dragging her around the circle while the rest pound the ground and their chests.

"CALISSSSSTA!" I roar, leaping high in the air and pulling my lochaber off my back as I spread my wings to gain height.

My feet hit the baoba tree several feet up, and I use it to spring higher still. My scream draws the attention of the majmun, and they look up. The tribe cries out, some in fear and some in defiance.

The alpha stops dragging Calista. He rises on his hind legs and pounds his chest, roaring at me. I raise my lochaber over my head, holding it in both hands and swing down, intending to bury it in his skull. As I swing towards his head, he surprises me with a punch that strikes in my gut.

I'm thrown backwards and my air is knocked out. I flap my wings trying to regain control while whipping my tail wildly from side to side. I slam into a baoba tree before I do. I hit hard enough to hurt, but my scales save me from anything breaking. I pull my wings closed and let myself slide down the tree trunk to land in a crouch with my lochaber ready. The alpha barks and pounds the ground, a sound that almost mimics laughter.

"Lafitupfuzbal thatsmyLadon," Calista says, words that I don't understand, but I recognize my name at the end.

Calista grabs a large branch and swings at the alpha. The beast's attention is on what it perceives to be the greater threat, me, so it doesn't see it coming until right before impact. It leans to the side, and the branch she's wielding slams against its side.

The alpha howls in surprise and pain, and Calista yelps loudly. The alpha grabs the branch, ripping it from her grip, and throws it aside. It turns towards her, and she holds up her hands, speaking words I don't understand while making patting gestures and slowly retreating.

"Here!" I yell, and the alpha whirls back to face me.

I keep my eyes on the alpha. He stomps forward, threatening by pounding the ground, baring his teeth, and roaring. I hold still and don't take my eyes off him. If I look away, he'll feel dominant. He's in my territory—nothing here is dominant over me.

I rise from my crouch, lochaber pointing towards him. I take a step forward and he retreats, grunting. I make a wordless hiss. The alpha shakes his head, hits the ground, then takes several quick steps forward, pounding the sand again. I hold my ground still, and he retreats.

The majmun around him hoot, seeing their alpha challenged. They pound their fists and egg him on. He looks around, then at me. Majmun are not intelligent, but they have primal instincts that they operate on. Much like when the bijass lays claim to my mind.

We stare for a long time then I step forward, my lochaber at the ready. I'd rather not kill him. They're not bad animals, and keep the guster packs from getting too thick. Their meat is not good for eating either, so there's nothing for me to gain by his death. All I need is for him to figure that out for himself.

He pounds the ground and then rises on his hind legs and throws his hands wide to either side. Calista watches from behind him and scoots back.

"Ladon!" she cries out.

My eyes dart to her for an instant, and then the alpha is rushing me. I whirl my lochaber and drop to a crouch with it held in front of me, ready to receive his attack. He slides to a stop just short of the point. He growls then beats the ground.

I take one hand off my lochaber and pound the ground then point up into the trees. The alpha shakes his head back and forth, so I repeat the motions. He backs up slowly then makes a noise. He leaps backwards, flying over Calista and grabbing onto one of the baoba trees. The rest of the pack joins him, and in moments they disappear into the sheltering canopy.

My treasure runs and throws her arms around my neck before I finish standing up. I wrap my arms around her, feeling a rush of relief that holds my anger at bay. We hold each other silent for a moment, then I grab her by the waist and set her firmly away.

"You could have been killed!" I yell, fear for her safety and anger at the majmun still roiling. She ran away and put herself in mortal danger. I don't understand why she did this. She shakes her head and moisture wells in her eyes, which just makes me even more confused.

"No! You cannot do this, do you not realize how dangerous what you just did is? What if I hadn't come in time? That alpha was claiming you as his own. You could be dead!"

I want her to understand, to know that she can't do this again. The moisture in the corners of her eyes falls down her cheeks, and she steps back away from me, bringing her arms up and crossing them over her chest. I step forward, pointing a finger at the trees. "Danger!"

I speak loudly, trying to drive in the word, desperate for her to understand. She stumbles backwards, and then I see it. She's afraid. Of me.

I stop moving as a heavy sensation settles in the pit of my stomach, then chills spread through my limbs. The moisture runs down her cheeks and she shakes her head, saying something over and over. It's the same word, so I listen to the sound of it closely until the roll of it becomes familiar.

"Sorry, sorry, sorry," she's saying, shaking as the drops continue rolling down her face.

Anger is gone in a flash, leaving regret in its wake. I've caused her grief and pain by acting out of fear. Fear she would be hurt or worse, but that makes no excuse for the way I treated her.

She's shaking, and each shudder of her body feels like my own heart is breaking with it. She crosses her arms over her chest, uncrosses, then recrosses them again and stares at the ground, saying that same word over and over. I move slowly so as not to startle her until I'm close enough to take her in my arms. She throws hers around me, puts her head against my chest, and continues sobbing. I hold her tightly against me and stroke her head, making soothing sounds. She clings to me until at last the sobs stop. She continues to hold me tight.

I caress her hair and then down her back and back up. I like the way she feels in my arms. Desire pulses low in my stomach. I want her, but not if it will put her in danger again. I don't understand what is going on with her, but I do know she needs comforting. This is the least I can offer to make amends for losing my temper. I don't even mark how long we stand together, but it's long enough to make her calm.

"We should go back to camp," I say, glancing at the suns and motioning back towards our shelter.

It's late. We won't make it anywhere safer before nightfall. One glance and I see Calista is covered with cuts and bruises that need tending to avoid infection. I hold her at arm's length, carefully inspecting her until I'm satisfied there is no serious damage. She talks, saying lots of things, so I nod even though I don't understand. I sweep her off her feet to carry her. She stiffens in my arms for only a moment before relaxing and wrapping her arms around my neck.

It doesn't take long to return to our camp. Once we've arrived, I set her inside the shelter and motion for her to stay. I wait, repeating the motions until I'm satisfied that she seems to understand.

I make my way to the heart of the oasis, listening for any sound that might indicate she has decided to follow. I don't hear any, for which I'm thankful. Once I reach the water, I fill both our water bottles then turn to return to camp.

I feel a slight trepidation as I return, because it occurs to me she might have run away again. A feeling of relief floods through me when I clear the trees and see her sitting inside the shelter watching me emerge around the trees.

I take my pack and pull out the salve that I carry. I make it from the talons of the sismis. When I grind them down and mix them with the moisture from a cvet's leaves, it creates a paste that fights off infections and helps wounds to heal faster. It smells terrible but it's highly effective. I take the stopper out of the tube I store it in and then kneel beside Calista.

She speaks, and I wish I could understand what she's saying. The few words of her language I do know are insufficient for me to know what she's talking about. She doesn't stop talking, though. I like the fact that she has a lot to say. It's been a very long time since I've talked with any other being.

I take her left arm in my hand and look it over carefully. One scratch is particularly deep and the most likely to become infected. I dig my finger in the salve and slather it across the wound. As soon as I touch her with it, she jumps and lets out a yelp. She tries to pull away, but I tighten my grip and hold her still.

"This will help," I say, knowing she doesn't understand my words, but hoping the intention will come through.

She speaks quickly and shakes her head.

"No. Help," I say, using a mix of my own language and hers since the one word I do know is no. "Help," I repeat.

She stops talking and watches my mouth so I repeat the word slowly. It only takes six times before she sounds it out herself. I know she's understood when she holds her arm out and points at the wound then says help. I smile and nod then return to spreading the salve across her wound.

I know from experience how the salve feels. When it first touches an open wound, it burns but then turns cold. She deals with it well and I'm impressed with her strength. I finish her left arm then take her right, tending to each small cut. Any open wound is an invitation for infection.

When I finish with her arms, I motion to her shirt. She looks down, says something, then looks back up at me. I repeat my motions, then reach for her shirt and try to take it off. She leans away from me, and I frown, hissing. I don't like it when she denies my help. She says more words, but I don't care what they are; her wounds are more important.

"I have to look," I say, pointing at her shirt again and miming pulling it off.

She sighs, looks at the ground, then grabs the hem of her shirt and pulls it over her head. As the shirt rises up, it passes over her breasts, and they lift and then bounce down. The brown circles on top of the mounds hold my attention. Only when my lungs are burning in desperation do I realize that I'm not breathing. My hearts are beating in triple time and my tail is stiffening. She's fascinating and beautiful. I wonder what her breasts would taste like, and have to fight the urge to find out.

Her chest rises and falls quickly. The points at the center of the circles stiffen like they are reaching out to test the air. My body reacts at such an open display, my cock lengthening.

I force myself to breathe and pay attention to the task at hand. Beneath her right breast is a massive purple bruise that clearly indicates internal damage. I dip two fingers into the salve and touch her skin just over the bruise. She jumps, yelping in pain. I jerk my hand back and shake my head.

"Sorry," I say, holding my hands up, palms towards her.

She nods as if she understands, and I point again to the bruise then point at the salve on my fingers. She grits her teeth and nods. I reach over and touch her, being as gentle as I can while spreading the salve over the bruise. The moisture forms in the corner of her eyes again and some of the drops fall down her cheeks. Using my free hand, I catch one drop as it falls.

"Why?" I ask, holding it up between us.

She shakes her head. I nod, understanding on some instinctual level that maybe she doesn't know either. I finish spreading the salve over her bruise, then resume my inspection. She has other small cuts, each of which I tend to, until every part of her chest has been seen to, and I motion at her pants. She hesitates only for a moment, then pulls them off and sets them aside. As she does, the heady smell of her storms my senses, and my already-stiff cock hardens to what I would have thought an impossible rigidity. The scent of her is so enticing and exciting I almost dump my first load without even touching her or myself.

I close my eyes and inhale deeply, savoring the scent of her. My desire pulses like a third heartbeat low in my core. My need to have her is matched only by my desire to give her pleasure. I want her more than I can put into words. It's an overwhelming feeling, a need so deep it's part of who and what I am.

She lays her hand on my chest, and a shudder rips through my spine as my desire flames into a roaring sun. Now I will claim my treasure.

12

CALISTA

I run my hands over his chest. It's hard and cool to the touch. My stomach quivers with anticipation. Here I am naked with an alien-dragon man and seriously contemplating having sex with him. I don't know if I can do this. Not because I don't want to, but because I'm not sure it won't hurt me. His anatomy is familiar yet almost normal, but those ridges! And its size. I mean, I know from biology classes that some guys can be really big like that, but I've never been with one.

"Calissssta," he says.

His voice is deep and rich. When he says my name, even dragging out the 's' sounds, it's one of the hottest things I've ever heard. He's saved my life more than once now, but the way he saved me from those animals was so primal. Over the top incredible.

And the way he looks at me, how can I not want this man? And he is a man. No matter all the differences between us, no matter the scales, no matter the tail, or his strange, beautiful eyes. When I came upon him in the water and saw his cock, any doubts of his manliness were erased.

Wetness from my core slides down my thighs. The front of the loose cloth he wears as clothing is tented out by his big dick. We can't even talk, nothing more than a few words, but none of that changes the facts.

He saved me when I was passed out in the desert. He saved me when that lizard thing attacked me. And he literally flew and faced down an entire pack of animals who wanted to hurt me. And not once has he tried to force himself on me. Not once has he done anything untoward. The only problem we've had is him getting mad at me for doing something stupid that put my own life in danger. I don't think he was even mad at me; he was probably scared. Or confused. Or wondering if I'm nuts and why he keeps bothering to save me. My entire life has been lived on a spaceship surrounded by others of my own kind, and not once has any other man treated me so well.

I trace the line of his jaw. It's strong, well defined, and then I trace down across his shoulders. He's so big and strong. The way he fought to save me was fearless. Strong, dominant, with a bravery I've never seen before. He's heroic, like some kind of fictional character charging into the face of danger with a daring grin and outrageous smile.

I run my hands over his biceps and down his arms. Some parts of him are soft while others are hard and scaly. All of him is cool to the touch, which is soothing on my burning skin. He runs his hands along my back and down to cup my ass.

"Ladon," I whisper, leaning into him.

I love the feel of his hands on my body. He squeezes and then lifts me up. I wrap my legs around his waist, and he carries me easily, kneeling to sit me down inside the shelter that he built for us.

Our faces are inches apart. He hisses, a soft sound, then leans in and nibbles along my neck.

He moves across my collarbone and onto my shoulder. As he does, his hands roam across my stomach, leaving icy trails of his cool touch on my hot skin. I shudder and shift my hips.

His hands find my breasts, and he rises onto his elbows and looks down, lust burning in his eyes. He grabs the fabric of his loincloth with one hand, holding himself up with the other, and pulls, freeing himself. His massive cock springs up, and anticipation mixes with trepidation.

But I put my trust in him. If nothing else, if I can't take it, he'll stop. The decision is mine. I want him.

He inhales deeply, then he lowers himself and laps around the mound of my left breast. His fingers work the soft flesh until he takes my right nipple between his thumb and forefinger and slowly circles the areola. Electric thrills run through me and my hips buck up and down involuntarily.

"Ladon," I cry out.

He continues suckling around my breasts until at last he takes the nipple in his mouth. His tongue lavishes it with attention as he sucks and releases.

Ladon doesn't tire, doesn't stop, and the pleasure is mounting and mounting until I'm wound so tight, I can't wait any more. I grab onto him and thrust myself up. I can feel his hard cock pressing into my belly and I squirm, trying to work myself around to where I can rub my clit against its length.

He stops what he's doing to my nipple then licks and kisses down my stomach. He reaches the crease of my legs and kisses along it, passing across my mound and pausing at the top of my opening. His tongue, long, hard, and probing, reaches out and grazes across my clitoris. I lose control once more, bucking my hips, and he continues kissing across the other side. Ladon pauses and looks up at me.

"Calisssta," he says, waiting and looking for my permission.

Biting my lip, unable to form words, I nod. He parts my seam with his rough tongue. He does indescribable things to my body, creating sensations I've never had before.

He parts my folds with his tongue and teases my clit until I'm a quivering mess. I feel him moving up and down, circling, then driving his tongue deep. My hands tear at the ground underneath us as he continues to pleasure me. It builds and builds, and then I'm falling. Every muscle tenses, causing my back to arch, and drives my pussy straight into his face. He slides an arm under the arch of my back for supports without removing his tongue. My orgasm rushes through like a hurricane blowing away everything before it.

As it slowly passes with multiple small quakes after and my muscles relax, he lowers me to the ground. His fingers stroke my skin with surprising gentleness. He's so big, so strong and dominating, but then there's this other side of him. A gentle, kind, caring side that makes him perfect. I stare with half-lidded eyes.

"Damn," I say. "That was amazing. We can't even speak to each other, yet you're a masterfully cunning linguist."

I laugh at my own joke, knowing he won't get it. It doesn't matter, because he smiles, and that makes it worth it. He's not done, though. He rolls over and moves up across me, holding himself on his elbows. His hard cock is at my opening, and the moment I feel it, all the satisfaction of the orgasm I just had is replaced by need and desire. I want him so badly.

He stares into my eyes and then slowly, so slowly it's both a relief and a frustration, he begins to slide in. I close my eyes and bite my lip, nervous. He stops, and when I open my eyes, he is staring at me.

"Calissssta?"

It's a question. He's asking for my permission to continue. Nothing hurts, but he's barely inside, enough that it feels good. Really good but not nearly enough. I nod, still biting my lip, and close my eyes, prepared for pain or discomfort. If it's too bad, I'll make him stop. He will. He can do that, I'm sure. I have faith in him.

It feels like the head is in, and he stops. I know, having seen it, and judging by sensation that the first ridge is pressing against the top of my opening.

"Slow," I breathe out, my eyes still closed, and either he understands my words or does so instinctively, because that's exactly what he does.

Holding himself there, he kisses me. Soft, gentle kisses which I slowly give myself over to, the tension easing. As it does, I return the kiss. His lips are soft, moving against mine. As we continue kissing, my body relaxes and the first ridge slips in without effort.

I'm swept away by pleasure. It stretches me, because of both the size and the hard scale, but as it passes in, it pulls in such a way that my clitoris rolls down and brushes against the top of his cock. That sends pleasure waves roaring through me like white caps from a storm on a lake.

I cry out with surprise at the shocking intensity of the pleasure. He stops, pulling back from our kiss, and says my name again, along with a lot more words I don't understand. I shake my head, trying to let him know that it's okay.

"Good," I say, nodding my head up and down, exaggerating. "More, more."

I wrap my arms around his waist the best I can and gently pull forward to make sure he understands. He hisses and nods. He doesn't push in, but instead kisses me again.

His kissing is insistent. His tongue licks my lips. One hand trails along the side of my body. I'm swept away by his rapt attention to my pleasure.

Slowly, he resumes pushing in. Each inch of him expands and fills me. As each individual ridge reaches my opening, it becomes more and more pleasurable.

I'm acutely aware of those hard ridges inside, and they create an ongoing feeling of pleasure as he penetrates deeper and deeper.

At last our hips meet and he's fully inside. I feel stretched beyond all limits, which is enhanced by the ridges on top of his cock. He holds himself there deep inside, and then presses his forehead to mine.

On impulse, I wrap my arms around his neck and drive my tongue into his mouth. His eyes widen in surprise, then he reacts like any human man would. His tongue finds mine and they dance.

He shifts his hips, and a surprise round of pleasure explodes through as something adds pressure to my clit. The sensations are overwhelming, blasting away all thought but pleasure. His cock retreats, but he doesn't pull all the way out, just to the first ridge, then he slides in, burying his cock inside. It feels so fucking good, and nature takes over.

As our tongues wrestle, our hips find their own rhythm. It takes a few times before we settle into it, rising up to meet him and not cutting his thrust short.

He moves slowly, pushing his cock in, and those ridges really are there for my pleasure. They entice my body in ways I didn't know existed. The sensations are incredible.

Our bodies welcome each other while we slowly increase our speed. Having found our rhythm in each other, he pushes in a little faster. He breaks our kiss to pull back and study my face while pushing in and out. Half-lidded eyes, biting my lower lip, I moan.

He grunts as he buries himself in me. It's a deep sound that rumbles up from his belly. I feel it moving through him, and it's really sexy.

"Yes," I pant, nodding.

I grab his ass and pull him down faster. He moves faster and faster, building towards wild abandon. Pistoning in and out. I meet every thrust of his hips with a thrust of my own. As he drives his cock in and out, I wrap my arms around his neck, holding his face against mine.

We kiss, our tongues dancing as his cock pushes in and retreats over and over. He moans into my mouth, and it's the hottest thing I've ever heard. I press myself as hard as I can against him and shudder as another wave of release locks my body. I cry out his name, then suddenly he breaks our kiss. He arches his back, looking up at the roof of our shelter, and screams my name as he buries himself in me.

His cock swells and his tail stands stiff and straight behind him. He groans, shuddering, as he holds until the last wave of his orgasm is complete. When he's finished, he looks down into my eyes and warmth suffuses my chest, swelling through my body. It's a look of pure adoration that makes the sex feel so much more than physical.

I'm overwhelmed by how satisfied I feel. I smile, and he smiles back. He slides out of me and rises to his knees, so I raise up on my elbows. It gives me a good view for what comes next. His massive, ridged cock softens and then lowers, and as it does, another cock drops from beneath his tail and stiffens between the two of us.

I look from his new cock to him in complete shock, but then college bio crashes into my brain. Snakes on Earth have two penises to help ensure fertilization. I never would've suspected his genetics would be similar. He looks from his cock to me.

"Calisssta?" he asks.

Two cocks. Wow. Talk about double the pleasure! Grinning, I nod. I'm still wet and ready to accommodate him. On impulse I hold up a hand, stopping him mid-motion before he can get over me.

I slip past him outside the shelter. He moves to follow, but I stop him by putting my hands on his shoulders. I push and pull on him, awkwardly getting him to move under my control.

"Calisssta?"

"Go with it," I instruct.

At last I have him on his back inside the shelter. I climb over top of him and reach down between my legs to grab his second cock. I'm leaned over, adjusting my position, when my nipples graze against his scales.

"Oh," I gasp, seeing stars.

He takes hold of my arms, supporting me, and I laugh as the unexpectedly intense sensation passes. Shifting my hips around, I get the head of his dick lined up like I want then I slide back onto it.

I'm adjusted to him now and no longer nervous, so he slides in easily. I push down until he's fully seated, then I rise up. As I do, my clit rubs against his protruding knob, and once more the lightning strike of pleasure reacts.

I grind myself against him, getting past the initial burst. I run my hands through my hair as I twist on his dick. He fondles my tits, and we come together, letting the orgasms build slowly.

I close my eyes, biting my lip and grinding. Something moves down my back, and I startle. Popping my eyes open, his tail moves over my shoulders, stroking up and down my back.

His tail. Damn, I'm fucking an alien. What will Jolie say to this?

I'm carried away. I didn't know I was capable of having so many orgasms, but I feel a fresh one building. I shift and lean over, putting my hands on either side of him.

In my new position I work my hips, driving his dick in and out like a jackhammer. My orgasm builds and builds until it explodes. He thrusts in one last time as my orgasm breaks, and then he screams my name at the same time I cry out his.

I'm left shaking and breathless. I don't want the aching emptiness I know will come when I slide off him, so I drop onto his chest and rest there enjoying the feeling of him softening inside.

We cuddle this way for a long time, but eventually it becomes uncomfortable. I slide up and off then roll over to the side. We shift around until my head is on his shoulder. I drift in and out of sleep. It's dark again. My what, third day since the crash?

Well, in three days progress has been made. I've learned a few words of an alien language. Taught an alien a few of mine. Had the best sex of my life. Progress for sure. Now if I can only get him to go help all the other survivors.

The weight of my responsibility for their survival settles heavy on my shoulders.

13

CALISTA

I'm pleasantly sore as we walk. It a constant reminder of how amazing sex with Ladon was, a feeling of having been deeply satisfied. A craving that I never noticed having was filled. I can't stop thinking about it as we travel, not that there's a lot else to think about.

The landscape around us is unchanging for so long it's numbing. I never would have believed I could become tired of seeing a horizon, but I am. Sand, more sand, and oh yes, here's some more sand to get excited about. Traveling is hard, and I wouldn't cover nearly the difference without his help. The top layer of the sand is loose enough that I sink in almost to my knee with every step, but Ladon uses his wings and tail to glide along the top without difficulty. I'll freely admit I'm jealous.

We pass by a few plants, and I would like to check them out, but it's too much effort. It's so hot I see the waves of energy bouncing off the sand. When I dare to glance up at the barren reddish-orange sky, I pray for a cloud. Anything that would bring a moment's relief from the harsh stare of the two suns, one larger, one smaller, that glare on us like the misshapen eyes of an angry god.

There's a constant breeze, which could bring some hints of relief from the heat, but no, it's nothing more than even hotter air. Now I know what it must be like to be a piece of meat in a convection oven. Miserable.

My headache returns with a vengeance, and by what must be midday I'm struggling to stay upright. I retreat further into the pleasant memories of last night as an escape from the unending monotonous work of traveling across this corner of hell.

I'm dimly aware on some level that the landscape is changing, if subtly. The ground had been mostly flat since leaving the oasis, with only low dunes of sand left by the ever present blowing breeze, but now the dunes are becoming steeper. They cut off any view of the horizon. Moving up them is so hard that Ladon offers to carry me, but I refuse only because I think that if we don't come to a shelter soon I'll pass out and then there won't be a choice but for him to carry me. All I can do is conserve his strength until the inevitable happens.

We're working our way up the biggest dune yet, and it's slow going. Every time I step forward, the sand slips and I slide back half a step at least. So every two steps forward is one step back. My body hurts so much I've gone past pain to feeling numb. I can only experience so much, and I've gone into some kind of a shutdown, running on pure will alone.

When at long last—what seems like it might be days—we come to the top of the hill, we're high enough I see something glistening ahead. I straighten up, stretch my back, and groan as it responds with several cracks. I shield my eyes and blink several times, forcing my eyes to focus on the gleam.

"Is that...?" I speak aloud out of habit.

I look at Ladon and point. He points also and says a word which I try to mimic. It takes me a few tries before I get it right. Ladon smiles and nods excitedly then points at the horizon again.

"Home?" I ask. The gleam looks to be a reflection off something metal. As my eyes focus, I see tall shadows that look like spiny fingers stretching up towards the sky. "Home?"

I repeat the word he said and alternate my own word for home with it. He nods, and I think I we are on the same page. It's really hard to know, but I hope so. If that is his home, then that means shelter from the sun. Safety from all the things that have tried to kill me so far. It also means that there is plenty of room for my friends and the other survivors to take shelter. It's already there, waiting for us to move in.

I FIND MY SECOND OR THIRD WIND OR WHATEVER. Seeing a destination that promises at least some relief lifts my spirits. I'm no longer walking in a daze, more lost in my own circular thoughts and memories. We continue with him helping me.

It's incredibly obvious how well adapted to this environment he is. His wings aren't intended to let him fly but to let him move across the loose sand without trouble. Where every step I take I sink in and must fight my way free to take the next one, he walks as light as a feather.

Dark spots dance before my eyes and I'm sure I'm on the verge of heat exhaustion again. Water is not replacing the electrolytes in my system. My headache is unending, my throat is always dry, and I stopped sweating at some point. The meat from his kill helps more than anything, surprisingly enough. I don't understand how or why, but I'd love to have some time in my lab with samples of it. It helps, but it doesn't completely fix my body's need for hydration.

I keep pushing on, hoping that things will get better soon. The landscape is rolling dunes. As soon as we top one, another is there waiting. The good part is they are getting smaller as we go. I put all my attention into taking one step at a time and not falling.

When we crest one of the biggest we've climbed in a while, I get another look at what he is calling home. It really is a city. Or was one. It's now the remnants of what once was probably a nice, big city.

Once tall towers are now shells of their former glory. Everything looks like it was blackened and burnt or twisted by some extreme force. In school we studied Earth history, including the great wars that culminated in humanity's exodus from our home planet. I've seen vids taken in the aftermath of the anti-matter bombs used in the last wars on Earth. This city looks like those. Something terrible, devastating, happened here.

I slip and slide down the dune we're on. It's the last one before a flat open area that leads directly into the city itself. Closer now, I see new details. The sand drifts up against the buildings. The damage looks like it was done a long time ago. Everything has a decayed look to it. Some of the buildings have hardy plants sticking out of pieces.

Some buildings seem to have survived better than others. The structures were built to withstand a lot of force. The ones closest to the edge are in the worst shape. Some of them are nothing more than twisted frames of a steel-like material. Those look like the twisted bones of giant monsters.

Further into the city, which looks like it's laid out similar to an Earth city, with square blocks and streets running between the sections, the buildings are closer to being whole. There is obvious damage. Broken and missing coverings. Façade damage, but not as many that look completely destroyed.

The transition from desert to the city is stepping from the desert into a civilization after it's been abandoned. There's almost a distinct line between sand and city, though there is no visible barrier or reason for it. The sand thins, then I'm walking on a hard material that has a slight spring to it, which gives a buoyancy to each step I take. This material forms the roads that run between the buildings.

As we pass over, the shadows of the buildings fall with welcome coolness across us. I pause, taking in the enormity of it. Once, long ago, this was the home of a thriving people. Ladon's people, I assume. What happened here? Is this what would have happened on Earth if the generation ships hadn't been built? How many friends and family did Ladon lose when this happened? Was he alive when it did?

Hundreds of questions come and go without answer. I stop and look at Ladon. My eyes ache, and I'm sure if I wasn't so dehydrated, I'd be crying. The loss around is too close to the loss I experienced. I've lost my home, and so has he. The world as I knew it was blown up, and so has his. I touch his arm and shake my head. The lump in my throat is much too big for me to get words past it.

He frowns with obvious concern, placing his hand over the top of mine. I laugh, not out of humor. I don't know why I do. It's a choked noise, and I shake my head.

"Sorry," I say. He touches my cheek, and I lift my face to meet his. "Sorry for your loss."

I motion around us, shaking my head. Choked up and desperate for a good cry. The stupidest thing I could do, but I'm human. What else am I supposed to do with this overwhelming sense of loss and grief? I need to express it somehow. Let it out, not keep it bottled up inside.

Ladon says something, but of course I don't know what it is. I wish, with all my heart, we could talk to one another. Like people do. I want to tell him how bad I feel for him. How much it echoes my own hurt. I want to empathize with him, and I want to feel him empathizing with me.

But we can't. He pulls me into his arms and holds me. We can't speak, but on some primal level below words, he understands. I wrap my arms around him and hold on with all I've got. I hold him until the black emptiness of all we've lost recedes. It's not gone—it's much too soon for that —but it retreats back into the dark corners of my thoughts, and that's enough. For now.

I loosen my grip and step back. He lets me go, but the way he's watching it's clear he's trying to make sure I'm okay. I force a smile, rub my face, and run my hands through my hair.

"Yeah," I say, nodding, which I know he'll understand. "I'm fine. Let's go. Lots to do and all that."

Ladon smiles and offers me his hand. I take it and he leads the way deeper into this broken city he calls home. The devastation and loss becomes clearer the further we go. Rubble, debris, and trash fill the streets. We pick our way through it carefully. Even here he's alert, looking around us constantly.

The people who built this city were every bit as advanced as Earth. I wouldn't be surprised to find they also had space travel. Is that why I haven't seen any other intelligent life besides Ladon? Was he somehow left behind? I can't help but wonder if this isn't the future of Earth. What Earth might look like right now, even. I knew the idea of rescue was farfetched, but thinking about this makes it seem even more of an impossibility.

The city is huge, but eventually we come to a large open space. Perhaps once this was a communal market or a park. In the center of the large area is a square made of what looks like concrete rising several feet from the ground. In the middle of this square is a statue of a man—well, an alien-dragon man similar to Ladon, but sculpted in heroic proportions to dominate the space. His wings are spread, one hand holding a weapon similar to Ladon's at his side, while the other is raised towards the sky and holds long strands of something that looks like seaweed. As we move closer to the statue and the raised square, the statue is on a raised dais. The square around it is walls. If I had to guess, it looks to have once been a fountain.

Ladon barely spares a glance for it as he leads us past and to a large, mostly intact, building. The building has a wide awning across its front with double doors and clear walls that can't be glass but looks similar. There is a sign, but whatever message it once presented has been blasted off. He strides up and opens the door, holding it for me.

I smile and step inside. It's dark and cool, which is a welcome relief from the pounding heat. Ladon says something then continues ahead. I look around in awe, drawing comparisons to what I'm familiar and what is different.

It's more obvious than ever that at some time in the past an advanced civilization lived and worked here. What happened to them?

The inside of the building is covered with thick dirt lying in layers over the rubble. Part of the ceiling has fallen, leaving black holes and revealing broken frameworks. There are pieces sticking out, which look like they might have once been desks or furniture of similar function, but it's rotting away and barely recognizable as more than junk.

Ladon strides through the space and I follow him through another set of doors to a set of stairs. One set goes up and one goes down. He takes the one leading up, moving us around and through the building. The stairwell is dimly lit with sunlight streaming in through holes in the walls around it. He climbs with the easy certainty of familiarity. I'm a lot slower.

The steps are not designed for my height, as I figure out on the second one when I knock my shin into it by not lifting high enough. After that I figure out to pay more attention. After we make it up what I'd guess is a flight, the condition of them changes too. There's a massive hole, and while Ladon steps over it easily, my legs aren't nearly that long.

I press against the wall and work my way up sideways. Ladon stands at the top, keeping one hand pressed to my stomach so I won't fall. Once we're past that hole, there are some others but none as wide as that.

Thanks to everything being wrong sized, I'm not sure how high we've climbed when he exits the stairwell and we emerge into a long dark hallway.

At the end of the hall is a double set of doors that I can barely make out in the creeping shadows.

Ladon offers me a hand, which I take gratefully. This hallway is unsettling, to say the least. There's an oppressive weight to the city. Almost an emptiness, but not quite. As if I might listen too closely and hear the screaming ghosts of its past.

He suffers no such qualms. Striding confidently down the hall, I double time my steps to keep up with him. We pass doorways that I glance in on as we go. Some of the doors are open, some are missing. The rooms they open up onto are more of the same. Debris, decay, and every indication of having been long abandoned. I do see signs of technology, most of which I can only guess at the original purpose of. The remnants of machines have survived the ravages of time better than most of the other things in the rooms. I assume they are made of metal, or some similar material by the look, but lying in the dirt and debris near them I spot crystals. Without being able to stop and inspect closer, I'm fairly certain that the technology would be considered advanced by my own people's standards.

When we arrive at the end of the hall, he opens the double doors and it takes my breath away. Light floods out of the room, but it's not hot. The air is actually a little cooler than the hallway.

The room itself is big enough to hold hundreds of people at once. There are row after row of what look like complicated stations resembling cubicles surrounded by clear glass. Many of them have been destroyed, broken shards hanging or empty frames. Some, though, are still intact.

The light reflecting throughout the room streams through the ceiling, which is also made of a kind of glass. The sunlight is diffused and altered from its normal red state to a soft white light that is cool instead of warm.

Not far ahead is one station that sparkles as the light passes through the mostly whole glass around it. It highlights the surface, and I can see designs that seem to flow and move across the clear walls that define it.

Ladon walks through the room, ignoring the surrounding wonders. I follow along, but my attention is darting around the room like a leaping frog. I want to know more. What was this room? What purpose did it serve, how does it work? Are these machines as I think, or are they something beyond that I can't yet comprehend?

This building seems to be centrally located, and I have a suspicion that it was a central hub for the city. Are there are more people like Ladon? Does he live alone? What happened to his people? How did this once thriving city become reduced to this?

As we pass by the mostly whole cubicle, it brightens. The glass walls glow then spring to life. Moving images are spread across the three walls. It reminds me of vid sticks on the ship, but the rendering is flat, two dimensional. Vids on the ship project and form a holographic scene you watch.

Curious, I walk inside the booth, picking my way over and around the debris littering the floor. The images swirl then coalesce and form a more familiar three-dimension, but they're no longer on the walls. I blink and still see them. They're casting directly onto my retinas. Fascinating!

I don't understand the language being spoken, but it is similar enough to a newscast or a documentary I can guess its purpose. It starts by showing what must be daily life here before whatever happened to leave the city empty. Ladon stands off to one side. He watches me, but it's clear he's not looking at the images.

"Is this okay?" I ask.

He doesn't say anything, so I turn back and watch. It doesn't take long before my stomach turns and tears well in my eyes. The images panning across the screen tell the story, and now I know what happened to his people. It's horrifying. On my ship they want to make sure we don't repeat the mistakes of our past. The history of Earth is drilled into every child, including all the atrocities ever committed by man against man. Somehow what I'm watching here is worse.

Men, women, and children like Ladon living, working, and playing together. The camera pans through the city, giving a complete slice of life view. It's obvious their world is harsh, but their technology more than compensates for it. As the camera pans around, I can see that the city itself is covered by a glistening dome. I make an educated guess that it controlled the environment inside and protected from the harshness of the planet.

The scenes play on, and as they do, ships come out of the sky. Different races of other aliens. They interact with and trade with Ladon's people. Dozens of different races come and go. Spaceports appear, and while the narrator continues, the imagery returns repeatedly to ships being loaded with similar crates.

The scene shifts and I'm following a group of alien-dragon men, Ladon's race, out through the dome and across the desert outside. They ride on cars that don't have wheels but seem to flow on a cushion of air. They travel to a cavern where the men disembark, gather their gear, and enter a dark maw.

Inside the cave is beautiful. Some of the men appear to be standing guard and have weapons while the others carry tools. They also seem to stay close, traveling as a group, and all of them are alert.

The cave glows with a soft blue light, and as they get deeper, long strands of plant life grows from the ceiling and gives off a luminescence. The men with the tools work together and harvest the strands. The other men stand guard, and it's not long before I can see why.

Huge bat-like creatures swoop out of the darkness and attack. The defenders shoot with their weapons, but instead of projectiles, I think they fire sound waves. Whatever it is, it drives the bat-like creatures away, and the harvesters finish their work.

They load their harvest onto the cars, and then the men climb back on. The camera follows as they exit the cave. The guards stay at attention the entire time, eyes scanning the desert.

Suddenly, the ground jumps underneath them and the car tilts so far over I think it's going to roll. My stomach lurches with it and I reach out, touching the cold glass to steady myself. The ground rumbles and is breaking up like something is running underneath it, tunneling fast, racing towards the men.

The guards leap from the moving car and bring their weapons around. Suddenly the ground bursts open and a giant worm-like creature shoots up into the sky, towering over them. It waves back and forth in the air then opens a giant maw filled with razor sharp teeth. The worm slams down against the ground, and the car is thrown up into the air, tossing men and supplies across the desert. The guards fire as the camera circles, somehow shifting to an aerial view.

The monster kills two men, grabbing them up and swallowing them whole. The sound of their screams echoes in my ears as the guards' fire incessantly. The worm-thing jerks back and forth, reacting to the blasts, then retreats. The remaining men hurriedly gather the scattered harvest, load it back onto the cars, climb in and continue on their way.

The scenes change and I see the streets of the city once more, but now there are angry people marching. They carry signs that flash messages as they head towards a familiar building. The one we're in right now.

Ships hover in the sky above the dome as the protesters reach the square where the fountain is. Three men stand in front of the building with their wings spread and their fists raised. They're talking, yelling, and the crowd is responding. The one in the middle points to the ships in the sky then closes his hand into a fist and shakes it. The people respond making fists and shaking them at the sky.

As the images dance across my vision, my head begins to itch. Enthralled in what I'm watching, I absently scratch my scalp, but it doesn't bring relief. The itching feels like it's on the inside. I close my eyes and the images play across the back of my eyelids. Warmth floods through my head. It spreads down, chest flushing, limbs pulsing with life.

The crowds in the vid continue to yell, a swelling sound that resolves into a chant. I shiver as cold races down my back. One word comes up over and over. Krixian.

My skin tingles and the itching in my head increases until it's like there are a thousand tiny needles poking rapidly. The vid continues, the ships hovering above, the crowd chanting. Shots are fired. Another ship of different make races across the sky, firing on the hovering ones.

"Fight the Krix, freedom!" the crowd chants.

The scene changes again and Ladon's people are armed for war. Invaders march through the streets which are lined with the dead, both of Ladon's race and the other alien races. There are dozens of different alien forms marching in formation, killing all that they come across.

The ships in the sky fire down and bombs are exploding. A gas cloud floods the city, and everyone it reaches chokes and dies. At last, almost no one is left alive. There are drones floating through the city, and it becomes obvious what I'm watching is a vid taken by one of them. It zooms between the buildings, racing up around so fast it's disorienting.

There is only silence as it flies, then gunfire. The drone wobbles, knocked around by the impact of the weapon. It spins to face its attackers, and two aliens of the same race as Ladon stand atop a pile of rubble firing at it. One of them charges, wielding a bladed weapon similar to the one I've seen him use.

"For Zmaj! For freedom!" the one charging screams, wielding his weapon in a spiraling display of skill.

There's a whistling sound that grows louder still. The drone tilts the angle shifting up, but in the bottom of its view I see its two attackers also looking up. My vision flashes white then the vid ends.

"Are you kidding?" I ask, shaking my head and struggling with knees gone weak.

Absently I rub my arms, staring at the walls that are slowly losing their glow. My chest tingles as I scramble to understand. An entire race, destroyed in a senseless war. But how did he survive? Are there others like him? How long ago was this?Cold chills spread across my skin as I turn to Ladon. He's staring at the ground, waiting for it to finish. The icy cold hand of empathy clenches my heart in a death grip.

The pain and the loss he's felt is, in some ways, worse than my own. I'm choked up, can barely breathe. The urge to comfort him fights with the need to be comforted. I can't imagine how he survived.

On impulse, I run to him and throw my arms around him, smashing my lips against his. He returns my embrace and we hold each other, letting the harsh memories fade the best we can.

I want to hold him until the heartache is healed, his and mine, but I know that's not possible. How can I fix what he's been through? Losing all his people? As much as I've lost, there are others. More of my people. I'm not left alone on this hellhole of a planet. How many years has he lived here alone? I pull back at last and he speaks softly, saying my name, and I smile.

"Oh my poor prince of Vulcan, what am I going to do with you? You're like Spock, having lost your people, and yet you survive, all alone in the universe. I'm here for you. I know you don't understand me, not yet, but I'm here, Ladon."

I touch his cheek and he smiles, but it doesn't reach his eyes. Those are filled with sadness. Heartache and loss. All of which I understand too well. I kiss him, not with passion, but with something much deeper. Sympathy, empathy— no, understanding. Shared pain.

"That was the Devastation," he says, when I break the kiss.

"It was awful, I'm so sorry," I say, resting my fingers on his face. I jerk back and my eyes go wide. My heart leaps into my throat. "Say something. Say something now."

He stares, his brow furrowing.

"What would I say?" he asks.

"Oh," I gasp. I touch my face, run my hands over it, shake my head, then return my gaze to him.

"Again. Say something else."

"Calista," he says. "What is happening?"

My jaw rests on my chest. I blink rapidly.

"Zmaj," I say, testing the word. Ladon goes stock still in that way that I've never seen any other living creature do. He blinks then slowly tilts his head to one side. "You are a Zmaj. You understood that, didn't you?"

"Calista, you're speaking my language," he says.

"I am," I exclaim, bouncing on the balls of my feet.

I throw my arms around him and we kiss. This time there is passion, but the passion is fleeting. The excitement at understanding is quickly overshadowed by the enormity of what I now know. The loss and pain he's been through.

"How long?" I ask, stepping back while taking his hands in mine. He shakes his head as his shoulders drop and he looks to the ground. He says something, but my new understanding of his language must be limited somehow, because I don't understand the words. I squeeze his hands and shake my head. "I'm sorry, I didn't understand that."

He inhales deeply, and as his chest fills, he squares his shoulders and looks into my eyes. He frowns then points at the cubicle.

"Old," he says, followed by a word that doesn't make sense.

"It's old?" I ask and he nods. "Oh, you mean it's probably not working right. You had this technology before?"

"Yes," he says. "Before…"

"What happened was awful," I say. "I can't imagine. Or maybe I can."

An incredible weight settles onto my shoulders now, and I can barely hold my own head up. I've avoided as much as possible thinking about what I've lost, but sometimes, like now, it sucker punches me right in the gut. The hurt and the loss is so raw it's overwhelming. I can't even begin to process the enormity of it all.

Ladon senses my pain or feels the echo of it in his own. He pulls me into his arms and wraps himself around me. I return the embrace, and we hold each other for what might only be a moment, but it feels longer. When at last he eases his arms, the ache has faded enough it's no longer so hard to breathe. Even so, tears press hard against the backs of my eyes.

"Tell me," I say.

"Tell?"

"Are you okay?"

He nods. "It was long ago. Memory is dim."

"How long?"

He says some words that don't make sense again no matter how I try to figure them out. It's like they slide across my mind without sticking; they don't form any concept of what they mean. I shake my head and frown in frustration.

"That didn't... I didn't understand it," I say, changing what I was going to say mid-thought to make it more accurate.

"I see," he says. Holding my hand, he leads the way over to where there is a long bench and takes a seat. I sit next to him, waiting. "The technology isn't all good. Partial. Used to work better."

"After what it's been through, I'm amazed it works at all," I say. "How did you survive?"

The torment on his face and in his eyes is so clear, so poignant, a tear falls for him. Something catches in my throat, and I wish I hadn't asked. I never want to cause him pain like this.

"I don't know," he says, shrugging and holding his hands up. His wings rustle as his tail twitches, dragging across the floor.

"Are there others? Survivors like you?" I ask, then it occurs to me that there might be other women of his kind. What if there are? How am I supposed to compete with a woman like the ones I saw in the vid? Big, strong, and made to survive on this inhospitable planet?

"Some," he says. "Not many."

"Oh," I say, chewing on my lip. "Are there any... females?"

He shakes his head. "No. They didn't survive. Only males at the end."

We sit in a contemplative silence. Part of me feels I should say something, anything, but every time I open my mouth to speak, I've got nothing. The parallels of our experience float through my thoughts, but I can barely grasp them. It's too broad, too raw, too recent for consideration.

The moment stretches until at last he rises from the bench. I stand up, and hand in hand, he leads us away. We leave the room with the screens behind, but as we go, I think about the city I saw from before the war.

There might still be sources of power, and as I've seen, there is lots of space. I have to get Ladon to understand about my friends and help me bring them here. There's an entire city at hand just waiting to have life brought back to it. There's a lot of work to do, repairs, cleaning and all that, but it doesn't change the fact that we could build something amazing together. Something that might fill the hole in what all of us have lost.

If we can find the power source, then maybe I can figure out how to activate the dome again too. That would protect us from the creatures that roam the desert as well as the extremes of temperature.

It's a nebulous idea with a lot of ifs, but it's a start. I can return to my people with hope.

If they've survived. If I survive.

14

LADON

While we walk, memories tug at my thoughts. Images break free of the fog the bijass brings. When she watched the screens, Calista's eyes were wide, with lines of moisture leaking from her eyes, trailing down her cheeks. Her mouth moved but no sound emerged.

I watched her, waiting, prepared for her recriminations. For her to tell me how stupid we were.

We thought we were kings of the galaxy. Epis ruled the world—no one in the known galaxy could survive or operate without it, and we thought we controlled it.

No one else could harvest it. Only us. We were arrogant fools. We brought about our own downfall with our greed. When the labor unions organized and wrested away control of the supply, we thought it would serve to enrich us, to take control of our own lives. Our own destiny, no longer working at the control of massive off-world organizations that controlled the flow of epis. When we took control of the ports and restricted the flow of epis, we thought we had won.

Stupid. Naïve. Ignorant. We hadn't won, we'd lost. More than we could have imagined. Everything. We'd lost everything.

The other races didn't respond with diplomacy as we expected. They brought war. They joined together and all but wiped us from existence.

I was part of the unions and the rebellion that followed. I played my part in the destruction of my race. I'd blocked off my memories of the times before the Devastation. I'd forgotten the role I'd played. Hidden it, buried it so deep, I no longer thought that was me.

I was a different person, but seeing the replays through Calista's eyes—it wasn't gone or forgotten. Just hidden and waiting to come back. Waiting to remind me that I'm no different now than I was then. My curse is that I survived the Devastation. My punishment is to wander the empty, destroyed city and know the hand I played in its fall. All the lives lost, and my part in that too.

Calista stops walking. She shakes her head and steps towards me, raising her hand, and I expect her to slap my face. In some strange way I need her to. All of this destruction and loss I helped cause.

She looks up, straining her neck full back to stare straight into my face. My stomach clenches tight, but I don't move. I will accept whatever punishment she deems worthy. Her hand touches my face, not with a slap, but with surprising gentleness.

Her touch is pulsing waves of warmth that spreads across my cheek. Her lips, full and plush, press together, then she rises onto her toes, and those soft, beautiful, delightful lips are on mine.

I don't react for two beatings of my hearts. Thoughts race, swirling in confusion. She wraps her arms around my neck, pulling me down into her, and I give myself to her kiss.

She wraps her fingers in my hair as our kiss goes on. And on. We only break when at last we can hold it no longer, leaving us holding each other, panting.

"I'm sorry," she says.

"Sorry? You have nothing to be sorry for," I say.

She shakes her head and places two fingers on my lips.

"No, not..." she frowns. "Words aren't right. I feel," she places one hand on her chest, "I hurt too. I understand how much it must hurt." Her words are broken, but it's enough for me to understand. Or I think I do. "I lost my home too."

Water streams down her face. Wasteful, yet something about it is touching. A pang in my chest echoes the display. Moving slow, I catch one of the drops onto my finger and hold it up for inspection. It catches the light and refracts it. Curious, I taste it. It's salty, full of nutrients she needs inside her body, not outside.

"What are you doing?" she asks.

I rest the palm of my hand on her cheek. "Why?"

"Why? Why what?"

"Moisture," I say, pointing with my other hand. "Why? Wasteful."

She snorts then chuckles softly. "Yeah, I guess it is."

She says a word that doesn't translate. I sound it out, relating the word to the idea of water leaking from her eyes.

"T-ea-rass," I say.

She shakes her head and repeats the word. I sound it out a few more times until she smiles and nods. Tears. What a strange thing they are. I do not think I've ever seen such a thing before.

"Did you," she stops speaking, furrowing her brow, then shakes her head. "No. I shouldn't... it's fine. We should keep moving."

"What is it?" I ask.

"I shouldn't ask," she says.

"Calista," I say, my hearts quickening as the syllables of her name roll off my tongue so sweetly, like the most delicate and lightest of sweets. "Please. Do ask. Anything."

She blinks rapidly as more of the tears race down her cheeks. She swallows and nods.

"Did you lose people?"

She says people, but there's something to the way she says the word, as if she's choosing that word over some other word. Or something else she really wants to ask.

"I did," he says. "My family."

"Family?" her voice is tight, almost as if she is choking on the word.

"Yes," I say.

The pain surges out of the fog, and in its wake is memory. Memory of those I helped destroy. My role in the rebellion, fresh and raw as if it has only just happened, not so long ago as it is.

I want to hide it away, forget it again. Bury it where it belongs. All the mistakes of the past, the stupid decisions, none of them matter. The bijass roils, pouncing at the opportunity to take control. It offers respite, forgetfulness. In the bijass, there is no past nor is there any future. There is only the now. The most primal of needs and desires. Food, mating, sleeping. An endless cycle with no looking into the past or to the future that doesn't exist.

The future that didn't exist. Calista watches me, her eyes sparkling with brilliant intelligence, and her face an open display of affection and concern. I didn't have any hope of a future, but in her I do. She waits, patient.

"My pod mates passed before me," I say, trying to dodge the most painful of the memories that have been unleashed.

"Pod mate," she repeats.

"My father." The word blurts without thought. Flying from my mouth to hang between us and drop like a heavy stone.

"Your father? That's awful, I'm sorry."

"He told me not to join the rebellion. He didn't agree with it. Told me," my throat clenches tight as I recall the final time I saw him. The argument we had that day.

"It's okay," she says, her voice so soft it could be a breeze slipping through the cracks of the building. "You don't have to say it."

I take a deep breath, forcing myself to meet her gaze.

"We argued," I say, "the last time I saw him. He didn't want me to join the rebellion. He said it would be the end of our world. That nothing good could ever come of it."

"Oh," she says.

I stare at the floor as the weight of the past crushes me. I can't lift my head. I'm surprised the structure of the building isn't giving way beneath my feet, casting me down into the rubble.

Calista's soft hands cup my chin, and she tugs until I lift my head and our eyes meet. My stomach clenches as I do, preparing for the reproach that will be on her face. Now she knows my failure.

When our eyes meet, the look on her face is anything but reproach. The moisture, the tears she calls them, stream down her face in a wasteful display. They are a sacrifice. A sacrifice to pain and loss. Hers and mine too. She sheds them for both of us.

"Ladon," she says, "it's not your fault."

I am forgiven.

She doesn't blame me, she understands. She too is lost. Falling from the sky in a piece of a ship. I'm sure the ship itself was even bigger than the massive chunk resting in the desert. She probably lost friends and family too.

"Ladon," she repeats, and her voice is soft and soothing. Music to my ears, a balm to the aching pains of my soul.

The fog of bijass, that regressive state that came over the last of my kind after the Devastation, recedes. Memories, clearer than they have been in ages, are laid bare. She places both her hands on my face, brushing my hair back from my face, and then she smiles.

"Calista," I say her name as an affirmation. "My treasure."

A thank you. An expression of my love. The dragon rumbles, content in having laid its claim.

I can't continue standing, though. Painful memories and the pleasant present will not handle the longer-term problem. She must have epis and soon. Even here, in the cool shelter of the building, her skin is flushed an unnatural pinkish color. There is a tremble to her movement that she tries to hide. She is not doing well. She's growing weaker. Her inefficient body is not adjusting to the heat, and worse she has shed so much moisture to wash away the sins of my past.

Tonight we'll rest here, then early tomorrow we'll head for the caverns and I will harvest epis for Calista. It's dangerous, of course, but everything on Tajss is dangerous. It is the only way I can keep her safe, so I will succeed.

I take her hand and continue towards where I have made my home in another part of this building. I lead her through the halls to the room I've claimed, and unload my pack.

This once was an apartment for the city officials who would have to work late or be on call for city services. Over time I've scavenged all over the city and collected things that offer some little comforts.

A metal box that once was part of a machine serves for a fire container. I keep tinder and wood close at hand, which I use to get a fire going. I place the makeshift wire racking over the fire and set the last of the guster meat on it to grill. The meat should give her strength, hopefully enough.

Calista is not idle while I cook. She explores the area, peeking through the tanned leather divider hanging over the one interior door to see the space I've made my bedroom. Off of it there is a restroom. She disappears into there while I finish cooking. The furnishings will be big for her but should be serviceable.

There's no running water, of course, and water is too precious a resource to waste. The sewage system of old used chemicals, buckets of which I have gathered and stored in there. I will have to show her how to use them.

As the meat sizzles, she emerges and makes herself at home. My smile is so broad it hurts my cheeks. She picks up debris that has fallen from the ceiling and places it into one corner. I grab a piece of an old plate and wipe it off before placing the meat on it and offering it Calista.

She smiles and takes it gratefully. We sit on the floor together and eat our dinner, then I lead her to my bed, where we lie together. She snuggles up against me, and I stroke her softly, wanting to please her again.

The heat must be affecting her worse than I feared, as she falls too quickly into uneasy sleep. I wrap myself around her, hoping my body will cool hers, and also fall into restless dreams.

I WAKE BEFORE HER AND LIE VERY STILL, LISTENING to her breathe. Even here in the cool building, her skin is hot. It's okay, though, because today I'll get the epis. She stretches and rolls into me, throwing her arms wide. I smile in the dark as she runs her leg down mine.

"Good morning," I say.

She moans and stretches, then her eyelids flutter open, and I see her beautiful eyes. A peaceful calm spread through me. She is my greatest treasure. She says something, and I try to follow the words.

"Good morning," I repeat, speaking slowly and making gestures I hope convey the idea.

She mimics the sounds I make, and in moments she masters them.

"Good morning," she says in my language, grinning from ear to ear.

I kiss her forehead then climb out of bed and dress, motioning that she should do the same.

"Danger today," I say, pointing at my lochaber.

She looks from it to me, then nods. I fix our breakfast and then gather the supplies we'll need. The cavern is at least two-mark's walk. I can make it faster on my own, but it's not safe to leave her here. The protective dome has not worked in recent memory, and wandering packs of dangerous animals encroach frequently. My presence is the only way to make sure she remains safe.

I hitch the supplies over my shoulder, and we leave as the suns are barely breaking the horizon. When we reach the edge of the city and walk onto the sands, I pause and kneel, placing my palm flat on the ground.

"Tajss grant your bounty," I mutter the old prayer softly.

Calista mimics my action, clearly not understanding my words, but her intention is welcome. If I fail, she'll die, and the odds are against me. Today I will face the greatest threat that Tajss has.

15

LADON

The journey to the cavern is uneventful. Calista talks almost nonstop, but I love listening to the sound of her voice. I find it soothing, almost musical. Listening to her makes the journey go by quickly, and before long the rock protrusion rises above the distant hill. The closer we get the higher it looms. When we're close enough, it reveals the long black crack in the world that will lead down into the caverns.

The suns are rising in the sky, and with them the temperature. Calista is growing weaker, her constant chatter trailing off until we walk in silence. The hot winds of Tajss pick up, whistling in my ears and pelting us with pieces of sand. I wrap an arm around Calista and then close one wing across her to protect her delicate skin.

The land before the upthrust cliff is mostly flat, and the dunes grow less steep as we get closer. Soon we're walking across the open ground. The sand is not as loose here as it is on the dunes, making it much easier for Calista. When the shadow of the cliff falls over us, I pull Calista close and motion that she should stay by me.

"Close," I say slowly, gently pulling her towards me to convey my intent. "Very dangerous. Danger."

I point to the top of my lochaber sticking above my shoulder to indicate danger. She nods and her lips tremble. I hate making her feel afraid, but if I had any option, I would not take her with me down below.

I pull my lochaber off my back then retrieve a small torch from my bag. I breathe from my inner throat glands, lighting it aflame. I hold it high over my head so its light doesn't blind us. I look Calista over one last time then we walk into the wide crack in the cliff face and into darkness. The light of day fades behind us until the torch is our only illumination.

The first part of the cave is a wide-open space, but the floor is covered with debris. Rocks, small sandy dunes, and lots of sismis guano. I choose our way carefully to make sure we don't attract unwanted attention. Many of the hostile creatures of Tajss make their homes in the caverns because they're cool and a welcome retreat from the surface's constant heat.

Calista stumbles, kicking some loose stones. In the near-silent caverns the sound is huge, and it echoes off the stone walls. The echoes are met with screeches as sismis spring to life, awakened by the sound of intrusion. The air fills with the sound of their leathery wings.

The sismis sweep down as a horde—a flurry of wings, teeth, and claws. I grab Calista and dive to the ground. The sismis are mostly blind and hunt by sound. She struggles under me for a moment, and only goes still when I hiss. The sismis dive and fly around, searching for prey, until at last they return to their perches along the ceiling.

I wait until there is nothing but silence again, then roll off and let her stand. I clamp my hand over my own mouth to communicate 'quiet,' and then point at the ceiling. She stares up into the shadows before nodding her understanding.

Taking her hand, I lead the way deeper into the cavern. The floor slopes down, then the passageway narrows. I have to turn sideways and still am barely able to squeeze through.

Ahead is the soft, blue-purple glow of the epis. I exhale heavily, forcing as much air out as I can so I can squeeze through. When I emerge on the other side of the pinch point, the cavern opens again into a wide chamber. The ground is covered in shallow water that is rich with nutrients from the sismis droppings on the other side of the pinch point. The walls of the cavern are red and white, smoothly bored by the passing of a zemlja. The color striation looks like wavy ridges.

The epis grows on the ceiling and hangs in long, iridescent strands. There are so many strands growing here that I no longer need my torch. The plant itself illuminates the area with its iridescent glow.

"Wow," Calista gasps, and I smile.

The cave is quite beautiful. Imagining how it must look to her, I see it with fresh eyes. There are not many places on Tajss where life grows in abundance, but the epis cave is life itself. The beauty hides a terrible danger, however.

The epis is a fibrous plant that only grows in these subterranean pools and tunnels left by the passage of the giant sand worms. We stand a great risk of attack being underground in their domain. The vibrations of our efforts to harvest the epis will undoubtedly attract the closest ones. Our best chance of survival is to get what we came for and get out of here as quickly as possible.

She walks around, her feet making soft splashes in the water while she cranes her neck to see everything, whispering in a mix of my language and her own. I smile at her enjoyment. She takes one of the strands of epis in her hand and holds it with a reverence that surprises me.

"Beautiful," she says, raising it close to her face as she studies it. "It's similar to seaweed."

"C-weed?" I ask, not understanding the word she used.

She doesn't look up, continuing to intently study the plant.

"Seaweed," she says. "It's a plant that grows underwater, growing up towards the light. But this… no light to speak of, so it's more a lichen or a moss family, but with properties similar to the seaweed."

We cannot stay here long; the passing moments come with ever increasing danger. I don't know many of the words she's using as she's mixing my language with her own, but I do know we don't have time for her inspection.

I climb a nearby boulder and use my lochaber to reach as high as possible and cut one glowing filament. The light of it dims as it falls to the ground, and I climb down.

Laying my lochaber to one side, I kneel and lay a piece of oiled leather across the ground. Picking up the strand, I carefully work to coil it on the leather.

Once it's coiled, I wrap the leather then bind it closed with the strings designed for the purpose. Harvesting epis was once the lifeblood of Tajss. There is an art to it that must be observed. It cannot be done without many precautions. Once it's harvested, its properties fade. Improper harvesting or storage will cause it to lose them faster.

I'm almost done. Calista has moved to watch me work. I tie the final knot, and as I rise the earth rumbles. Dust drifts from the ceiling. I freeze, not daring to breathe. Calista must remember the prior encounter, and she too is still as stone. The rumbling increases, more dust falls.

Calista inhales sharply. She places one hand under her nose, her eyes wide. Moisture glistens in the corners of her eyes as her face turns pale. The rumblings subside, but then she sneezes.

The rumbling returns, and in an instant the ground bucks underneath us. It's too late. A zemlja bursts from the ground three wings-spread in front of me. It makes a screeching sound, its open maw revealing the rows of teeth.

It's a small one, probably a baby, but zemlja are the apex predators of Tajss and its age doesn't make it less dangerous. The zemlja burrow through the ground in constant motion. Always hunting. Always hungry.

It emerges further out of the ground until it towers over us, screeching. It's three times my own height that I can see, covered in thick protective scales. Tajss' perfect killing machine. It undulates as it snaps its jaws open and shut. Strands of epis are torn from the ceiling as it blindly seeks its prey.

There is no time to waste. They hunt by sound, and all that matters now is that I protect Calista. I throw the epis over my shoulder towards her.

"Calista, run," I yell, leaping to my feet and grabbing my lochaber, swinging it to an attack position.

I don't have time to look back as the worm targets me. It spits, so I duck and roll towards it. The rock where I was sizzles where the creature's acidic saliva lands and eats through it. Swinging the lochaber, I strike the worm right where it emerges from the ground. My blade barely scratches its protective hide as I miss the overlap between plates. I curse my misfortune.

Calista screams, and one heart quits beating while the other double times. Still in a crouch, I whirl on one foot. She's retreating towards the entrance to the cavern with the epis in her hand, but her scream has caught the monster's attention. It dives under the earth, and the ground rumbles as it races towards her.

"Run," I scream as I bend my knees and spread my wings.

I race along the path of the monster. The ground underneath my feet bucks and jumps as it burrows beneath me. I'm only a few feet away from her, so I leap, but as my foot leaves the ground, the worm emerges below me.

I'm on top of it as it rises towards the roof. It opens its mouth, and I'm balancing on either side, trying to avoid falling into its sharp teeth. The jaw snaps shut then opens again. I flap my wings furiously, gaining as much lift as I can to continue dancing on the edge of death.

I bounce on the tips of my feet from one side of its opening mouth to the other while slamming my tail against it, hurting it enough that its jaws snap shut. I lift my lochaber over my head before driving the point down, committing myself to the maneuver.

The blade slices through air, aimed for the unprotected flesh inside its mouth. Seconds tick past as the blade moves down. I bounce from the ball of one foot to the other, swinging my tail the opposite direction to keep my balance.

The zemlja mouth is open, rows of teeth glistening wetly. My blade passes what would be its lips. Its hot breath exhales, the stench of it making my nose burn. Its mouth begins closing too soon.

It's as if the air is fighting back, slowing the passage of my weapon. The mouth clamps on the blade faster than I expect. The zemlja slides down, slipping back into the earth, convinced it has its prey.

I roar, leaning onto the shaft of the lochaber, trying to drive it further in. If it makes it below the ground, this won't be over. She won't be safe. Muscles strain, burning as I push. It slides further but not far enough, barely a hand's width.

"No," Calista screams, throwing rocks at the zemlja from the crack in the wall which she has stepped out from.

The rocks bounce harmlessly off the zemlja's protective scales, but she attracts its attention. It leans towards her.

The threat to my treasure infuses fresh zeal into my muscles. I shift my position, moving with the monster beneath me. It opens its mouth, probably to hurl more of its acidic spit, but I'm ready. The blade of the lochaber slices deep, and I lean all my strength and weight into it. It finds soft, vulnerable flesh.

The zemlja whips wildly back and forth, screeching in pain. It tosses me to the side, and I lose my delicate balancing act. I'm tumbling head over heels.

Spreading my wings, I try to gain control of my spin, but the force is too much. My right wing collapses, and some of the small bones snap. Pain explodes in my head then the rest of my body as I slam up against a wall and slide down. Distantly, I hear Calista crying out.

I shake my head, trying to push past the pain. I'm unarmed, and one wing isn't functioning. I'm in trouble if that monster is still alive. Our best hope is to get out of the cavern with our prize. Calista kneels before me, her warm hands on my face. Moisture streams from her eyes. She's distraught, and her emotions are a storm beating against me.

"Run," I say again, straining to get on my feet.

Pain shoots from my wing and up my back. I'm bruised and broken, but behind Calista's caring face, I see the monster stirring. I get to my knees and touch her face. Leaning in, I kiss her soft lips then whisper in her ear.

"Calista, run," I say and point at the crack.

She shakes her head, the moisture falling from her face and onto her shirt.

"No," she says. "No, no, no."

Frowning, I grab her shoulders and turn her roughly towards the opening. I point with a harsh, sharp gesture then shove. As I do, the worm rises, its maw snapping open and shut with a loud clack. It shakes side to side, trying to work my lochaber free. Calista stumbles forward two steps, then turns and looks at me, shaking her head as she retreats. She's not moving fast enough; I have to draw the creature away. It's the only way I can protect her.

I shake my head, then turn to the zemlja. Throwing my arms wide, I hiss loudly, issuing a challenging cry. It whips back and forth, then turns its eyeless head and gaping mouth to me.

"Come, you spineless animated dung! I, Ladon, will take you!"

It drives up into the air, preparing to crush me under its massive weight, so I run towards it in a full charge. My eyes lock onto my lochaber where it protrudes from the thing's mouth. My aim was true but not deep enough. If I can drive the weapon further into the monster, it will finish it. If I fail, it will crush me, and I can only hope I will have bought enough time for Calista to escape. Surely she'll figure out to consume the epis on her own.

Each time my foot makes contact with the ground, pain shoots up my leg, causing my vision to blur. I push past it. I have to, for her. I will not be bested by a mindless creature from below. The dragon rages inside, and I let it loose with a primal roar. I will not let her see me defeated. I will protect her.

The worm senses my footsteps as I pound the ground closing, and it uses that to track me. It's big and doesn't move as agilely as I do, which is my only advantage.

It arcs back then swings forward, using its size and mass. As it slams towards the ground, I duck and roll to the side. It hits the ground where I was, and the force of its impact makes me bounce.

Flying through the air, I instinctively open my wings, and pain blinds me as the injured one snaps open then collapses. I pull them back tight and spread my arms to slow myself. I land on my feet, skidding to a stop.

My lochaber is buried part way in out of my reach, so I crouch and leap. I stretch, reaching for the haft, and my hand barely grips it. I hang in the air, trying to get a better grip.

I'm swinging back and forth, so I put my feet against the thing and then move myself around so I'm climbing over the top of the worm. At last I get both hands on the shaft of my lochaber.

Climbing hand over hand, I pull myself closer and closer to the beast. The lodged blade is sliding slowly out. I don't have long. It rears up and throws itself forward, so I loosen my knees and prepare for the impact. As the monster and I fly towards the ground, I catch a glimpse of Calista. She's retreated into the opening and is hiding there in relative safety. I want her completely safe, though.

"Run," I yell.

It's all I can do before the beast hits the ground. Shocking vibrations numb my limbs. My fingers slip as the numbness reaches my hand, but I manage to keep a grip on the haft.

The middle part of the beast arches up as it places its head against the ground. It's going to go under, which I can't allow. I leap up and place my feet on the monster then lean into the lochaber, driving the blade deeper towards the brain. The monster's mouth opens wide then slams shut, filling the cavern with the sound of clacking, razor-sharp teeth.

The shaft of my lochaber is bitten in half, leaving me holding the ragged bottom half of it. Using the piece I have, I beat the zemlja with it, slamming it again and again, knowing I'm not causing actual harm, but keeping its attention on me. Keeping it above ground.

My dragon rises, and I give voice to the effort with a wordless roar. The sound of burning rock reaches my ears as its acid spit opens the ground. I have only moments before it's too late.

The broken haft embedded in the thing's mouth is just out of my reach, taunting with its offers of hope. I'm out of options, so I do the only thing I can. I force my wings open. Pain explodes through my head and my vision is covered with blasting stars, but I know what I have to do.

Something snaps and pops as I flap my wings to gain height, closing the distance as I stretch for the shaft.

My fingers brush the splintered end. I can't grasp it. Forcing my wings to flap again, though they were never designed for flying, I strain. A little bit more. Close. So close.

I close my hand on it. I've got it!

Dangling one handed, the blade slips, and I drop with jerking force. The broken part of the shaft is still in my other hand. I hit the beast over and over, and it retreats down.

In a moment my feet touch the ground, and at last I have leverage. I bend my knees and drop the broken haft. Wrapping both hands around the remnants of the lochaber in its mouth, I move up with explosive force.

The blade slices up, through the protective muscle. It pauses when the tip hits the bone shell that protects the thing's brain. Growling, I push harder, and the blade breaks through into the brain.

The monster shudders, then collapses. I drop to the ground, unable to keep myself upright. Everything is pain. Blackness invades the edges of my vision, blacking out the world.

"Ladon," Calista yells.

I hear her voice as if it's coming from across a vast gulf of darkness. I latch onto it and claw my way back. The monster is defeated, but it's far from the only threat. I must protect her, and she needs to eat the epis. Hot hands are on my face, running across my chest, then she touches my wings. Sharp pain brings her into focus, and I'm looking into her eyes. Cool moisture falls from them, and a drop lands in my partially open mouth. Salty. It's salty and strange, but it tastes of her. She shakes her head. I smile and touch her face, then she leans in and presses her lips to mine.

Her mouth-mating makes the pain less, makes it bearable. She is worth it.

16

CALISTA

My heart pounds in my chest so hard I'm sure it will explode. I'm lightheaded as I run across the cavern to where Ladon lies motionless.

"No," I scream. "Ladon!"

He's a crumpled heap, like some child's broken and discarded toy. He has to be okay. Has to—what will I do without him?

My stomach clenches and a cold hand strokes down my spine, causing me to shiver. What if he's dead? Bile rises in my throat as an empty black pit consumes my thoughts.

This is so much more than mere survival. He's been kind and caring. He's fought for me. Stood up for me in ways no human ever has. If he's... no, I can't think it.

I need him, of that there is no doubt, but that's not all this is. I've only known him for a few days. We can barely talk, but none of that changes the way he makes me feel. As if we've been connected forever. As if he... no. This is crazy. I can't be thinking this or feeling this.

It's the adrenaline mixing with fear. It's nuts. There's no way I can possibly feel that for him. Is there?

The luminescent strand of the plant he called epis he threw drops to the ground as I run, all but forgotten. All that matters is him.

The monster-worm thing lies still on the ground, but I still give it a wide berth in case it's only playing dead. The nasty thing looks like a ginormous earthworm with thick scales, but instead of a closed end at the tip, there's a massive mouth filled with thousands of sharp teeth in concentric circles going down its throat. And it spit acid! The ground is pockmarked where it was throwing spit around.

I stumble on one of those pits and fall to my knees, sliding to his side. My pants tear and my knees are scraped raw, but I don't care. He stirs as I touch his face, turning his head towards me.

Tears are streaming down my face and falling on his. His eyes blink open. I'm so grateful I run my hands over him, touching his face, his arms, his chest, just feeling him. I feel his heart beating as I rest my hands on his chest, but the rhythm is odd.

Worried, I press my hand flat to his chest. Something is definitely not right, but I can't figure it out. I lay my ear against him and listen. Every thump of his heart has an echoing thump that shouldn't be there. It could be a murmur, but one strong enough for me to hear it without instruments? No, that can't be it.

I turn the problem over and over then it hits me, and I chuckle. It only now occurs to me that he has two hearts. There's no other way to explain the beat I feel under the palms of my hand and hear when I listen.

I rest my forehead against his. He touches my hair, my arms, then moves to sit up. He winces in pain, so I help him the best I can. He's so much bigger and heavier than I am, I'm not sure if I help or hinder, but it's the least I can do.

"Oh thank you, thank you. I'm so glad you're okay."

"Calista," he says, and for probably the first time he doesn't drag out the 's' in my name.

I smile and kiss him. He rests for a few more moments, then shifts and climbs to his feet. He looks around, obviously looking for something.

"Epis?" he asks.

"Epis?" I ask, not changing trains of thought as fast as he is.

He points to the plants that grow from the ceiling. Their soft glow illuminates his face.

"Oh, right, I'll get it, it's over here."

I lead Ladon to where I dropped the epis. He kneels, grabs the package, then slowly unwraps it. He inspects the coil of plant inside it carefully. Apparently satisfied, he glances over at the worm before taking my hand and leading the way out of the cavern.

On the far side of the small passage, he stops again and gently lays the plant out on a flat stone. He opens his bag, takes out a small knife, and cuts a small piece off the plant and hands it to me.

"Food," he says, motioning between the plant and my mouth. "Eat it."

I stare at the light blue, glowing plant. I arch an eyebrow, uncertain. "You sure? I'm not from around here. What if this isn't good for me?"

"It will help," he says insistently.

He motions again, but this time there's a harshness to his gestures. When I hesitate still, he takes my hand holding the fragment of leaf and raises it to my mouth, nodding sharply.

"Okay," I say, figuring what the hell.

My head hasn't stopped pounding for days, and I have to admit, if only to myself, that I am weak. I'm not stupid, and I know damn well that I've been suffering from heat exhaustion, which is growing worse. I also know that eventually my body will shut down. In all honesty, it probably should have happened before now.

I place the piece of plant in my mouth, letting it rest on my tongue. A sour, almost spicy flavor fills my mouth. It tastes like... dirty curry. Ladon watches closely, and when I don't swallow, he mimes chewing, running his fingers down his throat.

"Food," he insists, saying more, but he's talking fast and the words don't make sense.

At his urging, I chew. What else am I going to do? He's not led me wrong yet. When I bite for the first time, a cold chill runs down my throat and then explodes through my limbs.

It's shocking but not unpleasant. As I keep chewing, the sensations lose their intensity, but still it feels like my body comes alive. As if every last cell in my body wakes up at the same time.

I've been overheated since waking up from the crash. Now I feel cool. My headache recedes and then is gone. The mild nausea and cramping in my stomach fade away. I stare at Ladon as I finish chewing. This is amazing. I feel stronger, too. Like I could lift him over my head and carry him easily. I point at the rest of the harvested plant with a questioning look.

"Epis," he says again.

"I have to get this to my…" I pause, realizing I don't know a word in his language for what I want to say, "friends."

I say it in Common. He stares at me, obviously not understanding. I frown, trying to figure out how to communicate the idea of friends. Knowing the history of his planet, the concept may be foreign to him. How long ago did what I saw in that vid happen? Was he alive then? Has he been alone his whole life?

"Friends," I repeat.

I have to get this to them. I feel amazing, and the more I chew, the better I feel. Tingles run across my body and through my system. It literally feels like my body is repairing itself. I shake my head, almost crying with joy, it feels so good. Then it hits me how to say what I want to say.

"Friends," I say, but now I mime something falling from the sky.

He watches my hands. I point to myself then put my right hand up high, folding my fingers in, and mime crashing down while pointing from myself to the hand coming down.

"Friends," I repeat.

Ladon smiles. It feels like he gets it, and excitement wells up in me. I point at the epis, then repeat 'friends' to him. He shakes his head.

"Why? My friends need this. Why can't I take it to them?" I ask.

"It won't last," he says.

"That doesn't make sense," I argue, but now the glimmer of doubt takes root. "They're going to need this too. I feel amazing, and I want my friends to survive."

I wrap the leather cloth, carefully closing the epis inside. Ladon touches my hand, so I look up at him. He shakes his head and then points at the epis one more time.

"No," he says, shaking his head.

"But why? They need it."

He frowns, and it's clear from the look on his face that he's as frustrated as I am.

"It will not be strong enough by the time we reach them," he says again. "The first time they take it, it needs to be fresh."

I unwrap the epis and look. It's not glowing like the live ones hanging from the ceiling, but that shouldn't matter. Medicinal plants retain their properties once harvested. I take the end of the strand, tear a small piece off, then put it in my mouth.

It doesn't taste as strong. It's duller, and the sour spiciness is barely there; it's like a ghost of the flavor and sensation that it was fresh. I wait for the cool rush that I felt before, and it doesn't compare.

"Damn it!" I exclaim in frustration.

The effect fades once harvested. It has to be something to do with the way it's collected. Sitting back on my haunches, I stare up at the strands hanging from the cavern ceiling.

They're beautiful. The soft glow they emit is tranquil. Probably the most beautiful thing I've seen since crashing here. I need to study this plant. I need my lab. My tools. Microscopes and scopes to find out what makes it work. As it is, I can't take any for my friends.

It means I have no options but to bring my people to the city. I don't know how well they've survived, but they had supplies. It's more than I had when Ladon found me. Maybe they'll be okay. No, they *have* to be okay. I try not to think about all the creatures that Ladon has protected me from. They have weapons. They'll be okay.

"Friends?" he asks in Common.

"Yes!" I say, excited he's still learning words in my language even though I mostly can speak his. "Friends."

He nods, saying something, but it's too fast for me to get. I know his language, but I guess fluency is still going to take practice. Groaning, he rises to stand, then stops and crouches back down. His breath is shallow and there's a wet wheeze. When I touch his face, he smiles then stands up.

His wing has an odd bent to it. A sympathetic pain stabs into my own back looking at it. Despite his protective scales, he has several cuts and discolorations that must be bruising. He took a heck of a beating fighting that thing. On his feet, he takes my hand and leads the way out of the cave.

The sunlight is blinding, but my eyes adjust quickly. It seems quicker than they would have before. We're in the shadow of the rough cliff, which isn't as hot as it is in the direct light of the two suns, but I'm not hot. Well, I'm hot, but I'm not burning up to the point where I think I might die like it was before. It's a massive improvement.

Looking around, I feel light as if I can float across the sands. I'm smiling so much my mouth is hurting, but I can't stop it now. I can't recall the last time I felt this good. This alive.

I'm acutely aware of tiny details. The grains of sand. Tiny insects that move across the rough face of the cliff wall. I didn't pay attention when we arrived, but there is a sort of natural walkway that zigzags up the cliff face.

Ladon isn't taking time for sightseeing, though. He sets a quick pace across the desert, and it's so much easier to keep up with him now that I'm not hurting and exhausted. The harder packed sand close to the cave gives way to the soft blowing stuff, and he helps me along which I'm so grateful for.

It doesn't seem that long before I see the dark shapes of the city sitting on the horizon. My new sense of hope has set my imagination free. If I can get my friends here, we can survive. We can do more than survive. We can bring this dead city back to life. The power source that once operated the thriving city I saw in those vids must still be there, somewhere, and I'm sure we can repair it. Once we have, then the future becomes much brighter.

Ladon has slowed as we've traveled, and now is moving slower than he normally does, like each step causes him pain. The damaged wing is drooping further. His tail is not swishing left to right like it usually does. He's hurt and trying to hide it. I put my hand on his shoulder, pulling him to stop.

"Are you hurt?" I ask.

He frowns but doesn't answer. I'm not sure if I used a wrong word and he doesn't understand or if he's just putting on a brave face. Either way it doesn't matter; he's hurt. He's done so much for me I can't not help. When I was hurt back at that oasis, he had a jar of salve he used on my wounds. I'm sure that will help him too.

He shakes his head and takes a step back, trying to continue on the way to his home. I grab his arm and stop him, shaking my head firmly. His frown deepens.

"It's fine," he says, pointing towards the city. "We need to get back to my home."

I ignore him, reaching my hand into his bag and rummaging around. I find the jar of salve he used on my injuries and pull it out, holding it up between us.

"Let me help," I say, pointing at his wings. "Will this work?"

He shrugs, then nods his head. I open the jar and dip my fingers into the cool salve. It's warm on my fingers then cools, almost like how menthol works.

Moving so that I am behind Ladon, I slather it over his wings where they connect to his back. He sighs loudly in what can only be relief, and the tension in the drooping wing relaxes, but it is still hanging at an odd angle.

"Thank you," he says.

"Of course," I say. "This is still bad, though."

I lean in to study the wing and its structure. I understand human biology, but humans don't have wings. I didn't study animal structures beyond the minimum required for my education. Plants were my domain, not birds. Still, structure is structure.

Tentatively I touch the wing, alert for the slightest hint I'm hurting him. The outer edge of his wing is a thicker bone that forms the frame. The wing itself feels like supple leather. It's thin, folding on itself with what looks almost like pleats.

"Can you open it any?" I ask.

He grunts as the wing opens part way. His other wing extends fully, but this one he can't. Even so, I see the problem. Comparing the two wings, the uninjured one and the one he can't use, I see that there is a network of small bones. On the injured one, two of those bones are out of place.

"We need to go," Ladon says.

"You can wait," I say. "I'm going to fix this."

"The suns are dropping," he says. "It is not safe."

"It's safe enough," I say, mustering my courage. "This is going to hurt." He looks over his shoulder, but can't turn his head far enough to see what I'm looking at. "These bones are out of place; that's what's keeping you from opening it. I can fix it."

I say that as if it's the most natural thing in the world. As if I'm some kind of wing-fixing expert. Even if I was trained in chiropractic care, I wouldn't be qualified to act so confident, but I'm definitely in the 'fake it until you make it' territory.

I stare at the wing, chewing my lip, nerves clanging like an alarm bell as I try to steel my nerve. Ladon takes my hand in his. I look up into his warm eyes.

"I trust you," he says.

My heart stops. The world stops. I'm on a precipice, and in the next instant I'm going to fall but time has frozen us here on the edge. There was no hesitation in his words. No sliver of doubt. Nothing but confidence. I nod then put my hands in place, fingertips touching one of the out of place bones.

A river wants to run in its banks. Bones want to be in their place. Things in the world have a place and they gravitate towards them. Natural order and all that. I close my eyes, take a deep breath, then in one motion I open my eyes and push. Ladon grunts, breathing harshly.

"I'm sorry," I exclaim, looking at his face as I try to judge how bad I hurt him.

He's gritting his teeth, his eyes are closed, his breathing is almost ragged. He huffs, exhaling heavily, then nods and opens his eyes.

"It's fine," he says as his jaw relaxes. "It feels better."

"Okay," I say, feeling tentative. "There's one more. I need to do it too."

The cold hardness that settles over his face is scary, but he nods and grits his teeth. I study the good wing once more then look at the injured one, memorizing the position I want to push the out of place bone into. Satisfied I've got it, I place my hands and look into his eyes.

"Ready?" I ask. He nods, and I push without warning. His eyes widen, his face darkens with pain, then he exhales, heavily panting. "That's it." I take his face in my hands and kiss his forehead over and over. "I'm sorry. Is it better?"

He opens his wing, and though he does grimace, it opens fully. He closes his wings and sighs, leaning his head back until our lips meet and we kiss.

"Thank you," he whispers into my mouth. "My treasure."

Warmth stokes in my belly and radiates throughout me. My heart palpitates and I can barely breathe. I stare into his eyes for a long moment, but the suns are low enough that they're shining into my eyes, and I know now is not the time for me to sort out all these feelings.

"I'm glad," I say and smile.

He stands up and tests his wings. He's still hurt, but they are working now. Satisfied I've done what I can, I return the jar to his bag and we continue on our way to his home.

My thoughts are firmly on my friends and what I must do to save them. We're getting better at communicating, and I think he has the idea at least. All I have to do is convince my sweet alien savior to take me to them and let them come live in his city.

17

LADON

*C*alista's care has eased my pain, and we make good time across the desert. Calista is much better now that she's had epis. I'll have to make sure she has a steady supply until her body is fully adjusted. Dimly I recall that it had side effects if the doses weren't maintained.

When we crest another dune, Calista stops and takes out her water bottle. She offers it to me, a gesture of extreme kindness, but I refuse, saving the precious resource for her. After she places the cap firmly in place, she rolls her shoulders and studies me with a frown.

"Can we go get my friends?" she asks. "They need help."

The fog that eats at my past and memories surges, bringing with it primal instincts. She is mine. My treasure. I will not compete for her. She is the other half of me. We belong together. If I save her 'friends,' will one of them try to compete?

Not that any of them could challenge me, but the idea makes my dragon rumble angrily. I've been alone for so long; do I want more people around? As I turn the problem over, the answer becomes clear.

It's not about what I want; what does she want? I lost everything so long ago I barely recall that sense of loss. It's not the same for her. Her loss is recent. She doesn't want to live alone, she wants friends and others of her kind. Can I deny this to her? Can I deny her anything?

"Friends," I say, using her word for it.

I place my arm around her waist and resume walking, changing direction towards where I originally found Calista.

I'm taking a more direct route and marking the sun as it travels across the sky, I figure if we make good time we'll be able to reach the oasis I took her to before by nightfall. After that it is less than half a day to where I found her.

As we travel, my biggest concern is if other Zmaj have found the wreck yet. I know they are out there still, though it's been ages since I've seen another. After the Devastation was over, the bijass rose to prominence and we began fighting each other, always seeking to establish dominance. It didn't take long before we went our separate ways, each laying claim to our own territory and avoiding one another.

The wreck, though, will attract them as it did me. I was close when it happened, so I arrived first and thank Tajss I did. If some other Zmaj had laid a hand on Calista... A growl slips out before I realize it's happening. Calista stops and looks up with concern on her face. I shake my head and push her to keep walking.

We talk as we walk, making the time pass quickly. As she talks in a mix of her language and mine, I decipher new words in what she calls Common. I mimic her words until she smiles and nods with excitement, then I share the same word in my own language. It's getting easier to share more complex ideas. She's smart and learns very quickly. Everything about her is impressive.

As the sun drops to the horizon, I think about making camp. We're not close enough to the oasis to push on; we'll have to sleep in the open. I have some cloth with me that I can use for camouflage and enough small bits of wood for a tiny fire. I can use that to cook some meat for our dinner. We have enough water as well.

She's doing much better now that she has eaten epis. She'll have to keep taking it, which she probably doesn't know yet, but that's fine. It just means she won't be leaving me. She's mine, my greatest treasure.

"We need to camp," I say, pointing at the sky.

I slip my pack off and pull out the cloth and the bits of wood. It only takes a short time before I have a small fire, and the succulent smell of bivo meat fills the air. It's not the treat that guster meat is, but it's hardy and lasts longer when traveling.

I lay out the cloth for us to sit on while it cooks. She nestles close so that we're constantly touching. Her hands are warm, but not burning like they were before. It's exciting when she touches me. Desire blossoms, and my testicles tighten against my body. I run my fingers along her soft skin and touch the hair on her head. We lean in and mate with our mouths while my prime cock stiffens and hardens. I trail my fingers along her leg towards her center of pleasure.

I want to bury my tongue inside her strange, pink folds and seek out that nub of flesh which gives her so much pleasure. I catch whiffs of her smell, and it pulls me in until the scent of burning flesh intrudes, and I remember the forgotten meat cooking over our fire. I jump around and retrieve it, laughing, and she laughs as well. One of the sticks holding the meat dropped lower and is on fire. I blow on it, trying to put the fire out before I lose the meat. She leans in and blows as well, and together we get the flames out.

"Damn it," she says, laughing.

"Dam-mmmmm-t?" I ask.

She shakes her head and laughs, then says the word slowly. "Da-mm-it."

She puts an emphasis on the end of the word, so I repeat it and she nods, clapping her hands together.

"Yes," she exclaims.

Happiness fills me when she laughs. I feel light and alive. I feel things I haven't felt since before the Devastation. A connection with another being. A sense of working together to ensure our mutual survival.

I touch her arm, then trail my fingers up to her mouth. She smiles, then takes my fingers into her mouth and sucks. Her mouth is wet and hot, and she moves her head up and down, causing a shudder to run through me and a stiffening in my tail. My cock feels like it's already about to explode with pent-up passion.

A moan slips past my lips. I've never felt anything like this before. She stares into my eyes as she moves up and down my fingers, sliding them in and out of her mouth. Her tongue moves around, licking, stroking, and it feels amazing. She grabs my other hand and pulls it towards her, placing it over her breast while her free hand dives between my legs to my cock.

I shudder and command my penis to not react as it tries to dump my first load at her touch. No Zmaj female ever did anything like what she is doing to me. Mating with a Zmaj was more straightforward, albeit much rougher than taking pleasure with Calista has been. Zmaj are not soft like her. Their fleshy bits are protected by scales and exposed only during the mating and for that purpose only. Sex was pleasurable, but I never felt this drive to have sex simply for the sake of having it.

Calista runs her hand up and down, lightly gripping my cock while sucking on my fingers. My testicles tighten more, pulling up against my tail, and I don't know how much longer I can hold off. I pull her shirt up, exposing her flat, soft stomach and the delectable mounds of her breasts. She moans around my fingers in her mouth, and I lose control, my seed bursting forth and across both of us.

As my prime penis softens, it folds back under and the second emerges from my tail, ready. She smiles and slides my fingers out of her mouth, shifting to lie on her back. She wiggles out of her pants, and the delightful, heady scent of her fills the air.

Without hesitation, I move over her and place my cock at her entrance. I do go slowly—she's not well-designed for my size and I don't want to hurt her—but that's the extent of my control. My desire for her is too high.

I slide in and she screams my name, her arms locking around my neck. I give her body just enough time to adjust then pull back, and she screams once more, but it's a new word.

"Fuck!"

I don't know what it means, but I know what I want and need. I thrust back, and then I'm lost in the pleasure of being in her. My mind is consumed with the push and the pull. Friction, moisture, and pleasure mix until all rational thought is gone. Her body conforms around my cock, squeezing and pulling, milking it as her pleasure begs for my seed. I hold off, biting down on my lip, focusing on her face. Her mouth opens and her eyes shut. She screams my name as I thrust deeply, and then I burst, filling her.

Her body arches to meet mine, and I hold myself deep inside until in a last, shuddering pump, I finish. My cock softens, but I remain close until she relaxes her own arch and lowers herself back to the ground. I kiss her soft, beautiful lips, then pull out and roll to lie beside her on the cloth.

It's now fully dark and stars twinkle in the sky. I wonder which of those stars was her home? Where did she come from, and how did she end up here? I can't count the number of marks it's been since the Devastation. Years, suddenly I remember the term. Years, it's been years. I haven't used that word in so long, it had become forgotten. As I remember it, another word comes back. Decades. It's been many decades.

Remembering the terms, a sense of my own age and my time alone enters my awareness. I've been alone for a really long time. Epis extends life, but it's addictive until your body is fully adjusted. Or so it was for others. Zmaj were never addicted to the plant like the other races. Once other races had it, they couldn't go without it. If they'd taken it for any length of time, more than a handful of tastes, it would kill them with the withdrawals.

Less than that, they might survive, but wish they hadn't because it hurt so much. It is a powerful drug, but it's the only thing that will help her adapt to survival on Tajss. I haven't needed it regularly in my memory, but I seem to recall taking it at some point. Having been alone and lost so much of my past to the fog of the bijass, I don't recall if Zmaj are naturally long lived or if it is because of the epis.

I hear a shifting of sand from behind us and roll to my knees. We're at the base of a dune, which is blocking my view so I don't see anything, but I know to trust my instincts. Calista sits up and looks where I'm looking.

"Ladon?" she whispers.

I put one finger over my lips, then point up the dune. She nods, looking worried. I pat her shoulder, then point at the ground. She nods once more, and I crawl off the cloth. On the sand, I lay flat and use my tail and arms to bury myself. Once I'm mostly covered, I work my way up the dune to the top. Looking down the side, there's a large, cylinder-shaped piece of metal that is buried most of the way in the sand. It's large, large enough to hold a person, and foreign.

I keep myself buried as I look around for any signs of trouble. I spot where the sand on the dune has been disturbed. The way it lies, it's clear to me that someone was watching us from that side of the dune.

"Ladon," Calista yelps from behind.

I don't bother with cover any longer. I leap to my feet, red sand pouring off, and I turn in mid-air to destroy whatever threatens her. A nasty-looking creature is holding her in front of it like a shield. Its skin has an orange tint and a leathery look. Its mouth is filled with sharp teeth, and there are two spiky protrusions coming out on either side. The top of its head is bald, but there are black, thick ropes hanging down which have metallic bands crimped around them here and there. It has one arm wrapped around her neck, and in the other hand is a club with metal spikes. Something about it tugs at memories.

It makes a clicking sound then points the club at me. I hiss, crouching low. No one and no thing threatens her. Nothing. I will make this creature regret its actions. I slide to one side and it turns, forcing Calista to stay between the two of us. It's afraid—and it should be. I will tear it limb from limb. I keep sliding to the side but not moving closer. I watch, patient, for an opening. Any mistake, one misstep will give me the opportunity I need.

"Ladon, no," Calista says, and the thing jerks back on her neck, forcing her chin up.

I hiss and step forward, but it tightens its grip. It motions towards the ground again, and an idea occurs to me. I comply with its motions, crouching down until I can rest my hands on the sand. I'm leaning forward in my crouch, ready to spring. My tail lashes back and forth. My wings are still tender or else I'd leap and take him, but I can't trust them.

I grip handfuls of sand, waiting. It clicks and makes guttural sounds. I hiss softly watching it. We're in a standoff and it knows it. It also seems to know instinctively that it's at a disadvantage.

It forces Calista towards me, keeping her between us. Closer... It's almost close enough. One more step. I need it to be one more step closer. Calista fights against its grip and it pauses, adjusting its grip even tighter, forcing her smaller frame up until her toes are barely touching the ground and she yelps. Adrenaline pumps through me along with anger. The dragon roars inside, but I keep my mouth firmly shut, holding its rage back. The creature forces her forward one step.

I throw sand up with both my hands and whirl, swinging my tail and hitting its legs. The blow knocks them from beneath it, and it crashes to the ground. It loses its grip as it falls, setting Calista free. She stumbles to one side and falls into the soft sand. I continue spinning until I'm facing the creature, and I leap onto it while it's struggling to regain its footing.

I slam my fist into its ugly face and feel the bones break under the force of my blow. Its head rocks to one side and I hit it with my other fist, then I'm pounding on it. Rage sweeps away all reason as I pummel this thing that would threaten my Calista. Nothing will harm her. She is mine, mine to protect and to care for. It has no right to touch her. I hit it again and again until at last my rage is spent and I'm left empty, looking down at the mess I've made.

I stand up and turn around. Calista runs into my arms and throws hers around me, and I take her in my embrace. I can't recall this creature or know where it came from, but there is a sense of having seen one before.

I look around, turning in a circle to see if there are more. Satisfied that it was alone, I put my attention on Calista. I lift her chin and see the purple and red bruising on her throat. I pull out some salve and spread it along her neck. I look at the monster and point then point at her.

"You know this?" I ask.

She shakes her head, but whether it's a denial or an indication of not understanding, I don't know.

"It's one of the things that attacked us." She says a word at the end in her own language that I don't understand.

"Attacked you? Where?"

She frowns, then points at the sky and repeats the word in her language. I understand. This is the thing that caused her to fall out of the sky.

"Your ship?" I ask, sharing the word she was missing with her.

She repeats the word ship until she has it. Wrapping my arm around her, I look at the remains of the creature. If I hadn't killed it for hurting her, I might have had to thank it. If it hadn't attacked her ship, she would not be here with me. It does mean, though, that there are probably more of them somewhere. I won't sleep tonight.

18

CALISTA

*T*raveling is so much easier now than it was before. The heat doesn't feel as bad, the sand doesn't seem to pull as hard—everything is just easier. Minutes felt like hours before the epis, now hours fly by as we travel, and I barely notice.

Ladon and I talk as we walk. Well, *I* talk, a lot, and he says words every so often. He's really picking up my language. Basic things, at least.

When we reach the top of another dune, I shield my eyes and look into the distance. I notice a black spot on the horizon. Butterflies dance in my stomach. Is it… could it be? I drop my hands and look at Ladon. The smile on his face says it all. That is the ship! I point to it, and Ladon nods.

"Your friends," he says.

"Yes!" I exclaim throwing my fist into the air.

Leaping onto him, I throw my arms around his neck and wrap my legs around his waist, then kiss him with every ounce of passion and gratitude I have. He returns my kiss, but there's no time to waste. I drop to my feet and look towards the ship once more.

"We're almost there. I hope they're okay."

Ladon nods. I haven't discussed my idea of all of us living in his city with him. It's not like we've had a lot of time, and communicating complex ideas is still a challenge. I don't think enough of the ship is intact to be good for a long term habitat, and besides, the city is empty.

Catching a second wind, I pick up my pace and so does Ladon. The epis may have helped me in dealing with the heat, and it feels like it's made me stronger overall, but I'm still not as well-adapted to this environment as he is. Even with his damaged wing, he moves across the sand with an easy grace. He's so big and muscular, and god, is he strong, but he moves like a delicate ballerina. Light on his feet and quick.

It isn't long at all before we top another rising dune and we're looking down on the hulk of the crashed spaceship. We're coming up from behind the opening, the same direction I'd left in what now feels like so long ago.

The debris that had scattered around the wreck has been cleaned. Crates are now neatly stacked against the ship instead of being strewn around. A hundred yards or so to my left are mounds in the sand. Graves for those who didn't make it.

Two people are visible as we come down the side of the dune. They see us and shout running around the ship to the far side. Ladon looks askance at me, but I don't have an answer, so I shrug and we continue marching towards the ship.

As we come around the edge, I see that the rip in the hull has been covered over with tarps. One of the runners ducks inside, still yelling. The other glares as we approach, holding a rifle in his arms. We approach, but already it's not the welcome home I expected. Ladon watches everything silently, but I feel his tension.

A group emerges from the shipwreck. At the head is Rosalind, still dressed in her impeccable white space leathers, three men I don't know, and one I do.

Gershom.

My stomach drops to the sands seeing his smug face. He's talking to Rosalind and she seems to be listening. We're not close enough for me to hear their words, but I squint and try to read his lips. That slimy son of a bitch. Obviously he's been busy worming his way towards more power while I was gone.

The suns are behind us which I'm sure makes it hard to see that it's me, but still, they could be more welcoming. I can't make out what Gershom is saying. My lip-reading skills suck, apparently. Another smaller figure emerges from the wreck. When I shift my attention, I see it's Jolie, and my spirits lift. She shields her eyes, sees me, then she's jumping up and down, pointing.

"Calista," she screams across the sand, still jumping up and down.

"Jolie," I yell, waving my arms over my head wildly.

I grab Ladon's arm and pull him along as I run down the dune towards my friends and the other survivors. Ladon doesn't resist, but he doesn't break into a full run either. I see his eyes darting around and evaluating, taking in everything and deciding if it's friend or foe.

"That's far enough," Rosalind says, holding her hand up when we're about thirty feet away.

I stumble to a stop in surprise. "What? What's going on?" I ask as the men with her bring their weapons to bear on Ladon.

Ladon stands still, but I feel his muscles tense under my hand on his arm. He's ready for action, much more ready than he would appear to anyone who doesn't know him.

"What is that?" Rosalind says, pointing at Ladon.

"Well 'that' is not a 'that,' it's a he. And *he* saved my life."

Rosalind narrows her eyes, and the men with her grip their weapons tighter. The tension is rising, and I don't understand why they're reacting this way.

"It's a damn monster, another one!" Gershom says from beside her. "Kill it before it kills us."

"No," I scream, and Ladon's arm tenses harder under my grip.

He steps forward and hisses, one hand over his shoulder close to his weapon. This is going bad fast.

"Damn, Calista," Lana says, stepping out of the hull.

She looks Ladon up and down with an easy smile. "We land in hell, and you manage to find a hot hunk." Lana's smile turns to me with a mischievous grin. "Yours, I take it?"

Ladon glances at her, but keeps his attention on the men and their weapons. I tell myself it doesn't matter; she doesn't mean anything by it, but I still have to fight an urge to push her away. I'm just projecting my own insecurity on her, and picking a fight won't help defuse the situation.

"Stand back, Lana," Rosalind orders before I can respond.

"Rosalind, what's going on? What's happened?" I ask, more comfortable talking to the Lady General than Lana.

"A lot. Where have you been?" Rosalind asks, turning my own question back on me.

Other people have emerged from the ship and still more are peeking out through the tarps and plastic. I look at those gathered, and no one meets my eyes. As I come to each, they look down or away into the distance.

Jolie frowns when I get to her and starts to say something, then her mouth snaps shut. They're all waiting for me to say something.

"I passed out. This is Ladon, he's a… native. He…" I stumble over what to say. I can't tell them we've had sex. They are already tense. I don't want them assuming the wrong thing. My cheeks burn hot, too hot, as I fumble trying to find words.

"He what?" Rosalind asks.

More people come out of the wreck, some of whom I know. Amara climbs up on a crate and looks imperiously down at all of us. Mei pushes through the crowd and moves towards me, then stops, looking around uncomfortably. Gershom is the only one smiling. He moves from Rosalind's side to Mei and puts an arm protectively in front of her. This is all going so wrong!

"Look, there's a city, it's abandoned, or—well, mostly, and we can go there and I think we can—"

"A city? What? Where! Is there water? Are there monsters? Are there more like him?!"

A dozen voices speak at once, asking questions and making exclamations. It's a cacophony of noise drowning out anything else I might say. I snap my mouth shut. An urge to find some place to hide hits me, and I'm looking around for an escape before I can stop myself. I've never missed my quiet lab where no one yells and no one bothers me more than right now.

I step back and wrap my arms around myself. The noise of everyone talking is growing louder as they shout to be heard over one another. It's so loud there's no longer words, only noise. Someone pushes someone else then the crowd is edging forward. An ice-cold hand clenches my chest. I'm acutely aware of my heartbeat, loud in my ears, and it's hard to breathe. It's too much, I'm overwhelmed.

Ladon steps between the approaching crowd and me, blocking them. He hisses and spreads his arms, his tail shifts back and forth, and his wings flutter on his back. One hand over his shoulder grips the haft of his weapon as he points with the other hand at my people.

Time slows to a crawl. Everything is going wrong. The armed guards bring their guns up, the mob's fear clearly written on their faces. I'm here with the best news ever, and they're threatening to kill him.

My own fear batters at me like dark wings. Uncertainty and doubts plague my thoughts. Insecurity washing over me like surging waves on a beach. The crowd is getting louder. The tension in the air is escalating. The rattle of guns being brought to bear fills my head.

The next few moments are going to decide the future of my entire race. It's on me to make that future brighter or to let fear rule.

"Stop!" I scream at the top of my lungs, my voice cracking as it bursts out. Now everyone is looking, some are glaring at me.

Pressure on my head and in my chest is making it hard to think. A combination of anger, fear, and disbelief converging. I have one chance to turn this around, and it's right now. I have to stop this insanity before it goes any further. He's not a monster, he's my friend—my lover even, not that that's any of their business. I have to find the right words to make them stop.

"This is Ladon," I say, forcing the words out. "He's a native of this planet and is willing to help us." The men with guns look at each other, unimpressed. "Seriously? Is this the way we're going to treat him? He came to help us and believe me, from what I've seen, we're going to need it. This place is harsher than you can possibly imagine."

Rosalind steps away from the people crowded around her. She's so perfect, imperious, her white outfit immaculate where my own clothes are grimy and torn from my adventures with Ladon. Intentionally or not, I feel inadequate in her presence. She's everything a leader and a woman should be.

All my life I've been a lab rat. The book-smart, more interested in my studies girl, and definitely not the girl who gets the guy. Ladon doesn't see me that way. He makes me feel... so much more. Valued. Loved. Desirable. All those feelings form a knot in my throat and swell behind my eyes.

Rosalind walks closer until there's only two feet between us, and places a hand on my shoulder. Ladon hisses loudly. The guns rattle as the guards lift and thrust them forward, prepared to fire.

"Is this a friend?" he asks in his own language, wanting to know if I'm okay with her touching me.

He's protecting me, and I'm not sure whether I deserve it or not. What have I brought him into? He deserves better than this. I wanted to bring these people into his home, to invade his haven, his space, and did I consider or ask what his opinion might be? Not once.

I felt obligated to save them, but now I'm not so sure. I could have stayed away, stayed with him and let them deal with their own lives the best they could. If this is the welcome they offer him and me when I return to offer hope, why bother?

I glance quickly around, then see Jolie. She smiles, a soft smile, supportive and filled with love. She mimes a hug. Something stabs the back of my throat as my stomach clenches with nausea. How could I have even thought of leaving her and the others behind? I close my eyes and take in a deep, calming breath before I try to speak. I swallow hard, forcing the lump of unexpressed emotions out of the way.

"She's a friend," I say in his language. "She is a leader; her opinion matters."

He doesn't relax, but he also doesn't attack, so it's clear he's not convinced. I can't blame him. I wouldn't be either. This certainly isn't welcoming or the way even the alien expects friends to act.

"Are you talking to it?" Gershom asks, his voice rising. "You're speaking with this monster? What the hell is wrong with you? How do you know its language?"

"I know some. He saved my life and then he took me to a place with old technology that sort of works. It taught me some of his language."

I'm back on the defense, having to explain myself to my old boss, exactly where I didn't want to be. The murmur of the crowd intensifies, and any second we'll be back to the rampant shouting and recriminations.

"Technology?"

"Saved your life?"

"Bet that's not all he did."

"It's a monster."

"Enough," Rosalind says, making a swiping motion with her hand and silencing the crowd.

Gershom steps forward and tightens his grip on his weapon. He has it pointed at Ladon and mutters something, but I can't make out the words. The way he's glaring at Ladon with a cold, calculating look on his face... He hates Ladon, it's clear as day. The waves of nausea hit so hard I'm rocked to my core. Sweat breaks out on my forehead and I clench my arms over my stomach, keeping my mouth shut to try and hold back being sick.

I don't understand what his problem is. How he can be this way? How can anyone hate someone they haven't even met? Hate on sight? It's unreal. I stare at Gershom until his glare meets my gaze. I want to look away from the hate, but something inside snaps.

"What is your malfunction?" I ask. It's almost as if the words come from someone else, but it's only me here. I meet his glare, and now I've got one of my own. I'm done with this. "You don't know him. How can you look at him like that? He's our best hope."

"We have questions," Rosalind says, stopping the growing confrontation. "This isn't the place to ask them, though. Everyone inside. I will handle this, but let's get out of the heat first."

The crowd has swelled and must include almost all the survivors, there are so many of them. They mutter and talk, but they do slowly disperse until only Rosalind, Ladon and I are left along with four guards.

I'm thankful that Gershom isn't among those that remain. Jolie peeks past the tarps, hiding in the corner of the entrance to the ship. Her wide eyes and fast smile lift my spirits so fast that I have to suppress a giggle despite the gravity of the situation.

"Rosalind, what's happened? Why is everyone so angry?" I ask.

She stares for a long moment, then shakes her head. "Let's get inside, we'll talk where it's cooler."

She turns and walks, and I fall in behind her, placing one hand on Ladon's arm.

"She wants to talk to us, inside," I say.

He looks at the remains of the ship with a calculating glance and a frown.

"You want this?" he asks.

My breath hitches. Me. He's always thinking of me. I smile and nod.

"With you," I say.

Together, arm in arm, we walk into the cool darkness of the hull.

19

CALISTA

*O*nly now that the tension of the situation has eased am I able to look at my fellow humans with anything resembling a clear mind. They look terrible. Their movements are sluggish, their skin is lax, their lips are chapped, and their eyes are sunken. The heat of the planet is draining them, and it's obvious that they won't survive much longer without help.

Rosalind leads us through the hull. I think this was one of the ship's hangars. A big warehouse-like space that was huge, but now it's tipped on end and partially buried in the sand. They've organized everything, making walls with crates of supplies and using blankets for doors. Even so, it's tight quarters for the survivors, and there's no real privacy. We walk into a cubicle area with a desk. The guards with us stop at the entrance while Rosalind walks in, stops, then turns to face Ladon and I.

"All right, I want to know what's going on. I want details. I want to know everything that's happened since I sent you out to catalog plants."

I swallow, uncomfortable under her gaze and her demanding demeanor. Next to me, Ladon tenses, and his eyes are roaming. I have to remain calm or I know that he'll go on the offense. I tell Rosalind everything that happened, leaving out the part about waking up to Ladon between my legs and our later sexual encounters. That's private, and I don't feel the need to share with anyone who I take to my bed. When I finish, Rosalind sighs.

"Okay," she says, her fingers drumming on the desk. No matter that her uniform is clean and crisp, this close she doesn't look well either. She hides it better than anyone else, but she seems to let her mask slip. Her lips purse and she's staring past us at the wall for a moment before she continues. "Things here have been rough. We've lost almost a dozen."

"Lost?" I ask.

"Dead," Rosalind says coldly.

"What? How?"

"Accidents, monsters, creatures, and stupidity. No one is feeling up to the welcoming of yet another strange alien." Rosalind eyes Ladon up and down. "Tell me more about this city."

I tell her everything I know. I hear people milling around on the other side of the crates and then footsteps moving away. I'm not finished telling her what I observed before judging by the sound of shuffling and heavy breathing there must be a dozen or more people on the other side of the crates listening. I can't blame them; this is our one great hope of survival on this planet.

"There's one more thing," I say.

"Just one?" Rosalind asks, arching an eyebrow.

"Well, yeah, I guess," I say and Ladon hisses.

"You're sure she is a friend?" he asks in his language, looking from me to Rosalind.

I shrug because I don't feel very friendly with her. Hell, I barely feel like I belong here with my own people right now. I can't tell him that, though.

"Yeah, she's a friend," I confirm.

She is the Lady General, if I can't trust her then who can I? Gershom? Ugh.

Rosalind watches our exchange closely but doesn't say anything, so I continue.

"There's a plant, very dangerous to get and it doesn't last very long once it's harvested, but it... I don't know exactly. I need to study it in a lab, but it makes things here bearable."

"A plant? Bearable? What do you mean exactly?"

I frown, trying to figure out how to explain epis when I don't really know what it does, just how it's made me feel. I don't want to sound like some kind of drug addict or something.

"It seems to interact with the body on a genetic level. Since he got some for me, I'm not... well, not as hot. My head isn't hurting, my stomach cramps are gone. I'm no longer suffering from heat exhaustion."

Rosalind's eyes go wide and her mouth drops into an O.

"You're kidding," she says, leaning over the desk and placing both her hands on it.

"No," I shrug.

"We have to have that. We're going to lose at least three more tomorrow without help. We don't have enough electrolytes to go around, nor enough food to last. Over half our people are stuck in bed, struck down with heatstroke and unable to do anything."

"Yeah, well, like I said, it's dangerous to get, and it doesn't last long after you harvest it. I'm not sure how to get enough, but give me a little time, and I think I can figure something out."

"Time is something we don't have," she says.

"Calista," Ladon says. "You are talking about epis?"

"Yes," I say to him. "My people, they can't take the heat." A deep frown forms on his face. He seems upset, and I don't understand. "What is it?"

"There is something you—they—should know," he says. "Once you take epis, you can't stop."

Cold coalesces in my belly and slowly stretches icy fingers along my limbs.

"Huh?" I ask.

"What is it?" Rosalind asks, but I barely register her.

"What do you mean?" I ask again, a little more intelligently than huh this time.

"It has… properties. Once you take it, you must continue taking it," Ladon says.

"For how long?"

"Forever," he says, his tail shifting across the steel floor of the makeshift office.

"You… you didn't tell me," I whisper.

He makes an all too human gesture with a shrug, though his wings protruding over his shoulders makes it looks weird. His eyes drop from mine for a breath then he meets my gaze.

"I did not consider it," he says heavily.

"Right," I say, trying to process what he's telling me. "What happens if I don't take it?"

"That won't happen," he says. "I will make sure of it."

"Right, but what if?"

"You will die," he says, his tail going still as his words fall on my ears with a weight words should never carry.

"Calista," Rosalind asserts, authority in her voice.

"Sorry," I apologize instinctively. "It seems there's something else, something I didn't know."

"Go on," she says, the corners of her mouth dropping into a frown.

"Once you take it, you can't not take it."

"Explain."

"I haven't been able to analyze it myself. He could be wrong. I want to study it myself because I don't—"

"Calista," Rosalind cuts me off. "It's addictive, but how addictive?"

"He believes it's one hundred percent," I frown.

"And the withdrawals?"

"Fatal."

Rosalind nods. I look at Ladon, who watches the exchange silently.

"I'm explaining it to her," I say to fill him in.

"I see," Rosalind says, frowning. She still has her hands on the desk, and one of them trembles. She clenches it into a fist then straightens. Her face is a mask, but in her eyes there's a storm of thoughts. "Do not share this information."

"But I can't—we can't let them take it without knowing," I protest.

"I did not say I would," she says sharply. "We are teetering on the edge, and the last thing I need right now is something that will further divide the survivors."

I fill Ladon in on what's being said.

"It will be almost impossible to get epis for this many," he says.

I think about how hard it was to get the epis for me, and remember the meat that Ladon kept feeding me and how I'd feel a little better when I ate it.

"Ladon, that one meat that helped me," I try to remember the right word, "gu-s-tur?"

I sound it out. He makes a gesture that looks like a shrug.

"Guster, yes," he repeats. "What of it?"

Rosalind watches the exchange between us but remains quiet.

"Can you help us get that in bigger quantities? Is it as addictive?"

"It would be easier," he says. "It's not epis, but the guster feed on epis, it infuses their meat. I don't know if it is addictive or not."

"There's meat from a certain animal, I don't know how it works, but Ladon fed it to me until he was able to get epis for me. It should help keep everyone alive until I can figure it out."

"Okay, well then, that's that," Rosalind says, straightening and wiping sweat from her brow. "We don't have any other viable options. We have to trust this," she pauses, pursing her lips. She stares at Ladon with an appraising look, then with a barest nod she continues. "We have to trust Ladon. Can you two get us to this city?"

This is it. We haven't discussed this idea of mine. The way my fellow humans acted when we showed up was terrible, acting like he was a monster. How can I even ask him about this now?

I look at Ladon, debating how to handle this. It's strange, but I feel as much loyalty to him as I do my own people. I hope he's really ready for this. I wish desperately that I could talk this over.

"Ladon, are you okay with moving the humans to the city?" I ask.

I press my hands to my stomach, waiting his answer. He frowns, furrowing his brow as his tail twitches rapidly. The sound of it shifting across the floor scrapes on my nerves as what feels like an eternity passes. He looks at Rosalind then over his shoulder.

"My city?" he asks.

"Yeah, your city," I say. "They—no, we—need a place to live. To make a home if we're going to survive."

I can only imagine what he's thinking. Why let these people who only a moment ago threatened him into his home?

"You wish this?" he asks.

I hesitate. It's only for a second, less than the time of a breath, but in that second a dozen scenarios play out in my head but there's only one way forward. One way that feels right, even though I already see it won't be easy.

"I do," I say.

"Then yes," he says, his voice soft, barely a whisper.

"Yes," I say to Rosalind.

"Good, we leave in the morning," she says decisively, and from outside the crate walls comes the sound of people moving and whispering. There aren't going to be any secrets in this new world.

I look at Ladon and give him a tentative smile. He watches quietly. I have no idea what he's thinking, but I hope it's not terrible thoughts or wondering what he has gotten himself in to.

Dismissed by Rosalind, we walk out of her office, and immediately we're surrounded by dozens of people. They stare at Ladon with a weird mix of resentment, fear, and awe. They are all talking at once, creating a cacophony of sound instead of words.

Ladon looks to me for guidance on how to act. He towers over the humans, his scales reflecting the rays of light off his muscled chest and incredible abs. The way the light hits him, he's statuesque. Like some alien god who's deigned to appear among mere mortals.

Lana steps out of the crowd to stand right in front of Ladon. She looks from him to me, and her eyes widen, then she smiles from ear to ear.

"Oh my god, you two have had sex," she says, pointing at me, and the crowd gasps.

I shake my head no, unable to speak.

"You did! You and him did the procreation dance! The super extraterrestrial xenobopping!" she continues.

"No... no, it's not like that, it's..." I can't form an entire thought; lying has never come naturally.

"Come on, tell us, we all want to know. What's he like, you know, down there? Is it big? Little?" She keeps teasing me, and my skin is burning hot.

"No, I can't, I'm not going to talk about this," I say.

"You're not denying it," Lana says.

She's right, I'm not and I can't. With how terribly everyone has reacted, I find myself more on his side than theirs. What does that mean? If I'm on his side then, well, I must care about him. I do, I do care about him.

Sure, he saved my life more than once, which would endear someone to you, but I also like the way he is with me. The way he makes me feel when he looks at me. As if I'm the greatest thing in his life.

I swallow hard. The crowd murmurs, and I hear several comments being made.

"You couldn't pay me to fuck him," someone says.

"Hell, you wouldn't have to pay me," someone else says.

"He's probably more man than any of the ones we have," another voice says.

"It's not a he, it's an animal," another voice says.

"He's not an animal!" I yell, anger flushing my face as I whirl on the crowd. They fall silent, a sea of dirty, shocked faces staring. I'm so angry I can't see any one person, it's a gray mob of shapes.

No one speaks as I stand there glaring, hands balled into tight fists, shaking with rage. Ladon places a protective arm over my shoulders. He opens his wings part way, and his tail rises up behind his head. A low rumble emerges from his throat. The mob takes a step back, falling silent.

"He's a person like any of you," I say. I'm so angry. Tears blur my vision. "What is wrong with us? Haven't we been through enough? He's here to help."

Jolie pushes through the crowd and takes my arm. I look at her, grateful for any excuse to get out of here. Ladon hisses softly, and I know it's a warning whether the mob does or not.

"Can you get us out of here?" I whisper to Jolie.

"Sure," she says. "I know a place we can hide out."

As Jolie leads us away, I glance over my shoulder and see that Rosalind has been watching the entire incident. I have no idea what she's thinking, but I hope for whatever reason that she doesn't think less of me.

20

LADON

These people are so frustrating. They don't listen, they don't learn, and their curiosity causes more problems than it solves. They are her people, though, and I will help save them. For her.

Their alpha female in white walks beside Calista and me as we lead her people across the desert to my home. They move so slowly it will probably take us three days to herd them all. I'd almost rather be responsible for a dozen bivo than try to get this group moving.

We climb to the top of a dune, and the three of us turn to look back. Calista's people are spread out almost to the horizon. It's stupid and dangerous to be spread so far out, and it's only blind luck that's kept us from attracting a zemlja.

"Too spread out," I say to Calista. "They need to stay closer together."

She nods and turns to the female in white and speaks rapidly, but the chieftess shakes her head, and my irritation grows. Stupid. Calista shrugs, then speaks rapidly and motions emphatically. She at least understands the danger.

We travel all day until night falls. Each of them carry their own supplies, which is good. There is no way I could hunt enough to feed this many in any reasonable amount of time.

While some of them prepare food, others unfold large pieces of cloth that they prop up with metal poles. The cloth forms a shelter once they have it all up and together. There is only one door into each shelter and that they close with some kind of fastener.

Calista pulls me to join her in one, but I shake my head and pull her away. A shelter like that would be entirely too restricting if we were attacked, which is highly likely with this many people making noise.

They share their food with me, which has a disgusting metallic taste. I accept it, not wanting to appear ungracious, but once the majority of them settle down into their little shelters, I go a distance away and set up my own camp, laying cloth down for Calista and building a small fire. Calista comes along too and helps, having seen me do this before she understands what to do. I get out some bivo meat and cook it for us. She looks at me gratefully as she takes the piece of meat, blows on it, then pops it in her mouth.

"I'm sorry," she sighs.

Her shoulders slump as she stares into the fire. Dark circles swell under her eyes too. She's been quiet and withdrawn ever since the confrontation with the others like her.

"Why are you sorry?" I ask.

"Them," she says, gesturing towards the humans' sleeping forms.

"They are not your responsibility."

"No," she agrees. "But I feel bad. The way they acted. I thought we were better than that."

"What is it they said?"

She purses her lips, and for an instant I'm distracted from my train of thought. Her full lips glisten by the silvery light of the moon. I want to kiss her, touch her, make love to her until she is no longer depressed.

"Some of them, not all of them, but some of them think you're an animal. Somehow less than."

"Less than?" I ask.

This doesn't make sense. Before the Devastation many different species came and went from Tajss. I don't recall ever thinking any intelligent race was less than any other.

"Yeah. Less than, not the equal of," she says, trying to clarify without looking up from the fire.

I scoot closer and put my arm around her. She shifts until we're holding each other close.

"I understand the words," I say. "But the concept is not clear to me. Do they not see me as intelligent?"

"Some don't, no. One of them is my old boss. I worked under him on the ship. He's always been a jerk, but that was different. Extreme. Problem is, it isn't just him. Others are listening to him."

I understand the concept now, some at least, but if they feel that way, like I am no better than an animal, does she? I pull my arm back from around her. We sit in an uncomfortable silence, the first time since I found her that I've felt like this. She looks over. The thought persists. I can't shake it; what if she doesn't see me as a male? As worthy?

She touches my face, turning my head to face her. Her eyes glisten with moisture, though none falls down her cheeks yet. She places her other hand on my face too then leans in and kisses me. A soft, loving kiss.

"And you?" I ask the question weighing my heart down.

"Me?" she asks and I nod, studying her eyes and face. "No, of course not."

I nod and we fall silent, each lost in our own thoughts. We finish our food and lie down together. She doesn't cuddle up next to me like she has every other night. I lie still, waiting, but she doesn't move. She's lying on her side with her back to me, and I don't understand. I scoot across the cloth closer to her until our bodies are touching, and she stiffens.

I place my hand on her leg and trail it up to her hip. She grabs my hand and stops it, then takes it off her and sets it back on my leg. I'm confused and hurt. Ever since we returned to her friends, she has been different. Maybe she does think less of me? I don't know what is happening, but I do not like it, and it makes me not like them even more. As I think about it, it makes me angry. I put my hand back on her leg and hiss softly in her ear.

"Mine," I say.

"No." She says more words as well, but I can't follow them.

She said no. No, what? What does she mean, no? Why is she pushing me away?

"I do not understand," I say.

She rolls over until she is on her side facing me. She meets my gaze, looks away frowning and shakes her head, and my frustration grows. It is no different from any other night, except she is being different. It has to be something to do with these others. I wish they would all go away. Let a zemlja eat them for all I care. They're nothing but trouble, anyway.

"No. The others, they will hear," she says something else and taps at her ears.

She is mixing my language and her own more than she did before, making it hard to follow her thoughts. She says something more in her language and taps her ear again, a look of frustration on her face. All right, fine, but that does not mean we cannot sleep close like we have been.

I hold my hands palm out and try to show her I understand. I slowly reach out and stroke her hair, then her face, and ease myself down so that her back is to my chest. I pull her in tight and stroke her hair until she relaxes and falls asleep.

I WAKE EARLY, BEFORE THE SUNS CREST THE horizon, to hunt. The humans are slow, weak, and only getting worse. Their inefficient and poorly designed bodies can't handle the heat. The only way they're going to make the city is with the meat of a guster.

After a successful hunt, I return to Calista's people with my harvest. I can hear voices arguing even before the camp comes into view. My dragon, that embodiment of primal instinct that connects to Tajss on a deeper level than social constructs, rumbles. These fools, their feet are loud enough, now they add their voices? Do they want to die?

Then, over the din of their many voices, I hear Calista yelp. The dragon roars, and its breath is the red fog of the bijass clamping over rational thought. Something threatens my treasure, challenges my dominance. My one thought is to save her and destroy that which would hurt her. I spread my wings and run, long leaping bounds, crossing the desert faster than any human could imagine doing.

I top the last dune before the camp and look down. In the middle of a herd of the humans is Calista, surrounded by them. She is on the ground on her side, holding herself up on one arm. One of the males, the one with streaks of white in his dark hair who spoke closely with the chieftess, is waving his arms angrily and pointing.

Gershom. Calista told me his name, and it echoes in my head as if she is yelling it into a rock canyon.

Calista looks up at him with fear on her face. The bijass was rising and the dragon raging, but now I'm blind with it. No one and no thing harms my treasure. I drop my bag and run four long strides then leap. My wings catch the warm breeze of Tajss's breath, and I glide down on them like a falling rock. I'm almost on them before they see me.

I have one fist cocked back, and as I close with Gershom, my prey turns. His eyes go wide, his mouth drops open, and he screams like a baby majmun. He stumbles backwards, tripping over Calista, and falls on the ground. He is fortunate as it makes me miss, my punch whistling past his head.

I land hard, sand and dirt flying up at my impact. Snapping my wings shut, tail raised, I stalk towards him as he scrambles backwards. The crowd of humans fall over each other in their haste to get out of my way. I growl, intent on teaching this male a lesson.

"Ladon!" Calista screams, but her voice comes from down a long tunnel.

She's far away on the other side of the pounding rage that is making my hearts beat in double time. I open and close my fists, preparing to destroy my enemy. I will make an example of him, and they will all know that she is under my protection. They will not dare stand against me or try to harm what is mine again. If they are to be guests in my home, then they will show respect. I am the dominant male.

He babbles as he scrabbles. His hands move, and he struggles to bring his stick to bear. I reach and grab for him, but he rolls to one side. He's quick, I'll give him that. I keep stalking the one who would dare lay hands on Calista.

"Ladon, please!" she cries, and her voice is closer, then she's in front of me holding her hands up. "Ladon!"

I stop and hiss. She steps in close and puts her warm hands on my chest. My hearts beat hard and fast like they want to jump out into her hands. Calm spreads through from where she touches. I point at the male where he lies on the ground, resting on his elbows with moisture running from his eyes.

"No," I hiss. I step around Calista and stare down, pointing at him then her. "No." I say the word as she taught it to me, making it as clear as possible that he's to never touch her again. Ever. He nods, blabbering words that mean nothing to me. I shake my head then turn my attention to Calista. I run my hands down her arms then cup her face between them.

"Are you all right?" I ask, looking to see if she's hurt.

She makes a tight smile and nods. "I'm okay."

Satisfied, I take her hand and walk back up the hill to where I dropped my pack. The humans move out of my path fast. None of them want to be in my way, and I'm fine with that. They allowed him to touch her. They are as guilty as he is.

Reaching my pack, I pick it up then return to Calista where she waits at the bottom of the dune. I open it and show her the meat inside. I motion from it to the humans who mill around each other like a pack of bivo.

"The guster meat?" she asks, smiling.

"It is," I agree, returning her smile. I stare at the humans. The negative thought has taken root in my head. The dragon rumbles, causing the bijass to surge, making me feel primal. "Are you sure you want all of them to have this?"

She pauses and looks at them too. She places one arm around my waist and rests her head against my chest.

"Yeah," she says. "It's the right thing to do."

I set up a fire and we cook, then make sure all her people are fed. The male and most of the other humans avoid me, which is fine. I still want to end his life, but for her sake, I'll let him be.

I know others take him meat, and part of me wants to deny him, let the planet itself claim him, but that is small. I will not be small. If I want to defeat an enemy, I will do it openly. As we eat, Calista talks.

"Gershom isn't all bad," she says. "They're scared and he's... well, he's always been power hungry, I guess."

I hiss, unable to agree with her assessment. I used to know males like Gershom. Males filled with bravado until the time called for action. Males who swagger and control those weaker than they are, but they crumble in the face of a real opponent. I don't want to argue with her or try to explain this to her, though, so I remain silent.

"Let me explain what happened," she says.

21

CALISTA

I examine my memory, preparing to relate to Ladon exactly what happened. I don't want him to hate all the humans. Most of them are good—a lot of them are my friends. I need him to understand, to not hate Gershom and those who he's influencing.

~

"LADON IS HUNTING," I SAID FOR THE HUNDREDTH time. "Once he's back, we'll continue on the way."

A dozen people crowded in behind Gershom. They pushed in with no consideration of personal space.

"Ah, yes," Gershom said, crossing his arms over his chest. "But to where?"

"I told you this," I said and threw my hands up in exasperation. "His city, like I've said over and over."

More people crowded around as I raised my voice. Encircling Gershom and I. My stomach tightened, and something primal in my head screamed to run. *Bolt away, escape, get out of this situation any way I can.*

"All I'm saying," Gershom said, his voice booming across the crowding survivors, making sure everyone heard him, "is I don't think we should be blindly following this monster."

"You have a better idea?" I shouted. "You have some idea how we're going to survive this desert?" I waved my arm to take in the empty expanses of red sand dunes surrounding us. "We'd be dead without him."

"I don't agree. We don't know anything about him. Are there more like him?" Gershom asked. "What are their intentions for us? How are we supposed to trust these *animals*?"

Rage blasted away the remnants of rationality, overriding my fear.

"He's not an animal," I screamed so loud my voice cracked. Tears filled my eyes as my hands balled into fists. "He's kind and caring and willing to help us for no reason except I asked!"

"Or so he wants you to believe," Gershom said. "He's fooled you. It's understandable. You were hurt, suffering from heatstroke. He cared for you when you were weak. There's a term for it, Stockholm syndrome."

I slapped his face. It happened so fast even I was surprised. My hand stung sharply, the imprint of it left on Gershom's cheek. His eyes widened, but so did his smug smile. He wanted this. He planned this.

He touched his cheek. "See? She's spent what, a week with that beast and she resorts to violence!" Gershom said.

The crowd closed in tighter. They were talking all at once; I couldn't make out any one set of words, only bits and pieces, but they were agreeing with him.

"That's not what I meant," I said, stepping towards Gershom.

A man standing next to him thrust his arm between me and Gershom. I didn't see him moving before I ran into his arm, and he pushed me back. I tripped and fell onto my butt.

Gershom turned sideways so he was addressing the crowd. "All I'm saying," he said, waving his arms in the air to make sure that all the attention was on him, "is we need to be careful. We can't trust this *alien*. We don't know his intentions, or if there are more of them. They may be planning to enslave us, for all we know."

"No," I shouted, trying to climb to my feet.

A shadow crossed the suns, blocking out the pounding light. Ladon dropped from the sky like a descending angel of doom. He had one fist cocked back and was aiming for Gershom.

Gershom turned and saw Ladon dropping on him. He screamed, a high-pitched sound more fitting for a little girl than a middle-aged man. Gershom raced back but tripped over me and fell onto his back with a whuff as his breath rushed out. Ladon's fist sliced through the air where Gershom was but a moment before.

Ladon landed hard, sand and dirt blasting up and forming a cloud around him. He straightened and stalked towards Gershom. As Gershom scrambled away, I got onto my feet. I had to stop it.

"Ladon!" I screamed.

He didn't stop, barely reacting to the sound of my voice.

"Keep him away, stop him, stop him, no, no," Gershom babbled as he crawled away.

Gershom fumbled with the rifle he had slung over his shoulder, trying to bring it to bear. I don't know if it would have punctured Ladon's scales or not, but I wasn't willing to find out. As I rushed forward, Ladon grabbed for Gershom. Gershom managed to roll to the side and avoided his grasp.

"Ladon, please," I said, running to put myself between him and Gershom. "Ladon."

The eyes of the crowd watched with bated breath. They were scared. Terrified. We were attacked by aliens, our ship crashed. Most of them were probably still in some degree of shock; I didn't blame them for their fear. But Ladon was a friend —I had to get them to see it. If he didn't help us, we'd die. This place was too harsh, unfit for human life.

Ladon stopped, his eyes focused past me on Gershom, but he wasn't moving. I closed with him and placed my hands on his chest. His eyes shifted to me, and he took a deep breath that he then exhaled slowly. The rage cleared from his face. He pointed to Gershom.

"No," he hissed in our language. He stepped to my side and stabbed his finger in Gershom's direction then back at me. "No."

He said it in perfect Common so there couldn't be any doubt he was understood. Gershom had tears streaming down his face as he frantically nodded. Ladon turned his back.

I knew, understanding Ladon better than anyone else there, that it was the ultimate insult. He didn't see Gershom as any kind of a threat, and he was making it clear. You never give a threat your back.

He ran his hands down my arms, his eyes boring into me as he inspected my wellbeing. "Are you all right?"

"I'm okay," I agreed, smiling.

He took my hand and walked away from Gershom. The crowd parted around us easily, giving him plenty of berth. As we moved through, I tried to read their faces. It was such a broad mix I didn't know what the final verdict was. I saw fear, admiration, even a few that I could only call lust.

As we broke free of the crowd, I spotted Rosalind off to one side with a small group of people. She watched, her face and demeanor imperious, but cold calculation was writ on her expression. When our eyes met, she gave me an almost imperceptible nod.

"He's not!" I argue, trying to push Ladon out of the silence he fell into after I related the story.

I don't know if I'm using the wrong words and he doesn't understand, or if it's that he doesn't agree. I don't want him to hate Gershom, but I get it. I'm not sure why I care. It's not as if I like Gershom either, but my not liking him doesn't end up with him being beaten or worse.

"He's scared. They all are. Surely you understand that?"

"Only a weak male acts from fear. More?" he asks, offering me another piece of the meat he's prepared.

I don't want to argue with him, especially about something like this. He was defending me, after all, not that Gershom and the others see it that way. They think he's a threat.

"Promise you won't hurt him?" I ask, changing tack.

Ladon stares down the hill at the other survivors. His brow furrows and he frowns thoughtfully.

"Promise," he muses, "no, but I will not act first. That I will promise."

"You really are my knight in shining armor," I say in Common because I have no idea how to translate that idea into his language. I've gotten the best I'm going to get and it's enough, so I give up arguing with him about Gershom. I swallow a piece of meat. "Although it's kind of reversed. I mean, a knight in shining armor slays dragons, and you're kind of a dragon. Where the hell does that leave me? Am I the princess? This is getting deep."

"You're the treasure," Jolie says, startling me as she plops down next to me.

"It is kind of like that," I say, thinking it over as I translate her words for Ladon.

She laughs and nods. Ladon hisses and shrugs. Lana walks over and takes a seat. She sits too close to Ladon for my personal taste. I bite my tongue before I spout off something I'll regret. She's not done a thing to make me feel this way, but jealousy digs painfully into my chest. I can't not compare myself to her and find myself wanting, but as I struggle, Ladon shifts his eyes to mine. Warmth flushes my skin and my heart speeds up. I'm about to say something when Inga walks up.

"Can I join you?" she asks timidly.

"Of course you can," I say. Her exposed skin is bright pink and she looks somehow more wan than ever. "How are you?"

"This meat seems to help," she says, taking a seat next to Jolie.

"It will be better soon, I promise." I haven't told any of them how difficult it will be to harvest the epis. We'll cross that bridge when we get there.

Amara and Mei come over together.

"This a private party, or can anybody join in?" Amara asks.

"You're both welcome," I say, smiling.

It's nice to have my friends, old and new, with me again. Although thinking about that makes me wonder how long Ladon's been alone. As much as I've lost, all of us have lost, I can only imagine his loss. We've lost our home, but our race isn't gone. I'm not the last human in the universe, and for all I know Ladon might be the last of his kind. It makes my heart break thinking about it.

"So, how much longer to this fabled city of yours?" Amara asks.

"Probably one more day if we make good time," I say. As they talk, I translate for Ladon, but he's only giving us part of his attention—mostly he's staring out across the desert in his own thoughts.

"Good," she responds. "Some of us have been thinking. You said the city seems to be fairly advanced. Some high-tech stuff. We're hoping we can find a way to get off this planet."

"God, yes," Mei adds. "I hate it here."

"Oh, it's not so bad," Jolie says.

"I don't like it here either," Inga says. "It's hot and sand is everywhere. I have sand in parts of me that have no business having sand in it. I need a shower."

"Oh, a shower would be heaven," Mei agrees.

"I don't know. I didn't see anything like that," I say. "It's a framework, a base for us to build from. I kinda figured we could fix it up and have a home."

"A home? Like, forever home? Here? Why the hell would we want to live here?" Amara asks.

The secret Rosalind ordered me to keep sits heavy on my tongue. I want to tell them, but I can't. If they take epis, they'll be stuck here, like me. If they don't and they do find a way off the planet, I'll be alone.

"I don't know, I kind of like it," I say, staring at Ladon.

"I know exactly why you like it," Lana says, a wide grin on her face as she reaches over and touches the bulging bicep of Ladon's arm.

My cheeks burn. He looks at her hand then at me. He grabs her hand, stopping its motion, then softly places it in her lap. Her eyes widen and her mouth drops open. I don't think any male anywhere has ever so blatantly turned her down in her life.

"Seriously," Amara says. "We don't belong here; we need to get off this planet."

"I guess," I say, stopping myself from saying more.

The conversation turns to small talk as we finish eating our breakfast. Then the day is consumed with loading our packs and continuing the journey. We make better time now that the survivors have had the meat. The day moves on blessedly free of any excitement. Soon the city looms large on the horizon. Surprisingly, we should make it before nightfall. The sight of the city invigorates everyone, and we enter it well before dark.

Everyone stares in wonder until Rosalind walks up.

"Thank you," she says to Ladon and I. Ladon nods understanding, that being one of the phrases in Common he understands. "Are there any others of his species here?"

I look at Ladon, who is watching my face.

"She wants to know if there are others like you?" I ask.

His gaze shifts off into the distance. A deep frown precedes the way his face clouds like a pending storm. An overwhelming air of sadness flows from him.

"No," he shakes his head. "None close."

"I don't think so," I say. "There are not many of his race left and none close."

"Some of this looks like apartment buildings, like that one over there. Is it okay if we set up there as our home base? Get people shelter for the night at least, then see what we can do about fixing this place up?"

Ladon looks from her to me.

"Can the humans set up there?" I ask pointing at the building Rosalind had indicated.

Ladon looks around with his thoughtful frown. He's considering something but doesn't say what. I'm a bit caught up in how cute his face is when he frowns; it forms a line between his eyebrows that I think is sexy.

"Yes," he says in Common.

I look at Rosalind, and she smiles. "Where will you stay?" she asks, looking between Ladon and me.

My cheeks burn, and I can't meet her gaze. "I'll meet you in the morning."

She nods like she expected nothing less. "Okay, we'll have a lot of work to do."

"We'll need to get epis as well. The meat he got for us helps, but it's a temporary fix," I remind her.

She gives me a discerning look as if questioning without words whether or not I told anyone about the addictive nature of epis. While I haven't, I'm sure people were listening to our conversation on the ship. Rumors must be flying.

"Yes, it's on my list," Rosalind says at last.

She leaves, barking orders and organizing our people. I watch her for a couple minutes before Ladon puts his arm around my waist, and I lean into him. Safe, happy, and together. Once they are all in the building that Rosalind chose, Ladon and I head for his home at the heart of the city.

The walk gives me time to think. They want to leave. I hadn't thought about it since getting to know Ladon. Now that I've taken epis, by choice or not, I can't. At least, that's what he believes. I'm sure, given time and equipment, I can figure out a way to either grow epis elsewhere or duplicate its effects, but then what?

What about him, us? He won't leave, will he? Do I want to live without him? And leave for what? We were never intended to reach the new home world. That wasn't the purpose of our generation. We would have lived and died on the ship, and I would never have met him. I bite my lip, thinking it over. I don't know. I don't want to lose my friends, but if they do figure a way off the planet and I figure out the epis problem, I'm not sure I will go. Not if he doesn't go with us.

We walk into his home and through to the area where we slept before. I feel withdrawn and more than a bit lost in my thoughts. Ladon doesn't pressure me, either. He makes dinner, and we eat in comfortable silence as I watch him and think about the last few days.

I remember the argument with Gershom this morning before Ladon showed up. It was humiliating. My entire species let me down on some fundamental level. In ways I can't put into words, it's such a huge concept. Are we really no better than this? Hating because someone is different than us?

It wasn't all of them. Rosalind and my friends weren't buying into Gershom's tactics. Tactics. I see it now. It all comes clear in a flash. Gershom has always craved power. On the ship he was limited in what he could grab control of; the social structures kept him restrained. Those are gone and he knows it. He's playing on people's fear.

My stomach churns and bile burns up my throat. It can't be that simple. That awful. Can it? I swallow hard, forcing the acid back down, and cough to clear my throat. Ladon looks up from his food and smiles. As warmth floods my belly and suffuses my skin, Gershom becomes tomorrow's problem. When Ladon smiles, it makes me feel like the universe is okay. When I'm with him, everything will be fine because he's here. How could I ever leave him behind?

I scoot across the small distance to where he sits on the floor, leaning against a wall, and I crawl into his lap, laying my head on his chest. Listening to the sound of his hearts beating is both soothing and sexy. His hand runs up and down my back as he looks down into my eyes. He leans in and we kiss, one of those long, soft, endearing, beautiful kisses that I've only known with Ladon. His hand moves, soft and slow, along my skin.

I drop my hand between his legs and work my way under his loose pants to find his already rock-hard cock. I rub the smooth underside and he moans into my mouth, flaming my desire to even greater heights. One of his hands lands on my ass and squeezes gently, while his other one fumbles with my shirt until my breasts are freed.

I let him play with my tits for a few minutes while kissing and stroking, then I slide out of his arms. I get onto my knees and loosen the tie of his pants then move them out of my way.

His cock is free and erect like a tower rising from his middle. I lean low and lick along the soft, smooth underside to the tip. He inhales in a long hiss of surprise and says something low in his own language. It sounds like a question. Has no one ever done this for him before? Smiling from ear to ear, I move to do it again. I am going to blow his mind!

The taste of him excites my senses. His cocks tastes of white pepper-seasoned ahi tuna chased with a rum-infused tropical drink. It ignites my taste buds. Despite the heat of this planet, his cock is cool to the touch and smells of skin with the faintest hints of salt and musky desire.

When I reach the end of his length, his head is thrown back, his eyes are closed, he's moaning, and the first drops of precum gleam on the head of his cock. I lick it up, curious as to the flavor.

It's spicy with a tang of cool refreshment that reminds me of epis. It makes my whole mouth feel cool and fresh. I lower myself again and lick along his length, lavishing his shaft with my tongue.

He shifts his hips, then he reaches down with his long arms and fondles my breasts. My nipples stiffen at his attention as I continue to work his cock with my tongue and mouth. I can't take him in fully since it's too big for my mouth, but I use my tongue to great effect. It's not long before he slams his hands against the floor to either side, and then his cock jumps and his come floods hot into my mouth.

He throws his head back and hisses in a low, long sound that lasts as long as his orgasm. When it's done, he opens his eyes and looks at me in amazement. I grin and watch as his now-soft cock retreats only to be replaced by his second, which is more than ready to go.

I slide out of my pants and crawl across the length of his body. Moving up is against the lay of his scales, which gently scratch my skin in the most pleasing of ways. I position myself over him and slide onto his cock slowly, letting us both enjoy the moment of first entry. Each inch of him that slides into me with each hard ridge is a little release. The sensations are so overwhelmingly pleasurable it's like my brain shuts down with each one, an instant of being unable to process thought, only sensations.

He puts his hands on my hips to help support me, but he lets me set the pace. I slide down and down until he hits bottom and the hard ridge at the base of his shaft is pressing against my clitoris. I hold the position for a moment, letting my body adjust, then I ease myself forward and back. The constant pressure of that hard bone on my clit combines with the fullness of his ridged cock inside me, and in moments I lose all control.

I rock back and forth, then up a little and down. I lose all sense of anything but pleasure as an orgasm builds, grabs me in its hold, and sweeps me away. Fire burns through me, stars fill my head, and my breath is ragged gasps as I scream his name, and he comes with me, filling me with his seed. When it passes at last, I collapse against him, panting and exhausted but in a good way.

He wraps his cool arms around my back and his tail curls around my waist. We hold each other in comfortable silence. I'm sleepy, almost half-asleep, but my thoughts are in turmoil. Every time I'm about to drift to sleep, the other humans desire to leave pushes in and I'm awake again. Ladon is playing with my hair, his chest rising and falling evenly, obviously content.

"I wish I understood what I'm feeling," I say in Common, trying to work out what I feel and what I want to say, trying to fit these feelings and thoughts that are too big to be contained in the symbols of words of either of our languages. "There are things I want to tell you. Ask you. I think you're feeling this too; I mean, you must be, right? I'm sure you don't act this way with every girl you meet."

I sigh, letting the beating of his hearts fill the silence. Words. What are the words I would say if he could understand me? Maybe the problem isn't not knowing the words in his language, maybe it's that I don't know them in my own either.

"I think..." I trail off.

The words are there, on the tip of my tongue, but something stops me saying it. It's too bold. Too soon. I can't feel that or can't know I feel it. Can I? He doesn't stop stroking my hair or holding me. His tail shifts around my waist until the tip is resting on my breast.

"Damn it," I curse. "I must be crazy. How can I..."

He says something, a new word I don't get at first. I wait, silent, until he repeats it. I rise up to look into his face and watch his mouth as he repeats the word. It feels like I know the word, like I know what he's saying, but it's not creating a picture in my head. He says it again, but this time he places two fingers against the middle of his chest then presses them to the same spot on me. He repeats the motion and word over again.

"Love?" Understanding comes not with an explosion, but an implosion. A mental well of gravity in my thoughts that pulls all other thought into it. My mouth is dry as the desert sands outside the city. Tears pressure against my eyes and I struggle to hold them back. "Is that it?"

I'm choked up and can barely speak.

"Love," he repeats himself. "I love you, Calista. You are my treasure."

"I love you."

My heart refuses to beat as I realize I said the words. The three words that I've been holding back. I didn't mean to say them, really. They slipped out, but they are so right.

Truth. They are truth put into sound and syllables. I love him!

The scent of him is heady, musky and sweet, making my head spin more. I lie in his arms, my spinning fears and thoughts keeping me far from sleep's sweet escape.

22

CALISTA

*T*he next few days are a blur. If nothing else can be said of Rosalind, it's for sure that she doesn't waste time. She's got us moving so fast that there isn't time to waste with thinking —everyone is given duties.

In an initial meeting, she gathered a handful of us and named us to be the City Council. Since Gershom was at her side and judging by the grin on his face, I harbor no doubt he was instrumental in the formation of that body.

We came up with a list of projects, and in less than an hour the orders were flowing. It was an easy and unanimous decision to focus on three key areas to ensure our immediate survival. Food, power, and shelter.

I was able to get Ladon to agree to help on the food, which took a while. He was very resistant to leaving me alone. He was still acting surly when he left to lead a group of guys back to the ship for supplies.

They're on their third trip out now and he's been more amenable at least, though he always finds me as soon as he returns. The way he holds me and looks me over leaves no doubts he's worried someone might have hurt me. It doesn't seem to matter to him no matter how many times I tell him that no one would dare after the way he handled Gershom.

Jolie, Amara, and I take on the task of trying to get power running to the city. Our qualifications are not the best for the job necessarily, but from Rosalind's surveying of the survivors skills, we're the best that humanity has to offer.

"It's too damn hot," Jolie says.

She wipes the sweat away from her eyes. Her dark hair is hanging in damp strands, and her shirt is soaked, making it cling to her skin.

"I know," I agree. "I think we've almost got it, though."

"You said that an hour ago," she says.

"Yeah, but that means we're an hour closer," I say, trying to pump a bright sound into my voice.

"Sometimes I hate you," she laughs.

"Would you two shut up?" Amara says, pulling her head out from under the massive machine that we think is a generator. "Hand me that spanner wrench."

Jolie picks up a tool out of the box and holds it up, waving it at Amara.

"This?" Jolie asks.

"Were you dropped on your head as a baby?" Amara grouses.

"Uh, no, botanist here, what do I know about spanner wrenches?" Jolie says.

"Nothing, apparently," Amara says, sliding out from under the machine and getting the tool herself while I laugh. "What are you laughing about?" She targets me. "You're no better."

"Hey, I'm not involved!"

"And don't I know it," she says.

Amara crawls back under the machine, and there's the sound of metal on metal then something crashes. She curses loudly.

"Are you okay?" I ask.

She slides out from under the machine, and her face is crimson. She climbs to her feet with a growl, then kicks the machine. She cries out in pain, holding her foot and hopping on the other. Jolie and I exchange a look, having lived with Amara long enough to know to let her be until she gets her cool back.

"I don't get it," Amara says at last. "This isn't put together like anything on the ship. I'm not a damn engineer. Hell, I'm not a mechanic! I'm a freaking pilot."

"It's okay," I say, putting an arm around her shoulders.

She shakes her head then sighs heavily. "No, it's not. They're counting on us. All of them, and we've made no headway."

"That's not true," Jolie says. "We've figured out that it runs on crystals. Which is weird, sure, but the basic theory is like a piezoelectric. So somehow the crystals inside this massive thing have to come under pressure. We figure that out, then they should generate at least some power."

"Blah, blah, sciency-talk, big words, no freaking clue," Amara says. "None of that makes sense to me."

Jolie stares at the machine. Ladon showed us how to get down into these tunnels that run under the city, but he didn't seem to understand the machines here any better than we do. Probably less so.

"What is that pipe there?" Jolie asks, pointing up.

"No clue," I say.

Jolie chews her lips and has a faraway look on her face I've seen before, usually before she has some groundbreaking idea.

"What if they used oxygen to apply the pressure?" she murmurs, walking away while staring up at the pipe that runs along the ceiling. "If this carries oxygen or some other gas, anything that would create pressure…"

She trails off, and I pick up her idea. "You're thinking that this is the key. It applies the pressure, and these machines are giant piezoelectric conduits."

"Basically," she agrees.

"Amara, if we can figure out where this pipe goes and what it carries, we might have the answer."

"Sure, why not," she agrees. "Everything inside the thing's guts seems to be in order. As if I'd actually know if it wasn't. I'm working off instinct and logic. How do I know these people used logic? What if they have some completely other type of thinking?"

Jolie and I exchange a glance but don't bother engaging Amara on that point. At times it's better to let it be than to dig in with her.

It takes what must be over an hour to trace the pipe around. It goes through walls where we have to find a doorway to keep going then find the right pipe again. At last we come to a section of it that is broken.

"There!" Jolie says excitedly.

The broken pipe hangs partway off the ceiling. One side of it is hissing, which lends credence to Jolie's theory.

"Now we need parts," Amara says. "Tools and a way to get up there to fix it."

We set to work, and it kills the rest of the day. When we finally call it quits for the day we're all dirty and exhausted, but close to a breakthrough. Amara is standing on top of the makeshift ladder, which is really piles of boxes and crates that if either Jolie or I don't hold steady will dump her off.

"Come on down, we'll finish it tomorrow," I say.

"One minute," Amara says. "I think I've almost got it tight."

"We need better tools," Jolie says. "Let's call it. I'm starving and exhausted."

"Give me a damn minute," Amara grumps. Metal screeches, and the crates I'm holding wobble away from my grip.

"Jolie!" I yell, needing her to help.

She rushes to grab them, but there's not enough time. Amara yelps as the crates slide out from under her, falling around us. Amara drops onto Jolie and the two of them hit the ground hard. I throw crates out of my way to get to them.

"Son of a," Amara doesn't finish swearing because she begins laughing instead. "Oh, damn it." She rolls off Jolie. "Thanks for breaking my fall."

"Yeah," Jolie says. "No problem. Happy to be your cushion."

As I take their hands to help them to their feet, there's a loud clang, a bang, and then a thrumming hum. We've been working by battery-powered lights from the ship but now I see them. Clearly.

"You did it," I exclaim. The overhead lights flicker and are dim, but they're working.

"Yeah, all thanks to me," Amara says, standing up.

"Yes, your highness," Jolie quips, mocking a bow to Amara.

Amara smiles and wipes the dirt away from her face. "Okay, okay, that's enough of that now."

"Is it really fixed?" I ask.

"I think so," Amara says, looking at the lights too. "Let's go check on the machine."

We rush back to where we started, taking a couple of wrong turns on the way, but soon we find our way back. The machine is humming; though there is a low whine and an occasional screech, it does seem to be working.

"I don't think it's running at full power, but at least parts of the city will be functioning now," Amara says.

"That's amazing," I say.

"Well, it is for now," Amara says. "I'm sure it won't be long before something breaks down. It looks like this equipment has been sitting here for a thousand years or more."

"It very well may have."

"Are you serious?"

"Yeah," I say and tell them about the vid I saw.

"Where did you see that?" Jolie asks.

"In the building where Ladon and I live. I think it might have been a library or whatever the alien equivalent of that is here. It had some power to it still and the one vid cubicle was working."

"A library? Let's check it out!" Jolie says, forgetting her hunger and exhaustion. "Maybe it will do more now that Amara has fixed the generators!"

"Okay," I say. "Let's check it out."

I hope she's right, so I lead my friends to the library. As soon as we enter the room, more of the intact glass panels light up. Nothing else happens though, so I lead them to the one that I saw the vid on when I was with Ladon.

"This looks cool," Jolie says.

"Are you kidding? It's trashed in here," Amara says.

"I meant the technology," Jolie clarifies. "The cubicles and stuff."

"Oh," Amara says, picking her way over a pile of debris.

"This is the one that showed me the vid," I say, and step inside the cubicle.

It lights up and the same vid plays, but this time a shelf slides out from the wall. The shelf is also clear but lines of light trace designs over its surface. Amara and Jolie crowd into the confined space to get a look at it too.

Tentatively I touch the shelf. Where my finger makes contact lights up brighter. As I move my finger around the surface it reacts, the brighter light moving along with it.

"Oh, that did something," Amara says, calling our attention up to the screen.

The vid stops, and shapes scroll up then sideways across. Strange. I continue fiddling. My scientific mind wants to give a much more formal term to it, but the truth is, none of us knows what we're doing. I'm randomly poking at things and hoping I don't blow us up.

I move my hand along, back and forth, then I make circles, which seems to get a reaction, changing the vid again. It takes a while longer, and finally in frustration, I press both my hands against the tray.

Two lines of blue light up below the palms of my hands on either side. The lines of light scan up and down, and then the panel flashes rapidly. It changes color so fast I can't track it. The colors coalesce and then a beam shoots straight into my eyes.

"Calista!" Jolie and Amara cry out, but their voices are distant.

Colors dance in my head. It feels like I'm expanding, growing bigger, too big for my body, even. I can't let go of the shelf. My friends pull on my shoulders, but I don't move. I'm stuck to it.

I blink rapidly, but can't keep my eyes closed. The beams flash so fast that it feels like they're telling me something. On some weird level I feel like I understand, but at the same time I don't know what I understand. Then it's over. Text scrolls across the screen.

It hits me that I'm reading it. I can understand the symbols that Zmaj used for words. It taught me to understand it before, but now it's taught me the written language.

We don't have any tech this cool. How advanced were these guys? It seems to have finished what began when I touched it the first time.

The screen flashes, there's a pop, and an acrid scent fills my nose. I jerk my hands away from the table a moment before the blue lines pulse once then disappear. Smoke rises from the now dark screen.

"Oh," I yell, stumbling back.

"Are you okay?" Jolie asks as I bump into her.

I blink and shake my head. "Yeah, yeah, I am."

"What happened?" Jolie asks.

Tendrils of smoke stretch out of the glass-looking walls like incorporeal fingers trying to break into our reality. I feel out of sorts, my head is thick, and even Jolie's concerned face doesn't seem quite real.

"I'm not, uhm, I'm not sure," I say, rubbing my face. "It was different this time."

"Looks like you broke it," Amara says.

A dull ache throbs in my head, hurting worse when I nod.

"Screw that, are you okay?" Jolie asks, leaning close and staring into my eyes. "Your eyes are weirdly dilated right now."

"I'm fine," I say, rubbing my forehead to try and ease the pain. "I think I know to how not only understand but read the written form of the native language now."

"I want to understand it too," Jolie says. "How did you get it to work?"

"Well…" I trail off. "I'm not one hundred percent sure, but I put both hands on it like this." I repeat the motion, and no glow happens. "Nothing, you try."

Jolie steps in and tries herself. It still doesn't glow.

"What now?" Jolie asks.

"I don't know, that's all I did," I say. "But you saw it flash, right? I think something burned out. A breaker or a circuit or something."

"Well, shoot," Jolie says. "You try, Amara."

Amara tries and still nothing.

"Maybe Ladon can figure it out," I shrug. "I don't know. There's something that happened, I don't know why, though. Why don't we try to get another one of the cubicles working?"

They agree, and we separate to do the work.

"I'm hungry," Amara says after we try with no luck at all.

"Yeah, I'm hungry too," Jolie says from beside her.

I turn to them. "Yeah, me too."

Standing here with my friends, the two people I've been closest to for most of my life, the secret Rosalind told me to keep is too heavy. I can't not tell them. I've never been bad at keeping secrets, but this is so much more than a secret. This is life or death. I've never had to hide anything this enormous before.

"What's wrong?" Jolie asks.

I bite my lip, trying to keep it secret, but I can't.

"I know some people were talking about leaving the planet," I trail off, unsure how they're going to react.

"Yeah?" Amara asks, and Jolie nods.

"I can't. I can never leave."

"What do you mean?" Jolie asks, placing a hand on my arm, concern on her face.

"I'm not supposed to say anything yet. Rosalind told me to keep quiet on this for now, but I can't not tell you two. That plant I told you all about, the one that lets me survive the heat better than you?"

"Yeah," Jolie says, encouraging me to keep talking.

"It has a side effect."

"Oh shit," Jolie says, her eyes widening as she makes the leap to the answer faster than Amara does.

"Yeah."

"Well, what is it?" Amara asks.

"It's highly addictive. Once you've taken it, there's no way to not have to take it again."

"Well, you can detox," Jolie says. "We can set up a celebrity rehab for you."

"It's not that easy," I say.

"Why not?" Amara asks.

"Because it changes your DNA, doesn't it?" Jolie asks, ever the scientist, as everything clicks into place for her.

"Yeah," I confirm. "I think so, anyway. It's the only thing that makes sense. It changes you at a cellular level. It doesn't help you adjust to the heat, it rewrites parts of your genetic coding. It extends your life, gives you strength, and lets you adapt to any environment, but you can ever not take it."

"How often do you have to take it?" Jolie asks.

"I'm not sure."

"Well, maybe we can grow some and take it with us. I mean, botanists, right? It's what we do," Jolie says.

"Yeah, that would work, wouldn't it?" Amara asks.

"Maybe," I say, not having the heart to tell them that I don't think we can.

If Jolie and I had our lab, all of our equipment and supplies, we might be able to work it out, but as it is, I don't see any way we can.

"Okay, we'll figure it out," Jolie says and hugs me.

"Yeah, right, we will."

We hug it out, and then my belly grumbles.

"Yeah!" Jolie laughs. "Let's eat, one problem at a time."

"Okay, dinner time," I agree.

I walk them out of the library and send them on their way home. They'll report to Rosalind about all we've learned.

I muse about my life. I may be stuck on this strange alien planet forever.

23

CALISTA

I find Ladon on the roof of the building he calls home.

"Ladon?"

"Hmmm?" he asks, still gazing into the distance.

I wonder what he's thinking about. What he dreams of. He's said there were others of his race out there, somewhere. What if a female survived? Would he prefer a woman of his own race? They way my people have treated him, I wouldn't be able to blame him.

"Are you happy?"

He turns and faces me, tilting his head to one side as he does when he's thinking something over. That now familiar crease in his brow as his lips turn down at the corners. I appreciate that he isn't giving me a flippant answer, but actually considering what I'm asking, though it makes me worry too.

What if he isn't happy? I didn't get to consult with him in depth before bringing all my friends and the other survivors into his home. The way they've treated him... well, not all of them. My fellow survivors are clearly dividing into two camps, those who are accepting of Ladon and those who are falling in with Gershom.

Those falling into that camp haven't acted out openly, but they move away from him. Cast fearful or even hateful looks at him when he's near. They refuse to be around him if at all possible.

What could I do, though? If I didn't act, they would be dead. I couldn't let that happen, but I don't want him to be upset or resentful. If he is, he hasn't said so to me, but I couldn't blame him.

"Yes, I am happy," he answers at last.

"Even with all of," I motion back towards the building the other humans have made their home, "them?"

He frowns and thinks. "It is... different. Change is not easy, but it is not bad."

"But different, different better? Different worse?"

He shakes his head. "Different is just different. You, my treasure, you make it okay."

I nod, accepting his simple answer. Holding his hand, I lead us to the edge of the building away from the desert, so that we can look out over the city. As I take it in, my attention is drawn out to the horizon. My chest swells as a smile spreads across my face. The setting suns turn the sweeping sands into a dazzling light show of sparkles.

"I want to fix this," I make a sweeping motion. "All of it. We can bring this back to life. Recover all your people had before and combine it with what my people know. Together we can make this place beautiful again. I can see it all laid out before us. These buildings repaired, cared for, shiny, and like new. The dome, like I saw in the videos, that will keep the weather and any predators out. It will make us safe."

"Yes," he agrees.

"It will be perfect," I say.

"You are perfect. It will be an extension of you. You are my greatest treasure," he says.

I turn to him and smile, then rise up for a kiss.

"We need to get epis," I say as I lower back onto my feet. "The others aren't going to survive without it."

"Yes," he agrees.

"Will you lead an expedition?"

"Lead? Them?" He frowns.

"And me," I say.

"No," he says, shaking his head. "You will not go."

"I will, too!" I argue.

"No. It is too dangerous. You will stay here where your work is more important."

Anger flashes like a bolt of lightning in my head. I step out of his arms and glare. "I don't know how your women were," I snap, "but I'm not someone you can order around."

His frown forms deep lines along the sides of his mouth, but his eyes flash dangerously. He's stock still, even his tail isn't shifting.

"Zmaj females knew their limits," he says coldly. "You are my treasure. I will protect you."

"Protect me, sure—this planet is harsh, I get it, but everything here is dangerous. The only way I'm going to survive is to learn. I need to be with you for you to teach me."

"No," he makes a swift motion left to right with his hand. "You do not need to learn how to face a zemlja or other predators. You saw how dangerous they are. I will not put you at risk again. You will stay here."

"That's not happening," I retort. "Are you going to lock me in my room and then sneak off?" It was meant as a smart-ass comment, but he looks like he's seriously contemplating it. "You wouldn't dare…"

"You would be safe," he says, tilting his head back and looking down on me from his much greater height.

"And I'd never forgive you."

He frowns, starts to say something, and then his shoulders slump. I've won, obviously, but he's not happy about it.

"Fine," he says. "However, this is not wise."

"I get it, and I can live with that. It's important, though, if I don't know the dangers; if we all don't know them, we'll never make it. You're one male, you can't be everywhere always."

"I will make sure you live, and I don't need to be everywhere, only with you," he says.

My face flushes as blood rushes to my head and my lady bits. He's so protective, and that argument takes the wind right out of my sails. I'm not sure how to respond to that, so I let it go.

"You said the epis is addictive, but how long can I go without it?"

He frowns and touches my cheek with the tips of his fingers, drawing them down along my jaw.

"Does that worry you? I will make sure you have what you need."

"It... does," I say. "But it doesn't, too." He nods his understanding. "Some of the others, they want to get off this planet. They hope to find a ship or think we're going to be rescued or something."

"Will you be?" he asks, and there's an edge to his voice that I can only think is concern.

"No," I say. "It's impossible. Even if Earth did send a rescue, which they won't, it wouldn't arrive in our lifetime. Like it or not, this is our home now."

"Do you?"

"Do I what?"

"Like it."

That stops my train of thought. Do I like it? This place is hell, sure, but does that matter? I've never felt what I feel when I'm with him. I've never felt... lighter, more alive, more... me. How can I not like that? Does the world around us matter if we're together?

"I..." more thoughts race through my head, and I can't form the words to express them. It takes me a moment before I can continue, but Ladon waits, patient. "Yeah. I mean, I don't like Tajss, sorry. This place sucks. Too much sand, too many things want to kill you, and the heat. Even with the epis, the heat sucks. But…"

I don't finish with words; instead, I wrap my arms around his neck and kiss him. Actions really are louder, and I'm going to back up my feelings and thoughts, expressing them in the best way I can.

Judging by his reaction and the look on his face, he gets it. We break the kiss and I drop back onto the flats of my feet. He places his arm around my shoulders and I lean into him. We watch the city below us, together.

"Before they take it, I'll need to explain to them about the addictive nature of the epis. They need to make an informed decision before they take it."

"Yes," he says thoughtfully. "They will die without it, however."

"Yes, probably, maybe. I don't know. I can't trick them into it, you know? They need to know that if they take it, that's it. They're stuck here, forever."

"The choice you didn't have," he says, watching me closely.

"Yeah."

"I am sorry," he says. "I couldn't explain it to you. I had to save you. I knew, the moment I found you, I knew."

"Knew?"

"You are my one. The one I'm meant to be with forever. The one I've lived for, waited for."

My throat clenches shut. A warm breeze carries the scent of something sweet as tears fill my eyes. I cover my mouth with my hands, unable to speak as my heart races.

"Oh Ladon," I choke out the words and throw my arms around him.

"You are okay with it? With me?"

I nod against his chest as tears stream down my face. He holds me until the pressure eases and my throat unclenches.

"Yeah," I say, stepping back and drying my tears with the palms of my hands. "Yeah, I am. But I have to tell them. I'm not sure what Rosalind's plan is, but I can't let my friends or any of them take it without knowing. It doesn't feel right."

He nods, and we walk to the door and down. Getting every one of the survivors into one place is all but impossible. Since we've been in the city, Rosalind has been organizing teams of people based on their skills to work on projects to either insure or enhance our survival here. They're gone all day long, every day, out on their work details. My friends are easier to gather, so I decide to start with them. Word should spread fast enough after that.

As Ladon and I pass through the library to our apartment, I see Jolie tinkering in one of the booths.

"Hey, Jolie!"

"What?" she asks, looking up with a grin on her face.

"Hey, I'm going to brief the others about epis. You want to tag along in case there's any questions?"

"You mean like ones you couldn't answer for yourself?" she asks. "Cause you know, you're *not* the nerdy one of the two of us now?"

Jolie glances suggestively at Ladon who, I'm supremely thankful, doesn't get her implications. My cheeks burn hot as I shake my head.

"Uh, yeah, exactly that," I laugh, trying to hide my embarrassment.

"You're red!" she laughs, pointing.

"So, are you going to help or…"

"Sure, I'll tag along. You know, you turn the loveliest shade of pink."

"Thanks," I say, leading the way to the others.

I walk into the survivors' building and find Inga, Amara, and Lana working as a team, cleaning the place up.

"Did you two live in a pigsty?" Amara barks. "Seriously, you call this clean?"

Amara points imperiously at a section of the floor that looks clean to me. The other two hang their heads and roll their eyes.

"Sure, Amara, when were you going to do some of the work yourself?" Inga asks.

"Hey! We've got a big strong man coming to our rescue. Maybe he could help us out?" Lana grins.

Jealousy is a green monster inside that wants to roar out at her. Damnit, she's so pretty. And confident, never forget that confidence.

Everything about her exudes sex appeal and the kind of poise and self-assurance I've never had for one second. I close my eyes and set all that aside.

It's not her, it's me. I'm projecting my insecurity onto her. Looking up at Ladon, it still doesn't feel real. Him choosing me no matter that I know, beyond the shadow of any doubt, he has.

"Hey guys," I say, trying to push past my own awful feelings. "I need to talk to Rosalind, is she around?"

"I'm here," Rosalind says, and I have to look around to find out where she is.

Finally, I look up. She's actually up in the ceiling doing something. She grabs the lip of the opening through which she must have entered and does a drop hang down to land gracefully on her feet. Now I'm jealous for an entirely different reason.

Something I barely recognize flutters in my chest. Fear, nothing like what I would have felt before, though. Before it would have stopped me, I'd never have stood up to the Lady General like this, but a lot has changed. I'm not the same girl I was on the ship.

"Can we talk?" I ask.

"Yes," Rosalind says, walking off to a far corner of the room.

"You guys mind waiting?" I ask Ladon and Jolie individually, and they both give their agreement.

I join Rosalind, fully aware of the interested stares of my friends who are now pretending to do their work.

"I have to tell them," I say. Rosalind's face is a perfect mask. I can't get a read on her thoughts or any hint of her reaction. She doesn't say anything in response. I count my heart beats waiting until I can't stand it. "The epis, I have to tell them before they take it."

"Go on," Rosalind says.

All my words disappear. I had played out a dozen scenarios in my head, worked out every possible argument she might have, but not this. She's supposed to disagree with me. Supposed to fight me, but she's standing here staring at me with her austere, imperious look, and I've got nothing.

"Well," I say, reaching for something. "That's it, I guess. I can't be a part of giving anyone epis without them knowing that if they take it, the odds are they're going to be stuck here. Forever."

"I agree," Rosalind says.

"It wouldn't be—wait, what?"

"I agree," Rosalind repeats herself.

"You do?"

"I do."

"Oh. Okay, yeah, right. I'm going to tell my friends here, then I'm sure the word will spread, but we can tell them before anyone takes it."

"Fine," Rosalind says.

"Good, thanks," I say.

Rosalind smiles and places a hand on my shoulder.

"You have a good heart, Calista," she says. "I'll be leaning on that as we work to survive this planet."

My chest swells with pride. I feel like I'm twelve feet tall and ready to take on a zemlja in hand to hand with every bit of confidence.

"Thank you," I say.

Rosalind motions that I should go talk to the waiting people. I rejoin my friends. They stop pretending to work as I approach. I move to stand between Jolie and Ladon then address them.

"So, yeah. We wanted to talk to you about the epis," I begin.

"That's the plant you said would help us survive on the planet?" Inga asks.

"Yes," I say. "Thing is, it's highly addictive."

"How addictive? What are the side effects?" Mei asks.

I take a deep breath and organize my thoughts.

"One hundred percent. It seems to, well... it, I don't have my lab to confirm this, but I think it works by changing your DNA. It makes adjustments to adapt you to this planet, as near as I can figure. Over time, of course."

"Okay. There's something you're not saying, though. How does that affect us if we do try to leave?" Lana asks.

The others defer to her and wait for me to answer. This is the part I didn't want to have to tell them. I look at the ground, the walls, anywhere but them, unable to meet their eyes.

"We won't be able to leave," I say.

Someone gasps, and the others murmur softly.

"Why, exactly?" Mei asks.

"Once you take it, I believe the effects begin immediately. Then you must take it on a regular basis, or you will die from the withdrawals," Jolie chimes in.

"Damn," Lana says.

"That can't be right," Inga cuts in. "We'll just grow some and take it with us. You two are the most brilliant botanists I know. Why can't you just do that?"

"It's not that simple—" Jolie starts.

"Bullshit," Lana cuts her off. "You have to fix it."

"We can't. The epis grows only in tunnels left behind by these giant sand worms that the Zmaj call zemlja. We don't have any of our equipment. I don't know if any of our lab on the ship survived, or if it will work. It would take years to figure out a way to replicate it, if we ever did," I say.

"And whatever all those science-y words mean," Lana says. "I get it's addictive, but this is you and Jolie's wheelhouse. Figure it out."

I look at Jolie in desperation. This is going wrong. I thought this group would be more understanding. A powerful urge to run away surges, and it's all I can do to stand here. I've never been good at confrontation.

Ladon steps in front of me, and I feel his pulsing anger. He may not be able to understand the conversation, but he's getting the tone of their words, and it's not sitting well.

"It's not that easy," Jolie repeats.

"I don't give a damn about easy!" Lana yells, her face turning red with anger. The others with her murmur their assent and support. "It's your job to fix it, so fix it! I don't want to be stuck on this second ring of hell for the rest of my life! We'll find a ship or something, and I want to be able to go someplace, any place, that isn't here."

"Lana, enough," Rosalind says.

Rosalind doesn't raise her voice, but Lana's mouth snaps shut. Rosalind has that effect on people. Charisma, fear, or pure good leadership. Whatever it is, people listen to her.

"I understand," I say. "This isn't great news, but look. This is where we are. We're here, and before any of you take epis for yourselves, I want you to know what it will mean."

I meet the confused and angry looks of the group, and behind it all I see and feel their fear. Seeing it, I understand, and where before I would have cowered and been afraid, I'm not now. I step past Ladon so I'm standing on my own. I look at each of the women, one at a time, and meet their gaze.

"We'll do our best," I say. "But the choice is yours, and I want you to make it with all the knowledge I have."

Rosalind walks up to Ladon and meets his eyes. They stare at each other in silence for a long moment, and then he steps aside with a nod. She then walks up to me and takes my hands. When I meet her gaze, there is a strength and reassurance that flows from her to me.

"Do what you can," she says. "Everyone will have to make their choice and roll the dice."

"Okay," I say softly. "I'll do my best."

A growing familiar heaviness settles on me, the responsibility of all these lives and futures.

24

CALISTA

"I should go alone," he says for the millionth time, looking up from sharpening his lochaber.

"We've discussed that."

We've been discussing it for two days, I think but don't say out loud.

He returns his attention to the blade, inspecting its edge.

"You stay behind then," he says after a few moments.

"No!" I say. "I'm not going to sit here worrying whether you're coming back."

"I will worry about you," he says, shaking his head. "I'll be fine on my own."

"I'm sure you will, but the answer is still no. I'm here now, we're together, and we'll do it together. I've told you if I'm going to figure this epis problem out, I need to study it where it grows."

He sighs and then stands, putting the lochaber through the leather loops that hold it on his back. He smiles and I return it, then he holds out his hand and we walk out to meet the others.

"The other Zmaj, how many are there? Are they close? Would they help us?" I ask on impulse.

The question has been on my mind for a while, but I've been hesitant to bring it up. He hisses softly, a sound I've come to recognize he makes when he's unsure what to say.

"Yes," he says at last.

"Where?" I ask, the strangest mix of excitement and trepidation making my nerves jangle.

"Other places, other cities, not in my territory."

"Are there... females?"

"No, I do not think so," he says. "Only a handful of males survived the Devastation."

I don't know what to say to that. We walk a while in silence while I chew on the information. I don't want to feel better, because it's small and petty. My own insecurity trying to interweave into my thoughts, but still, I am relieved. How could I compare to a Zmaj female, someone bred to this planet and its harsh environment? I know he loves me. I know he's chosen me to be his one and only, but I don't want to risk ever losing him.

As we get close to the doors outside where we're going to meet the others, he stops and turns to me, taking both my hands in his large, strong ones. My stomach clenches when I see the concern on his face.

"They're dangerous," he says, his voice low, brow furrowed.

"Who are?" I ask, confused.

"Other Zmaj," he says, squeezing my hands. "Other males."

"I don't understand," I say. "Why would they be bad?"

"When the Devastation first happened, we lived in groups," he says. "We changed, something changed in us. We call it the bijass."

"Bijass? I don't understand that word."

"Inside each of us there is our dragon. It is the most primal instincts. The need to eat, protect, and to be dominant. The bijass is a... like a red cloud that covers your thoughts. When a Zmaj is in the grip of it, they act only on those needs."

"It sounds awful," I say, squeezing his hands in mine.

"I struggle with it still," he admits. "It eats memory. Until you, I barely recalled there was a before. Even now it is dim and fragmented. I don't know what happened exactly, but I do remember that the bijass became stronger after the Devastation."

"It sounds like regression, a survival mechanism."

"Perhaps," he says. "I recall fighting. More and more until at last we parted and stayed away from each other. This city has been mine ever since."

"Ladon, I'm so sorry," I say. "That sounds awful."

"You have to understand. If other Zmaj see these females, they'll steal them. You are a great treasure. They will want you and the others for themselves."

"What do you mean?" I ask, fear blossoming in me at the weight of his words and the intensity with which he says them.

"There is little of beauty left on Tajss. It was all destroyed in the Devastation, ruined by our arrogance and stupidity. We've been alone for so long. If others see you or those like you..." He trails off, running the fingers of his right hand along my jaw.

"They'll kidnap them?"

He nods.

"Like you did me?" I laugh, but his eyes widen with surprise.

"No!"

"I'm kidding," I say. "I understand. We'll have to figure that out. Warn them, I guess, make sure they stay close to the city."

He nods slowly, clearly still thinking about it.

We walk out into the bright sun and find the others waiting for us by the fountain statue. Rosalind stands in front, still dressed in her whites, which are immaculate as always. It must be magic that allows her to be so perfect. Never a hair out of place and not a smudge to be seen.

A few soldiers stand with her, and on her left is Gershom with two of his own men. I roll my eyes seeing him. He's such an ass. He has a knife on his hip and his graying hair is tucked under some kind of rag. He looks around imperiously like he's the one in charge.

"Ready?" I ask Rosalind, pointedly ignoring Gershom.

"Yes," she says.

She has a sword strapped to her side. I smile and point at it. "Coming prepared?"

"Better than not," she replies, nodding at Ladon's lochaber.

We walk to the cavern where Ladon took me before. My stomach alternates between nervous flutters and clenching into tight knots as we travel across the red sand. Last time Ladon was seriously injured trying to harvest the epis. No matter that we have an entire team with us now, I've seen what can happen, and I'm worried.

No one talks as we walk. I made sure they all saw the vids and have some idea of the challenges we will face. We have to succeed. The survival of our group depends on it. We make good time overall, but humans traveling across the desert are slow.

We make camp the first night. Ladon makes a small fire and cooks meat for us. The others have all brought rations from the scavenged ship supplies. I offer them meat, and only Rosalind and her soldiers accept. Gershom and the two men with him keep their distance, setting up their blankets as far as they reasonably can from Ladon and I. Rosalind has no such qualms. She establishes a series of watches and we all sleep, although mine is fitful and not restful at all.

The night was uneventful, and the next day we're at it before the suns break the horizon. Eventually the opening to the cave approaches fast, and as I see it looming before us, my heart beats faster. I tighten my grip on Ladon's arm, and he places his hand over mine. He smiles and it reassures me, even though I know the situation hasn't changed. His confidence bolsters me.

We stop outside the entrance, and everyone gathers around Ladon. He looks around and frowns.

"Tell them to be quiet, zemlja hunt by sound," he says so I can translate.

Everyone nods, then we head into the quiet of the cavern. It's exactly as I remember. As the darkness engulfs us, each person lights a torch that cuts through the blackness.

"Damn," Gershom says softly.

Rosalind takes him by the shoulder and turns him towards her. She puts a finger across her lips and shakes her head. Gershom looks pissed, but he shuts up, which is all I care about. Ladon watches the exchange without speaking before moving forward in a crouch, leading the way to the pinch point we have to pass to get to where the epis grows. He disappears into the darkness where I can't see him. He and Rosalind insisted I stay in the middle of the group, since I have the least experience with weapons and fighting.

"Ow, shit!" someone behinds me yells, and the sound echoes off the stone walls.

Others makes shushing noises, but it's too late. The air is filled with the sound of leathery wings as sismis wake from their daytime slumber and attack. As I crouch down to make myself a smaller target, Gershom's two flunkies randomly swing their weapons and scream.

"Stop!" I yell, but they don't hear me over the noise.

One of the soldiers screams and I hear a body hit the floor, but can't see who it is. The cry causes the others to panic. I've got one hand on the ground, through which I feel a rumble. This is going to be bad. Standing up, I run into the pinch point, hoping to be clear of where the zemlja will be coming through.

"Run," I yell. "Disperse! It's coming, damn it!"

Gershom turns and looks at me just as the ground explodes and the zemlja bursts up. It's big, much bigger than the one Ladon fought before. It dominates the space of the cavern, filling it to capacity. The humans are knocked away and slam into the outer walls.

My stomach is a tight knot as I back my way deeper into the crevasse, trying to get to Ladon and Rosalind. Anywhere that is away from that thing. It whips back and forth seeking food, prey, or just to cause destruction. Its massive maw opens then snaps shut over and over. Cold sweat runs over my skin, just like the chills of fear that race through my limbs. A hand touches me, and I scream.

"Calista!" Ladon yells.

His hand is on my shoulder, then he leaps in front of me, out of the crevasse, and lands in front of the zemlja. A few of the humans are stirring. They grab their weapons and are trying to bring them to bear, but there's barely room because the monster fills so much of the space. Ladon brandishes his lochaber and stabs, pulling its attention. He dances out of my view from the crevasse, and at the same time he moves aside, Rosalind leaps over me.

"Stay there," she orders, stepping out with her own weapon drawn.

She stabs at the zemlja then twirls to the opposite side from where Ladon disappeared. I'm terrified, but the best thing I can do is to get to some kind of safety. Anywhere away from the monster.

I scoot forward, crawling closer to the edge of the opening, keeping myself low. The zemlja makes a sound that causes the entire cavern to vibrate, then it sounds like it's choking. It whips around in a circle, then a glob of slimy spit flies out of its mouth and lands on one of its attackers.

It hits one of the soldiers, and he screams. A pitch so high and so horrifying that it makes my skin crawl as he literally melts in front of my eyes. I scream too, unable to contain it. I'm far enough forward now to have a good view of the chamber. Ladon and Rosalind are on opposite sides of the monster. They dance in and out, stabbing the thing with careful upward thrusts that slide between the protective plates. The zemlja rises higher until it hits the ceiling, then it retreats, pulling down into the ground.

Everyone is staring at the hole it left behind, waiting to see what happens next. I'm afraid to even breathe in the silence that dominates the space. Ladon is in a crouch with his weapon in front of him, and Rosalind could be a mirror of his pose on the opposite side. Minus the wings and tail, of course.

A minute passes, then two. Gershom's remaining men climb to their feet from where they were tossed against the wall, then walk over and look down the hole. Ladon and Rosalind hold their positions, ready to spring into action. At last, they seem satisfied that it's safe, and as one, they stand.

Rosalind looks at the surviving soldiers.

"Who started that?" she asks in a whisper. No one meets her gaze, and at last she shakes her head and turns back to Ladon. "Let's finish before someone else does something stupid."

Ladon nods as if he not only understands but agrees. He leads the way through the crevasse to the other side. The soft blue glow of epis lights the room. It's every bit as beautiful as I remember. Several people gasp and stop to admire the beauty, then we get to work. We collect the life-giving plant and get out without further incident.

The walk back is done in silence. We journeyed here in fear, and now going home we've lost another of our own. The somber mood is palpable. At camp, Gershom and his surviving man whisper to one another, but our group ignores them.

When at last we reach the city center, those who stayed behind are gathered and waiting. Rosalind steps to the front of the group and climbs up on the fountain. The crowd circles around, and she lets them push in close.

I watch her, so easily in control. I want to go hide somewhere myself. Too many people too close, pushing in, looking for answers. She stands imperiously, waiting until silence has fallen before she speaks.

"We have the epis," she says, her voice carrying easily. She holds up a small portion of a strand of the plant. "The rumors you've heard are true. This plant will make life on this planet bearable. It reduces the effects of the heat and increases your odds of survival."

"Great, give it to us."

Voices merge and mingle but not all of them are raised in agreement. Some dissenters are among those gathering around. I don't know if I realized how many people survived in our section of the ship. There must be close to a thousand bodies pressing around, maybe more.

"It's not without side effects," Rosalind continues. "I have no doubt you've heard stories of this too. The truth is, we don't know the long-term effects. The one thing we are mostly certain of though is that once you've taken it, you can't stop. It has a highly addictive property, and if you don't take it, it will most likely kill you."

People gasp, and now the dissenting voices are louder. The crowd shifts and moves, then Gershom steps out in front. Boldly he climbs onto the fountain to stand next to Rosalind. Rosalind's eyes dart towards him but she gives no other acknowledgement of his presence.

"What does this mean?" a voice asks.

"What if rescue comes?" someone asks.

"Or we find a ship?" someone else asks.

"It is your choice. If you take the epis, you will never be able to leave this planet," Rosalind answers. "If rescue was to come or we were to find a ship, those who have taken it won't be able to leave."

My stomach drops. I hadn't thought about that for a while. If they find a way off the planet, I won't be going with them. I'll be left behind. I didn't have a choice. Ladon couldn't explain to me the risk of what I was taking. These people should be grateful that they're getting to make an informed decision.

"I'm not doing that!"

"We don't have a choice!"

"I want off this Vulcan hellhole!"

"My fellow *Humans*," Gershom says. The way he says the word humans, emphasizing it, making it into a title, not a statement of species, rubs me wrong. Anger surges, but I can't let it go. The crowd that was working itself into an outrage stops and gives him their attention. "Many of you know me. My name is Gershom. Believe me, I understand your fears. I feel them too."

"Thank you, Gershom," Rosalind says. "But this is a personal decision for each person."

"I agree," he says, pitching his voice to carry over those assembled. "Very personal. One they should not make without *all* the information."

"I have told them all that we know," Rosalind says through tight lips.

Gershom smiles, a slimy condescending smile that makes my hand twitch with the desire to slap his stupid face.

"I am a member of the newly formed City Council," Gershom says, addressing the group. "As such, I have nothing but *your* interest at heart. I, like so many of you, am concerned. It's not only our survival that is in question, but also the survival of our entire species!"

"Gershom, don't," Rosalind hisses. Her eyes narrow, and the bags under her eyes look like massive weights, pulling her face down into hard lines. Gershom shakes his head sadly, still playing to his audience.

"How can we, the *Human* race, walk quietly into the dark?" he asks. "Is this to be our end? Following that..." he frowns and shakes his head as if looking for the right word, "thing? Is that what we are going to do?"

"No." "No way." "Humans first."

"Exactly," Gershom's smile is so broad I'm amazed his head doesn't split in two. "Humans first. I'm all for helping those who are less than us, but we need to care for ourselves first."

"As I was saying, it's personal choice," Rosalind says.

"Yes," Gershom agrees, sliding right in with her. "It's your choice. Do you want to take this drug that, by the Lady General's own words, we don't know the effects of, or do you want to put your own species first?"

No matter how much I hate to admit it, the bastard is good. He's manipulating the crowd, and while I think the majority of people see through his show, a lot of people don't. They're desperate and scared. He's playing on that fear and forming a following.

"The likelihood of any chance of escaping this planet are minimal," Rosalind says. "There isn't going to be a rescue. Survival is what we need to focus on."

"But they aren't none," Gershom says. "We don't know what technology we will find any more than we know the side effects of this drug. Or the true intentions of that alien."

"Yeah! What are his intentions?"

"What if there are more of them?"

"They could hurt us."

"He's done nothing but help us!" I yell.

"Now, I'm not saying he has bad intentions," Gershom says. "But I am saying, we don't know what the future holds. How can we commit ourselves to this place, to some alien's intentions, before we know for sure?"

No matter there are two giant red suns beating down on us, I'm cold. I've never have believed this could be us. Gershom is playing their fear and giving it a focus, Ladon. He's using the love of my life as a catalyst to build power for himself.

"Listen," Rosalind says, but they don't quiet. "Listen!" Everyone goes silent, turning their attention to her. "Good. It's your choice. You have to make it. The epis will adjust your body so you can survive here. In trade, you can't leave. The choice is yours to make, do so now. Our harvest won't last long."

She climbs down, and the crowding people fall to discussing with each other. Gershom, having lost his foil, is left standing alone, but the damage is done. The survivors have had the seeds of doubt sewn in their minds, and more than I would like are following Gershom.

The bright future I'd dreamed of with Ladon, fixing this city, seeing it gleaming and populated with life, feels like it was nothing more than a dream. We're fracturing under the pressure of surviving. Of making the choice to commit to Tajss or not. And it's not happening without help. Gershom is pulling the strings.

Crossing my arms over my chest and struggling to not let myself cry, I realize that Rosalind did the best thing she could by leaving. Gershom was using her to counterpoint his arguments. Once she walked away he was on his own, no one to argue with, so he fizzled out.

People either line up or walk away in small groups. Those who line up look anxious. I can't blame them for that; they're making a choice. One that will last forever. That's no easy thing.

The first of them walks forward, taking the epis in his hand. I don't know him; he didn't work in my department on the ship. He's an older gentleman, gray at the temples with wrinkles at the corners of his eyes. He looks at the piece of plant, holding it up before his face and turning it this way and that.

No one says a word. We all watch in silence as he inspects it and comes to terms with what he's about to do. When he puts it in his mouth, the silence is a heavy blanket laying across the watching crowd. As he chews his skin loses the angry red flush we all suffer. He stands straighter.

"Not bad," he says, to no one in particular. The crowd breathes a sigh of relief. "It's kind of spicy."

He holds his arms out and turns his hands, inspecting them.

"What's happening?" a girl asks, her voice tight and nervous.

"Huh," he says. "It's kind of... tingly."

"Is that right?" the same girls asks. "Is it supposed to do that?"

"That's normal," I assure them.

Rosalind stands to one side watching and gives me a grateful look. The man steps to one side and the next in line comes forward. One by one they take the epis. Each of them that does is accepting our fate.

25

CALISTA

*H*ome. When did this become home? The thought of it makes me smile. This is home, here with him. Because of us, he and I and my friends will make this place something wonderful. Our futures are tied together now.

"Food is ready," I say as he nuzzles my neck.

"Good, I'm starving."

"Then you'll have to let me go," I laugh as his cool breath tickles me. "Soon we should have vegetables to go with our meals."

"Hmm," he says with a distinct lack of interest.

"I know, I know, me man, me eat meat, but vegetables are an important part of a balanced diet."

"As you wish, my love," he says.

"Are you quoting *The Princess Bride?*"

"What is prince's bride?" he asks.

"Never mind, it's a vid. Was a vid. I wonder if any of the vids survived on the shipwreck," I muse.

It's not like I didn't see it all a million times. Nothing new was being produced on the ship. All the entertainment came from old books, movies, and television from Earth that came with us when the ship launched.

Ladon smiles as his eyes roam over me, and I know where his thoughts are. Mine aren't far from the same place. His strong hands massage my shoulders so gently. His gentleness, when his power and strength are so obvious... well, it never fails to surprise me every time. Surprise me and turn me on.

"Mmmm," I moan as the tension fades from my muscles.

I relax until I'm nothing but jelly under his touch.

"More?" he asks.

"Yes!" I say, and before I can finish the single syllable, he sweeps me into his arms and carries me to our bed.

He lays me gently down, then motions for me to roll onto my stomach. I slip my clothes off, then stretch out for him. The bed of hides and furs shifts as he straddles me. His strong, hard hands work the muscles of my back, starting between my shoulder blades, then working lower.

My mind drifts as the tension and knots from the day's labor give way to his touch. Relaxation flows from his fingers and through me. He massages across my ass and down my legs. Slow, long touches, sensual and full of love—they make me feel special. At last, he reaches my feet, which he gives extra attention to. As he slowly works his way back up my legs, I wiggle my ass, and he hisses a sound of pleasure.

"See something you like?" I tease, wiggling again.

"Yessss," he says, one of the few words he knows of Common, dragging out the 's' in excitement.

His hands massage as he pulls apart the mounds of my ass. Wetness, proof of my desire, slides down my thighs. He leans in and kisses each cheek then comes up my back to the base of my neck, kissing his way along. A thrill runs down my spine like an electrical touch, and I wiggle again. As he moves higher, his cock drags its way along my leg until it's pressing hard between my thighs, straining towards my opening.

I push up with my hips until the head of his impressive dick is at my slick entrance. I'm ready for him, so I push back harder, trying to get him inside, but he places a hand on my lower back and pushes down, forcing me away from the object of my desire.

"Ahhh," I groan.

"My greatest treasure, you have no patience," he says softly into my ear.

"I have all the patience I need! I love you inside me, I want you," I say.

"I want you to enjoy the experience. We have no rush."

He's stronger than I am by far, so I don't have much choice but to enjoy his touches, which I do.

He trails the tips of his fingers along my spine down to my ass then up to the nape of my neck. From there he trails along my arms to my hands and then down to my ass. It feels like tiny electric sparks follow his exploring fingers, creating a building storm through my nervous system.

My senses go into overdrive. Every touch is a thing of beauty and wonder. I shiver then shimmy under him, but still he doesn't stop. Instead, he adds his mouth and tongue to the light touches. Touching, then kissing and licking his way along. His cock throbs against my ass as he works, constantly pulling my attention and my wet desire to have him penetrate my depths.

"Ladon," I say, my voice tight with pent-up desire. "I need you, now."

"Soon," he whispers.

Another shiver rocks through my body. The electrical storm is building to a crescendo. It's like thunderclouds moving in closer. The hair on my arms and neck stands on end. The pounding pulse of my clitoris accents the storm, laying down a bass line underneath its building tempo. Each pulsing, pounding beat highlights the ache in my pussy, demanding to be filled.

Unable to hold off, I slide a hand underneath myself and down. I press against the top of my folds and make circling motions, but instead of giving me relief, it makes me need him more.

"Ladon, please!" I whimper. "I need you."

"You are my greatest treasure," he says, placing an arm to either side of me and sliding his cock forward so the head is just inside my silky outer folds. "You have saved me from emptiness and loneliness. When I saw you, I knew you were my treasure. I had to have you. Tell me you choose me."

"What?" I ask.

"Tell me your choice. Choose me," he says, holding himself back from penetration.

"Of course I do," I say, not understanding.

"No, the choice is yours. I choose you, Calista, I choose you to be mine, forever. You must choose, of your own free will, you must choose to be mine."

"I don't—"

"Choose," he cuts me off, whispering in my ear then licking my neck.

I shudder and shimmy, but he moves with me so that he still doesn't penetrate any further in.

"I do. I choose you. I'm yours."

Something changes. It's not something I can put my finger on or even put into words, but I sense it. When I place a hand on his chest, I feel his hearts beating strong, and my own heart falls into time with his. I feel connected to him in some new, deeper way. My desire doubles, becoming overwhelming. It floods through me. I'm stuck on a small island of sanity that I'm holding onto by the tips of my fingers alone, fighting to not be washed away in the storm that rages around me.

He wants me. Wants me more than anything I've ever experienced. He needs me in ways that I didn't know one person could need another. As he slides into me, I don't just feel full, I feel complete. As he enters me, everything in my life has been nothing but a prelude to this moment.

This instant I become one with him.

As he enters me from behind, the weight of him presses me into the soft furs, causing the ridges along the top of his cock to rub me differently.

"Oh!" I cry out in pleasure as he slides in deeper.

He reaches bottom and holds, letting me get used to the new sensations. The ridge at the very base of his penis presses between the cheeks of my ass, giving me new and interesting feelings that I'm only dimly aware of, his cock taking most of my attention. He pulls back, and as each ridge pulls free of my silky folds, the sensations pulse through.

"Calista," he moans, then he's sliding in to the hilt. "We are one."

"Yes!" I cry out as the raging storm takes me over, and I lose my grip on the small island.

I'm washed away. Carried on wild winds and knocked around by waves of sensation and pleasure. He grunts, and I buck up into him. I love the sounds he makes as we make love. I'm being tossed like a small ship on stormy seas, but he's there and I latch onto him. We're entwined on some level beyond our bodies.

I hear myself crying out his name, and he is moaning mine. Our voices wind up in each other's, then become one unified sound. Slowly my body pulls me back in, and as I rejoin my flesh, he collapses, then rolls to the side and we cuddle close.

I can't speak. My throat is too dry, and words are beyond me and unnecessary. My body is exhausted, so I lie next to him with one leg thrown over his and let it all just come. I sleep, minutes or hours I don't know, but I wake and he's still there, his chest rising and falling evenly. I stir, and he looks over and smiles.

"I love you," I say on impulse, and he smiles bigger.

"We are one," he says. "You are mine, I am yours. My treasure."

He brushes a stray hair away from my eyes.

"Is this..." I shake my head and laugh. So much joy is filling me that I don't know if I can contain it.

"It is us," he says. "We are joined. We are one. You are my treasure, I am your treasure; we chose."

I smile and he touches my cheek. "I get it," I say.

"I know," he says, smiling. "This is love."

I nod my agreement. This is what the poets wrote about and the songwriters tried to put into their music. This is what I was born for, to join him and be with him. I know that our future may bring hard times. This world is harsh and full of danger, but together there is nothing we can't overcome. "I love you, too."

26

EPILOGUE
CALISTA

*T*here is so much to do! Now that the city has at least a minimum of power, we're all busy with investigating and searching. Ladon and I spend most of our days apart, but every night we come home to each other. He cares so much and is so protective. He hates being apart during the day, but his attention is needed to supervise the teams exploring the city, and he's teaching some of the men how to hunt the bivo to supplement our food supplies.

Some of Jolie's and my work was salvaged from the wreckage of our crashed ship. Now we are working to see if we can adjust any of the seeds to grow in this harsher environment. Food is our biggest problem, ranking right next to safety from the monsters that roam the landscape.

Yesterday a pack of guster entered the city proper, and two people lost their lives before they could find shelter. A team that Jolie has been helping part time is working on the protective dome we saw in the vids from before the Devastation. If we can get that working, then at least there will be somewhere we can be safe.

"You know," Jolie says. "This place really looks like Gallifrey."

"If you get those domes working, I can see it," I say, looking up from the small pot of salvaged soil and the tiny sapling I'm working with.

Jolie wipes sweat from her brow and sighs.

"Why don't you take the epis?" I ask for what feels like the umpteenth time.

She frowns and looks away, crossing her arms over her chest. I didn't mean to upset her, so I go to her side and put my arm around her shoulders. "Hey, it's okay."

"Yeah," she says with a sniffle and wiping her eyes with her sleeve. "It's just... I don't know."

"I could guess a thousand reasons," I say, "but I don't want my guesses. You're my best friend. You can tell me. I'm sorry if I upset you; I only want you to be well."

She smiles, still sniffling and fighting back tears. I pull her around into a full hug and hold her, silent. She returns my embrace until her emotions have passed.

"Thanks," she says, stepping away and wiping her face dry. "I don't know, really... I guess, I'm... ugh."

"It's fine, you can tell me. I already know you're a weirdo."

Jolie snorts and a genuine smile lights up her face.

"Yeah, I guess you do," she says. "I haven't because I'm still holding out hope."

"Hope?"

"Stupid, huh?"

"Hope is never stupid," I say. "But hope for what?"

"A guy of my own," she sighs. "I want someone who looks at me the way Ladon does you. I need that, to feel... complete."

"Oh, Jolie—" As I reach out my arms to embrace her, a random wave of nausea passes over me, followed by cold chills. My stomach cramps, and the urge to vomit is so strong that bile rises into my throat.

"Are you okay?"

"I kn—" The words I was going to say are cut off by another wave of nausea, then I'm running for a bucket.

I get sick, violently so. My stomach feels like it's trying to squeeze out everything I ate in my entire life. Jolie races over and holds my hair back for me. Once I'm done, I feel better, like nothing at all is wrong. I stand up and wipe the cold sweat from my brow. Jolie hands me a scrap of cloth, and I clean myself up.

"Are you okay?" she asks.

"Uh, yeah, that was random," I say. "Maybe something I ate."

Jolie looks me up and down, frowning. Her eyes land on my stomach, and she frowns more.

"What?" I ask.

"Nothing," she says, turning away. "So yeah, Gallifrey, you know Doctor Who?"

"You're not getting off that easy; what?"

"Nothing. Seriously."

"It's not nothing, and it's not Doctor Who. What is it?"

"Well, it's just..." She trails off and her shoulders slump. "Have you put on some weight?"

"What? No! I mean, no!"

I'm flustered by her comment. It's certainly not what I expected to come out of her mouth. My hands go to my stomach, and as I touch it, I flatten them out.

"Maybe I'm a little bloated," I say.

"Uh huh," she says, not taking her attention off the microscope she's looking through.

"Okay, give. What?" I ask again.

"It's just... look—I'm just asking, but when did you last have your period?"

"My what? Um..." I think for a moment. "Before the crash."

"Which was over a month ago by ship time."

"No, that can't be, I mean, it's stress, right? All the stress of living here, surviving. Pressure can do that to a girl."

"Sure, it could be," she agrees. "Do you think that's all it is?"

"It has to be! I mean the only guy I've been with is Ladon and…"

We've never used any kind of protection. Our diets on the ship let us control pregnancy without thinking about it. When you were ready to have children, you took a pill to counteract the chemicals in our diet. It was so easy, I never even thought about not having that diet any longer.

"Uh-huh," Jolie says, smiling.

"Oh my god," I say, my voice dropping to a whisper.

Everything spins around, and then a wave of nausea is chased by dizziness. Grabbing onto the chair next to me, I plop down. Jolie runs over and takes both of my hands in hers.

She beams. "Yes! This is so exciting!"

"No, it's not," I say as fear threatens to overwhelm me. "I don't know... what if... how does his race..."

"Bah! We'll figure it out. You're brilliant and so am I. Cross that bridge when we get there."

"Easy for you to say."

My voice is barely above a whisper. I cross my arms over my belly and stare. Can this be? I mean, it has to be, right? Tears well up in my eyes, but then I'm happier than I've ever been.

I don't know if I'm going to laugh or cry. Jolie pulls me into a tight hug.

"It's fine," she says softly. "We got this."

Breathing in deeply, I nod and then straighten myself. "Yeah, it's just... scary, you know?"

"Yeah, sure, but it's fine. We got this. Besides, he dotes on you! Hell, I'm jealous. I want a guy who looks at me like he does you."

"Yeah, he does, doesn't he?" I say, a surprisingly calm feeling washing over me.

"Hell yes! He's over the moon for you and you know it. You see the way his eyes light up as soon as he sees you?"

I smile, knowing exactly what she's talking about. "I've got to tell him!"

"Yes, you do!" she says, just as excited as I am.

I hug her once more and then run off to find Ladon. It's only mid-afternoon, and it takes a while. When I do track him down, he's on the roof of our apartment building looking out across the desert wasteland. He's alone, and his tail is switching back and forth idly. I walk out onto the roof, and he looks over his shoulder.

"Calista," he says, smiling.

"What are you doing up here?"

"Peace and quiet," he chuckles. "All these people, it's strange and noisy."

"Do they bother you?"

"Bother?" he muses. "More, it's different."

"Okay," I say, putting my hand into his. "It's nice. We can fix all this and get it working again."

Ladon shrugs. "Different."

"Well, that's not all that's going to be different," I say, edging towards what I need to tell him.

"Hmm," he says, and it sounds more a hiss.

"I hope you don't mind…"

"Mind? Is it you or them? You, I never mind. You make me happy, repel my aloneness."

"Good," I say. "Someone else is going to be joining us soon."

"Someone? More of them?" he asks, pointing out at where the other survivors have set up their home.

I shake my head, my throat closing and unable to say the words. A tear falls, and he wipes it gently away.

"Calista, what is this?"

"I'm pregnant," I blurt it out.

His eyes widen, and he hisses loudly. "Pregnant?" He repeats the word, cocking his head. "This is the right word?"

"Yes," I laugh, looking down at my belly. "Pregnant."

"You're sure?" he says softly, placing his hands on my stomach.

I nod, unable to speak, uncertain what his reaction is going to be. He moves his hands in a circular motion around my belly. He kneels, then leans in and kisses my stomach through my shirt. He makes a soft sound like a hum, then low words reach my ears, and I realize he's singing.

I can't catch all the words, but the sound of it is so beautiful it brings fresh tears to my eyes. When he's finished, he turns his head and rests it against me, like he's listening for a heartbeat. I rest my hands on his head, holding him close, and he wraps his arms around me. At last, he stands up and blinks several times.

"I will prepare!" he says sharply.

"Prepare?"

"Yes, there is much to do. The dome must be fixed. Our child will not be threatened here in our home. We will need more living space. You will no longer go on the hunts with me. It is too dangerous, and you would risk two. I will train the others to be useful."

"I'm not broken," I say.

"No, not broken, perfect. You are perfect." He leans in and kisses me.

"Thank you," I say, feeling his love encircling me. "I love you." He leans back and looks into my eyes like he's searching.

I love the way he protects me, the way he touches me, the way he cares. I love the way he smiles, and my heart leaps at the sight of it. I love him! He stares into my eyes then he smiles, and it spreads across his face like the rays of the sun.

"I love you," he says and pulls me close. "My treasure."

I'm pressed into his coolness and encircled in his arms. He rests his head on top of mine, and we stare out at the desert. The wide sweeping vista of the desert is gorgeous. Traveling across it I'd become numb to its beauty, but here, comfortable and in the arms of my love, I appreciate it anew. His tail shifts back and forth, and his wings flutter, making the only sound close to us.

THE CITY IS A WRECK, BUT WE CAN FIX IT. WE'LL work as a team, all of us, and we'll create a home for our child. Our two races will merge as one, and the future will become something new and bright. That is what our love will create. I'm dreaming of what the future will look like, happy in his arms, in our new city that will be shiny and full of life. The future our children will have, and the world we will leave behind.

"I need to go see Jolie," I say, reluctant to leave his arms. "She'll want to know how you took it all."

"I will walk with you, my treasure," he says, and we head down together to the library where I left her.

"Jolie?" I call out, not seeing her.

Silence.

Ladon and I walk through the displays, but she's nowhere to be found.

"Perhaps she went to get food," he says.

"Maybe," I say, an uneasy feeling settling over me.

I stop as we emerge outside to let my eyes adjust to the brighter light. Mei is walking around the empty fountain.

"Mei!" I call out. "Have you seen Jolie?"

Mei stops walking and looks over at us. "No," she says. "Isn't she in the library?"

"No, I was just there."

"Hmmm, well I just got here to look at this fountain to see if I can figure out where its water supply came from. Sorry, I haven't seen her. She probably ran off to investigate some idea. You know how impetuous she can be."

"Yeah, maybe," I say, but worry gnaws at me.

"Try over at the barracks," she says, shrugging.

"The barracks?"

"Yeah, that's what we're calling the building we're sleeping in. It doesn't feel like a home yet so... well, yeah."

"Okay, thanks."

We walk towards the barracks. Ahead I see Amara and Inga. Amara is loud as always and abrasive, Inga is walking with her head down.

"All I'm saying is that if we just made sure that most of the water was going to the barracks, we wouldn't be having this problem."

"Hey, Amara," I call out as we come closer together.

"What?" she asks as Inga looks up, begging me to take her away with her eyes.

"Have either of you seen Jolie?" I ask.

"Nope, and I'm busy," Amara says, starting to walk past me.

"Hey! I can't find her," I say, upset at her brush-off.

Ladon steps in front of her, blocking her way forward.

"And that is my problem, how?" Amara asks over her shoulder.

"Well, it's not, but... I mean, you could just help out some," I say, feeling defeated.

"Yeah, I did. I haven't seen her. Anything else, Princess?" Amara snarls.

"No, that's all," I say. "Let her go," I say to Ladon in his language.

He steps to one side and Amara marches past, obviously upset, but not saying any more. She goes ten feet down the street, then turns around.

"Are you coming or what?" she yells at Inga.

"Sure," Inga says, sighing and hustling after her.

"What was that?" Ladon asks as we watch them go.

"I don't know," I say. "My only other idea is to check her bunk."

"Okay, my love."

"You don't have to come."

"I will," he says, looking back at Amara again.

It's obvious he's being protective, but I like that about him. We make our way to the barracks and inside, then up the stairs to Jolie's room. There are no locks on the doors, but I knock just to be sure. No one answers, so I push it open.

"Jolie?" I ask.

The room is empty. Frowning, I turn to Ladon. "You don't think she got kidnapped, do you?"

"No, no one would dare. You are in my city. It would be an affront. No Zmaj would dare trespass this far into my territory."

"Ladon, she's my best friend. We have to find her."

"She has probably just gone exploring," he says.

"Yeah, probably," I say, but I can't shake this sense of foreboding or of something being wrong.

He's right. I'm sure he's right. Nothing is out of place, and none of her things are missing. She probably just got caught up looking at something and hasn't come back. I convince myself of it, mostly, at last.

"If she's not here tomorrow, will you help find her?" I ask.

"Yes, of course."

"Thank you," I say, then we head towards home.

As we walk through the city, holding hands, I watch the people working. My people. Some look on Ladon and I with looks of anger or mutters of disgust, but most are nice. Grateful for what they've been given, even.

It's not a perfect world. It's not the world we were aiming for, but it's our world now. We can only work to make it better, one day at a time. Together. My heart swells and I look up at my unexpected, unlooked for, love, and pulling on his neck, bring him down into a kiss.

I may not have been given a choice about staying here, but being here, with him, is the only choice I could ever have made. I wouldn't change a thing.

"I love you," I say.

"I love you," he says, placing one hand protectively over my growing belly. "Forever."

"Forever," I repeat.

THANK YOU FOR READING! REVIEWS ARE THE lifeblood of indie publishing and if you enjoyed this edited and extended version of Dragon's Baby, I'd really appreciate it if you left a review.

The story continues in Dragon's Mate, keep reading for a look at Jolie's adventure.

Like being stranded on a desert alien planet wasn't enough...

All I ever wanted was someone to love. Now my best friend is knocked up by the only hunky alien-dragon available and I can't tell anyone how totally jealous I am. The handful of humans who survived our ship's crash are locked in a struggle to live in sweltering heat with dwindling supplies.

The others are taking the life giving, addictive epis but if I take it that means I'm stuck here. Forever. Which also means the chance of being rescued by a knight in shining armor would be zero.

If that weren't enough, I go and get myself kidnapped and he's another big, sexy, alien-dragon warrior.

Dragon's Mate is a full length, standalone scifi novel with a happily ever after ending, plenty of steam, bloody battles and alien-human intrigue.

JOLIE

MY HEAD ISN'T HURTING AS MUCH AS USUAL. That's nice, so much better than when I normally wake up. I lie still enjoying the freedom from pain before opening my eyes. The bed is unusually comfortable as well. Maybe I'll sleep a while longer. Shifting I pull the blanket up then stop. Something is weird, the blanket is too... furry? I crack one eye open to figure that out still hoping to go back to sleep.

Is it still night? The light is dim, like it's late evening or early in the morning. My room is only this dark during those times. The blanket over me isn't mine. What the hell is this? Fear freezes me in place for an instant gripping my stomach in a tight knot and sending chills racing through my limbs. Opening both eyes I look around without moving.

A furry blanket is on top of me and I'm lying on more furs. The wall next to me looks like it's made of stone, not the smooth metal and glass of my room. I'm lying on my side facing a stone wall that is illuminated with a soft orange glow from somewhere behind me. My heart pounds like a jackhammer in my chest and it's all I can do to keep myself from hyperventilating. Dim memories of being carried and bouncing emerge from the clutches of my mind. Wasn't that a dream? Am I dreaming now? That has to be it. One of those lucid dreams where you know you're dreaming and it all seems too real, right?

I make a very slow roll over to my back listening for any sound of disturbance at my movement. Now I'm staring at a ceiling that is maybe four feet over me. It's also plain rock with shadows dancing from the illumination source. Nothing happens, no sounds to clue me in and no idea how I got here. Rolling on to my side I'm face to face with a thin curtain. I can see a room on the other side of it that seems to be filled with things.

What do I do now? Okay Jolie what options do you have? One, lay here and wait. Wait for what? No clue. Okay that's not a great idea. Option two I climb out of here ready to face anything and everything. Well that at least has the temptation of being in motion. Lying here waiting just doesn't work for me and if whatever or whoever brought me here wanted to hurt me it isn't going to do any good to lie here until it happens.

Moving my body aches and I remember the guster. One of them hit me and I was flying then a Zmaj showed up except it wasn't Ladon! The memory of the Zmaj hits like a thunder stroke. A different Zmaj! Of course, well good, right? Ladon is cool so this guy is probably a nice guy too right? I mean he saved me and that is pretty much a re-creation of how Calista and Ladon met. So, so far so good.

Feelings of relief relax the knots of fear and tension in my stomach and muscles. I lie still a moment longer letting my muscles relax and as fear passes a low level of horniness floods in behind it. Great, I'm horny. Just what I need as a distraction. Okay, push that aside cause right now I need to meet this new Zmaj and figure out where the hell we are. And my friends will be worried. I need to get back to the city and let them know I'm okay. Looking back at it, leaving without telling someone what I was doing ranks in the top ten dumbest things I've ever done. If I had though they would have stopped me so that's a catch twenty-two if there ever was one.

Oh well. I'm here and hey I'm about to meet a new alien. So take the win and lets roll with it. Swinging my legs off the edge of the makeshift bed, my bruised muscles cry out in discomfort and a groan escapes my lips. Something scrapes outside the curtain as I drop my legs underneath the edge of it. I'm reaching for the curtain to pull it aside when it's jerked open and I'm inches away from my rescuer and I yelp.

I don't mean to. It slips out mostly because I'm startled and he's so big and so in my space without warning. His eyes widen and he hisses in response. Tilting his head to one side he leans down so that we're eye to eye. His eyes are fascinating, almost a turquoise color that is gorgeous and deep like a rich, sweet pool of water. His scales are different than Ladon's having a blue hue to them and the edges are a bright, rich, almost fluorescent green. The wings on his back rustle with a soft leathery sound.

"Hi!" I exclaim, raising a hand in greeting.

He says something. Of course I don't speak Zmaj so I have no clue what it is. I'm going to assume he's saying something like 'hi' back to me. It could be 'I want to eat you for dinner' but who wants to start a first meeting out on that note? We stare at each other for what starts to feel like forever. I'm waiting for him to move or say something and maybe he's waiting for the same. Either way I decide to take the bull by the horns.

"So," I say. "What's a sexy alien man like you doing in a place like this?"

I smile my best and most friendly smile and push myself forward. My feet barely touch the ground when I'm completely on the edge of the bed. He moves back enough that I'm able to slide the rest of the way out and stand. He towers over me but I'm used to that. Most everyone is taller than me.

The room looks like a converted cave that has been outfitted with at least the rudiments of comfort. Shelves line the stone walls filled with objects and a handful of what look like books. The floor is covered with dark brown furs that I recognize as coming from the bivo herds. On some of the cabinets are small bowls with a floating flame in them that is the source of illumination. A table is to the left and behind the Zmaj with two chairs. Several metal objects lie on it as well as some cloths and uh, goop?

I push past the Zmaj and walk over to one of the shelves. I pick up what looks like a tiny skull and look it over. The thing still has nasty looking fangs and looks like it might have come from a snake. The next piece I grab is metal, cylindrical in shape, with a diamond shaped end on one side and the other is a flat bottom. Turning it over in my hands I examine it but can't figure out any rhyme or reason to what it might be or do.

"This looks nifty, what is it?" I ask over my shoulder.

He watches me still standing where I left him. Smiling I wave the stick thing in his direction but he doesn't respond.

"Not the talkative type?" I ask. "That's okay, I'll talk for both of us."

He's big and imposing. Also there's something about him that excites the low level of desire I woke up with causing it to pull at my attention. To push thoughts like that aside I put all my attention on the objects in front of me. Suddenly it hits me and I look down at myself and realize I'm not wearing my clothes. The clothes I have on are loose, flowing, and definitely not what I was wearing when the guster attacked. Looking from them to him my skin burns hot knowing that he had to change them and that means he's seen me naked. Embarrassment burns while jealousy stabs in behind it because I'd really like to see his massive, well muscled and colorful body too. Only fair right?

"Uh, clothes?" I ask holding up a piece of the flowing cloth and pointing at it.

He shrugs then nods his head. Okay then. This language barrier sucks.

"Well yeah, uh, thanks?" I say.

We stare at each other and I debate whether anything got across to him or if he's just filling in blanks. Maybe he's just thinking I'm nuts. Or wondering what I am. I've seen his race before because I know Ladon but he's probably never seen a human before. Well crud, I hadn't thought about that.

"I'm Jolie," I say pointing at myself then I point at him. "You?"

He watches my motions, his head moving along with each one and he looks like he's studying me. I guess. I really didn't ever pay much attention to Ladon's mannerisms so I can't claim to be an expert. He hisses, a soft sound like air escaping from a balloon and then I realize he's talking. He speaks softer than Ladon does, very quiet, so I step closer to make sure I hear him.

There's a scent to him when I get closer. It's not musk, that's a human scent, this is something exotic, enticing, pulling at my olfactory. Smelling it makes my lizard brain jump into hyper drive. Hmm, bad choice of phrasing. Okay, it makes my primal urges much more prominent. It's almost like a spice, or really good food that you've never tasted but can't wait to savor. The odor pulls me in and I want to inhale more of it. I'm two paces away from him and close my eyes inhaling deeply through my nose, letting the scent fill me. He hisses and this time I can tell it's almost my name, if I was to drag out the J into a really long consonant sound and leave off the O. It sounds like Jjjjjjjlie. Opening my eyes I smile broadly and nod excited.

"Yes! J-O-lie," I say emphasizing the O sound for him.

He frowns, his thinly scaled lips purse and his eyes narrow giving him a definitive look of concentration. It's exciting watching him move his mouth to form the vowels.

"Jjjjj-oooo-leee," he says.

I jump up and down clapping my hands.

"Perfect!" I exclaim.

He smiles or at least partially smiles. It's not a full smile, I've seen Ladon smile most any time he's looking at Calista and it's not that so let's call it a grin. He grins. Yeah, I can go with that.

"Jjjjoooleee," he says again, smoothing out the sound of my name.

I clap and grin encouraging his efforts. "Jolie," I repeat after him pointing to myself.

He touches my chest between my breasts. My breath catches and my heart stops at his touch. All my attention goes to that mostly innocent point of contact between us. I don't drop my eyes, I don't dare to, desire is threatening to roar into a raging fire that I know will consume me and I'll do something stupid.

Buy DRAGON'S MATE to keep reading!

If you want to know more about how the survivors arrived on Tajss read the prequel Red Planet Dragons of Tajss (Red Planet Jungle).

JOIN MIRANDA'S READER LIST
USA TODAY BESTSELLING AUTHOR

Subscribe to get the Red Planet Dragons of Tajss prequel Dragon's Origins *PLUS* bonus freebie Ribbed For Her Pleasure!

http://tny.sh/mirandamartinlist

ABOUT THE AUTHOR

About Miranda Martin

USA Today bestselling author Miranda Martin writes fantasy and scifi romance featuring heroes with out-of-this-world anatomy that readers call 'larger than life' and smart heroines destined to save the world. As a little girl, she would sneak off with her nose in a book, dreaming of magical realms. Today she brings those fantasies to life and adores every fan who chooses to live in them for a while.

Though born and raised in southern Virginia, Miranda Martin is a veteran who's traveled to places like Korea, Hawaii, and good 'ole Texas. She's since settled in Kansas, the heart of America, with her husband and daughters, a cat, and wishes for a pet dragon or unicorn. When she's not writing, you can still find her tucked away somewhere with a warm blanket and her nose in a book.

Visit her website http://mirandamartinromance.com

www.ingramcontent.com/pod-product-compliance
Lightning Source LLC
Chambersburg PA
CBHW030910050726
47498CB00003BA/671